Praise for *The Runes of*

"What would your *Dungeons & Dragons* campaign look like the DM let you choose a squad of U.S. Marines for your characters? Most DMs know better, but Klecha and Buckell have shown us how that adventure might go. Spoiler alert: It will be fun, action-packed, occasionally gritty, and full of jokes for Geeks and Marines alike."
—Jim C. Hines, author of *Terminal Alliance*

"Tobias S. Buckell and Dave Klecha have crafted a portal fantasy that gleefully asks, 'What if we sent in the Marines?' Equal parts grounded and tongue-in-cheek, this swiftly moving military adventure will fit in perfectly before your next *D&D* campaign."
—Samantha Mills, author of *The Wings Upon Her Back*

"A story stitched from the greatest late-night dorm room debates. Who would win: Black Hawks versus dragons? Marines versus trolls? All the magic of Tolkien arrayed against the 21st-century American war machine?"
—Brian Staveley, author of *The Empire's Ruin*

"As a lifelong fan of both nerdy pursuits and action movies, *The Runes of Engagement* is exactly what I didn't know I needed! The Marines are a fun mix of jarhead and scholar (sometimes both in one), and the various characters they encounter—an artsy troll, a mysterious ranger, a suspiciously helpful child who attracts danger—are absolutely the kind of characters I hope to encounter every time I play *D&D*!"
—Rachel Copeland, Boswell Book Company

THE RUNES OF ENGAGEMENT
TOBIAS S. BUCKELL & DAVE KLECHA

Also by Tobias Buckell

The Xenowealth Books

Crystal Rain (2006)
Ragamuffin (2007)
Sly Mongoose (2008)
The Apocalypse Ocean (2012)

Novels

Arctic Rising (2012)
Hurricane Fever (2014)
The Trove (2017)
The Tangled Lands (with Paolo Bacigalupi, 2018)
A Stranger in the Citadel (2023)

Halo

Halo: The Cold Protocol (2008)
Halo: Envoy (2017)

THE RUNES OF ENGAGEMENT

TOBIAS S. BUCKELL   DAVE KLECHA

TACHYON

SAN FRANCISCO

Cover art "Dragon vs Soldiers" copyright © 2009 by Andree Wallin
Cover and interior design by Elizabeth Story
Tobias S. Buckell author photo copyright © Scott Edelman
Dave Klecha author photo copyright © Dave Scott, 4Scotts Photography

Tachyon Publications LLC
1459 18th Street #139
San Francisco, CA 94107
415.285.5615
www.tachyonpublications.com
tachyon@tachyonpublications.com

Series editor: Jacob Weisman
Project editor: Jaymee Goh

Print ISBN: 978-1-61696-416-0
Digital ISBN: 978-1-61696-417-7

Printed in the United States by Versa Press, Inc.

First Edition: 2024
9 8 7 6 5 4 3 2 1

CHAPTER ONE

ARROWS *SHOULD* HAVE BEEN SILENT compared to gunfire, Private First Class Sadiq Rashad thought, but there was no mistaking that bristly whistle as one whipped through the air just above his head and thwacked into someone's flak jacket behind him. Somehow it seemed to shatter the forest silence as effectively as any gunshot.

The entire squad ate dirt, and everyone checked their ammo. Rashad backed against a tree trunk and wondered how they'd gotten flanked, then realized how stupid a question that was: this was wood elf territory. They knew their own land more intimately than any human would, or even ever could.

Rashad was new to the squad, only a month in the Fleet, so he was still nervous. Every crack in the brush and shaken leaf had him jumpy. The squad had all been teasing him. *Boot* this and *newb* that. He knew he had to just keep eating it all up with a smile on his face, or at least keep his expression neutral.

But the most confusing thing about combat over here wasn't just the chaos of being under some kind of attack. It was the fact that the *voices* of everyone else in the squad were in his head and he wasn't used to it.

He'd thought magical forests would be unreal and full of ineffable beauty. Instead, he was missing the Badlands of North Dakota where he'd grown up.

Just because you read about this crap in books and thought it sounded amazing didn't mean living it was going to be *fun*. Everything in the forests kept shooting pointy objects and spells at them, the locals were inscrutable and dirty, and the squad spent most of its time hunkered down in a forward operating base, eating MREs.

Rashad hadn't even had a single hearty stew yet.

Another arrow smacked into a nearby tree and Rashad, weighed down with seventy pounds of gear, tried to make himself as small as possible.

Staff Sergeant Raymond Cale lay low about five meters away. He could see that Rashad's face was pale and shaken, but Rashad had his rifle cradled and ready, looking for orders. Good. The newb had paid attention in training. He'd been a bit out of sorts since joining. He'd come in with an adventurer's excitement that hadn't been blunted by boot camp, but once he'd realized that life on the other side at a FOB was all guard duty, moving shit from one place to another and filling sandbags, he'd started to wallow in his own head a bit.

Cale had to be careful to shield that thought, as he didn't want his impressions of his people leaking out all over the place. Not good for morale. All their minds were linked up into one single group mind via the Spell of Tactician's Weave, but Cale had a commander's training on how to use STW.

The rest of the squad spread out. Lance Corporal Alden Diaz pulled an arrow out from his body armor and looked a bit chagrined. Not too far away, LCpl Robert Orley crawled intently through dirt.

"Got eyes on the woodie," Orley reported.

"Hold," Cale whispered.

This was the rendezvous point. The whole squad had cloaks draped over their regular gear that made them look like peasant travelers. So why the sudden hostility? Cale suspected they were going to have to ditch the robes that had let them camouflage themselves, and see if they could de-escalate before a simple hand-off turned into a cluster fuck.

Through Tactician's Weave, Cale could tell Orley really didn't want to do any de-escalation. He wanted to *engage* the wood elves. But even though some Marine certified to cast a spell on them back at the FOB had joined their minds together to make a more effective combat unit, only one person here was in charge.

And that was Cale.

"Ditch the cloaks," Cale ordered the thirteen other members of his platoon.

Diaz had a memory to share with the entire platoon. It was a story he had been told about a couple of African American Special Forces who stumbled in out of the night with bows and arrows. They were scouts setting out to blend into the local land, and on the way back in, they'd ended up getting shot by jumpy sentries who thought they were orcs.

The realization that some people would see black skin, bows, right away think orc, and go straight to trigger-pulling—it left a bad taste in everyone's mouths. A lot of the bad taste was Diaz's, leaking out into the whole platoon via the spell. Diaz was half black; he was often pointing out stuff like that to them with the mental equivalent of a sigh.

Teachable moment about making assumptions aside—and Diaz had laid plenty of those thanks to the forced intimacy of the Tactician's Weave spell—Orley got Diaz's point and took his energy to engage down a notch so that the whole squad wasn't quivering with an eagerness to shoot at anything.

Now everyone was synching with Cale's reasoning: the elves were probably seeing The Enemy, not US Marines, due to the cloaks.

As one, they shrugged off the cloaks, displaying their standard Marine Corps digi-cammies and gear. Each of the three fire teams was clustered around a different tree, a corporal with an eagle eye making sure they had zones of fire in all directions for each team, and that they were ready for anything to happen next.

A bird whistle from the tree canopy pierced the air. More whistles came from all around the squad. The elves had marked the squad from the get-go, Cale realized. The arrow had been an exploratory shot to make sure they were actually Marines in disguise, not the start of a firefight.

Just because the folk out in the woods here were using arrows didn't mean they were stupid, and it certainly didn't mean they had no grasp of the differences in technology and force levels.

Cale felt Rashad grasp at a thought that several of the other Marines sent rattling at him. There was a grinning visage looking down the bark of the tree from over Rashad. It was a wood elf. Half the squad poked Rashad with rote lessons about high ground. The boot needed to clear up and down, not just in the two-dimensional plane. The elf had gotten the damn drop on him.

"Cheshire!" Cale shouted.

"Alice," came the reply in a purr from the wood elf above Rashad.

Good to go.

"Hello the shooters!" Cale shouted. "First Battalion, Ninth

Marines." He never gave their correct unit, and changed it every time he talked to any locals. 1/9 had a fearsome reputation, though, thanks to the Battle of the Low Gorge Keep. "You're expecting us? We're here as escort for the Lady Wíela."

Silence stretched on for a bit. Cale worried that maybe the translation spell every soldier on this side of the portal had been hit with as they came through had failed.

Rashad fidgeted, glancing away from the wood elf crouched on the tree above him and off into the foliage. More of the elves' child-like forms melted out from the shadows, their small bows slung on their backs and their hands resting on the hilts of knives. They were skeletal and lean, chiseled teeth glinting as they looked the squad over with cold eyes.

"I'm Achur. I have protected the Lady this far. Do you have the writ?" the elf above Rashad finally said, dropping nimbly from the tree and approaching Cale.

Cale held up the papyrus that he pulled from one of the many pockets at his thigh. The symbols on it glittered, and then blazed, as the elf's gaze passed over them.

Achur swallowed and nodded. "We turn the Lady over to your care."

And just like that, the elves melted back away. All that remained was a young woman in a cloak as black as the shadows, her green eyes peeking out from under the hood.

Lady Wíela.

Diaz and Orley bowed deeply toward her, as they'd been taught by battalion S-3 and the cultural liaison gurus. Cale was about to do so as well when the squad radio crackled. It was First Squad—Stormcrow—laid out five kilometers farther into enemy territory.

"You've got three trolls, Longshanks," they reported. "Headed your way like they know something's up."

Cale looked reflexively down at his watch. Eight hours before sunrise, a long way to go. He hadn't heard anything like trolls approaching. But the whole squad had been focused on the attacking wood elves and could have easily missed the distant popcorn sound of gunfire or trembling ground.

"Engage and slow them down, we have the package," Cale whispered into the handset, then strained to hear their reply.

"They're already past us, Longshanks," First Squad reported. "I've got two dead. I've already called for a casevac and we might be pinned down. I'd be calling *you* for help if—"

A brief burst of static cut off any further words.

"Stormcrow?"

Nothing. First Squad was dead or moving, and Cale needed to focus on what his people needed to do now.

Over the eerie feel of Tactician's Weave, Cale felt that Orley *thought* he could hear the sound of wood cracking. Diaz was sure he could feel a distant thudding.

Hell, Cale was half convinced he could as well.

"The night is young." Lady Wíela spoke up, her voice high and fair. "We'd better start running, unless any of your machines can hurt a troll."

"Trolls," Rashad repeated, and Cale felt him trying to remember his all-too-brief training before he'd suited up and come through the breach to this world.

"They'll be weak in the daylight. We just have to make it through the night," Lady Wíela said, as if reassuring them. Or maybe she was trying to convince herself. It was hard to say: her face was buried deep in the shadows of her cowl. No one in the squad found it easy to get a good look at her features. Their gazes just sort of slid away from the shadows hidden away there. Some kind of magical veil, or a glamour, made it hard to perceive her properly.

And Cale didn't have time to worry about it right now.

"Right," Cale said. "Get them to daylight."

But the whole squad, linked mind to mind, had the exact same thought: *It will be a miracle if we make it through the night.*

CHAPTER TWO

CALE ORDERED LCPL PHILIP ANTOINE to tap Rashad with a pre-packaged, one-use Wand of Night Seeing and they all took off, rolling through the woods at double-time. Rashad was on point, like a good little newbie, his rifle half-raised as he scanned the woods ahead. He would never be a night elf—no human from the Earth side of the rift could be that good—but the bottled spell gave him a good look at the terrain as they busted through it.

At this point, they figured anyone in the woods with half a lick of sense knew they were dragging a shit-ton of trouble behind them in the shape of three trolls. Anyone in front of them basically *wanted* to get trampled, if they were hanging around.

Didn't stop Rashad from jumping at every flickery shadow, though, Cale noticed.

Cale, and everyone else, could sense Rashad was feeling the sting of letting that wood elf get the jump on him and he was itching to prove himself.

"Jotun," Cale muttered to the boot. *Be cool. Cool as a frost giant.* It was a figure of speech that had percolated through the ranks from the stream of eager sign-ups who'd read tabletop gaming manuals and pored over old mythology with the enthu-siasm of a college prof. Now even lifers in command like Cale were getting infected with the language, no matter how hard he tried to resist all the other crap that came with it.

The woods opened up in front of him, which was the pro-verbial blessing and curse; they had better visibility, but then so did anyone looking for them. And whatever advantage they had flitting between the trees, where the trolls had to crash through obstacles, would be lost in the more open ground.

Hell of a view though, Cale thought briefly. And then: *Time to slow the trolls down.*

As Rashad hustled down off the ridge line, running along just below the crest, the trees thinned out. He could see the Medju Gorge, the twisted frontier between the wood elves' home and the land of the orcs. He glanced at the tortured rock formations as he ran. They rose up around him like charred souls trying to escape Hell, each larger, more misshapen, and unnatural than the last. The gorge deepened and widened, and the formations grew ever more massive.

"Almost anything could be hiding in there," Orley said out loud, voicing a thought ping-ponging around the squad.

The ridge sloped down toward the rim of the gorge, and Rashad felt a plan form in all their minds, almost at once under Cale's guidance. Pros and cons shot back and forth—without the need for pleasantries or protocol—as fast as the thoughts coalesced.

Within moments, the squad moved into position for a hasty ambush.

Rashad stopped and curled back, and the rest of first team followed him. He shook his head as he saw them picking their way over the flat, sparsely treed ground between the steep ridge and the gorge. They had the unenviable job of serving as bait.

Their run to safety would be short, though, and the trolls would be distracted with other things—like stampeding off a cliff into the gorge.

Still. . . .

The squad felt the trolls before they heard them. The ground shook, the earth itself reacting to the trolls. Then they heard it— the tree-cracking, metal-jangling, grunting and snorting of the biggest, dumbest animals on two legs. Branches jerked suddenly and toppled.

Then the trolls lumbered into view, massive arms and legs swinging through the foliage, huge bodies shoving gnarled trunks aside as if they were saplings. Rashad's mind had a hard time with it, even through the unreal vision of Night Seeing. Videos he'd watched from the first Rangers that had come through the breach were one thing—gunsight cameras another—but this almost burned out his brain.

Real. Fucking. Trolls.

The sight might have kept him frozen in that spot had it not been for the rest of the squad. Other than coordination, this was the thing Tactician's Weave was good for. They pushed Rashad through the initial shock and, as one, first team raised their weapons and fired. They weren't trying to bring down the trolls—only enrage them, draw them right into the beaten zone where all the overlapping fields of fire converged.

It worked, of course. They were big, dumb animals. They'd walked right into a withering wall of lead.

But, everyone noticed, that shower of fire looked utterly ineffective right now, and the plan started to make less sense as the trolls just got really, really pissed.

Still, they were committed.

"This is a bad idea," Lady Wíela hissed at Cale, just as first team started to move, spraying three-round bursts back at the lumbering beasts.

"Yeah, we know," Cale said, and brought his rifle up. There was an HEDP—High Explosive, Dual Purpose—grenade in the tube slung under the barrel, and he hoped it would do the trick.

"You won't get me back to your world this way," Lady Wíela said.

"We won't get you anywhere if we don't try to shake these assholes."

Three M27s opened up, the designated gunners concentrating on the closest troll, and whatever else she might have said was drowned in a cacophony of fire.

The rest of the squad, using regular night-vision scopes, saw greenish lumps, fragments of huge bodies, and the bright, actinic sparks of tracer rounds pinging off their impossibly thick hides.

A troll staggered into view and Cale took the shot, angling his rifle up and popping off the grenade. The rifle butt smacked him in the shoulder and he admired the shot for a moment—just like they say you shouldn't—a perfect arc that nailed the troll in its squat neck.

They all watched the explosion, then scattered like camouflage cockroaches when the lights turn on.

The troll Cale hit freaked out, broke off, and did a runner right toward the gorge. The other two flailed around, maddened and completely lost. While that was great for the squad trying to boogie out, Cale thought, it was shit for them trying to do so in one piece. Tree limbs, rocks, and clods of dirt the size of a person's torso flew through the air.

Someone screamed, that particular shock-and-fury sound of the initially wounded.

"Who's hit?" Cale shouted into the mayhem.

Rashad spotted LCpl Trent Marcel as Marcel dropped, run through with a couple of big shards of bole wood from a shattered tree trunk. Rashad grabbed Marcel by the drag strap on the back of his vest and pulled the senior lance corporal deeper into the woods. Rashad knew he might have been one of the biggest Tolkien nerds in his Boot Camp platoon, but he was also one of the strongest.

And thanks to Tactician's Weave, Rashad also knew the squad liked him like that.

"Leave him," Lady Wíela hissed as they all tried to regroup. She had stayed by Cale's side through the ambush. "He'll only slow us down, and the trolls' madness will pass. They *will* hunt us again."

"We don't leave a Marine behind!" several of them shouted automatically back at her, as one. It could have been the effect of the Tactician's Weave, or just the usual.

All accounted for, the platoon got back on the move, taking advantage of the trolls' confusion.

"You're jeopardizing this mission!" Lady Wíela said, lowering her voice. In order to eavesdrop, Rashad edged as close to Cale as he dared. "And the whole war besides. Your people stopped the invasion into your world, but you are barely keeping your enemies from staying on this side. I am the key to the alliance your forces need."

There was no denying that coalition forces had been stuck in a morass ever since pushing through to the other side, and everyone knew it. They had all watched The Event on TV, or been glued to shaky videos and live social media posts on the internet.

When the rifts had opened, no one had understood what was happening. At first, it was just tiny pockets where two worlds touched, showing glimpses of some foreign landscape. But then they grew wider, reaching beyond the woods and back alleys and caves where they'd first appeared. And the moment the governments started to investigate these portals to another world, realizing that you could step through them, *they* had poured out.

No one thought that a bunch of creatures out of old storybooks could stand up for long against cops, much less the Army or Marines, but they made a fight out of it the world would never forget. Or maybe the world would, Rashad thought, when given enough time. Maybe it would all fade to legends and fairy tales and great big hairy operas written by the descendants of the Germans. Maybe that was where all the old legends had originally come from.

Either way, one thing was for sure: everyone started looking at those old stories differently when orcs started beheading joggers in Central Park, and when trolls hammered at the foundations of the Empire State Building until it collapsed.

When coalition forces had stopped the invasion and pushed through to the other side of the fissures, they'd allied quickly with benevolent beings like the wood elves and humans like Lady Wíela, who had been humanity's allies and friends in the old stories.

And then they'd found out why scary creatures of forgotten legend were invading: there was something even scarier on this side they'd been running away from. Or—and intel was scrambled on this—some of them were acting on the scary thing's bidding.

Everyone on this side called it the "Corrupted One." A force of evil and mayhem, ancient and brooding, that had been spreading across the world like a virus.

Which was why the squad was on the edge of the wood elves' territory, running from trolls in enemy territory, far from home, skirting a gorge that looked like something out of Peter Jackson's wet dreams and hoping the trolls wouldn't take up the chase again.

"We know what's at stake," Cale told her. "We know you have information the brass is hot and heavy for."

They'd been told she was some sort of royalty on this side of the rift, and the squad was the anonymous security team delivering her to the safe location for talks.

Everyone here knew their role. Even the newb.

They didn't stop moving, trying to form back up as they left the thrashing noise of the trolls behind. They took advantage of the bond that Tactician's Weave brought to keep trucking generally toward the objective: their FOB. Home, as they knew it over here.

"You don't know what's really at stake," Lady Wíela said, her voice rising in pitch and volume. Yet it remained royal and commanding, even despite the fact that she was running alongside the Marines. She didn't seem to even be out of breath. "You haven't the first idea—"

"You could just tell us," Orley interrupted.

"I'll only speak to your leaders. Your minds are all bonded together: I can see the Weave. I'm not about to give information to warriors who might yet get captured, or have secrets dragged from them by ale. We have very little time to drag around the dying out of sentimentality!"

Rashad realized she must have no idea that people could actually recover from wounds like the gashes in Marcel's leg, much less survive them without some intense magic. But still, he wasn't feeling charitable toward her right now for her suggestion they abandon a Marine.

"He's not dying; he'll be fine if we get him to a surgeon soon." Cale sounded annoyed, too, but he was such a commensurate commander that none of those feelings leaked into the Tactician's Weave. Rashad was impressed with that, as he often was with Staff Sergeant.

"Quit being a suck-up," someone hissed at him, having heard his thoughts trickle out.

Cale glanced over, and Rashad flushed, embarrassed. Tactician's Weave could be a pain in the ass sometimes.

"We will all die if we don't get to safety, and soon," Cale growled.

He ordered them all to stop; they'd gotten enough distance to take a quick breather. Emphasis on quick: the thudding in the distance reminded them that death plodded toward them with stony implacability.

"Dooley, take a look at Marcel. Heath, you're with Doc on the stretcher."

Rashad, now back on point, came across a deep draw cutting across their path and draining down into the ravine. This was useful terrain. The whole platoon could feel Cale planning another ambush to slow the trolls down.

Rashad, through Tactician's Weave, could also hear LCpl Tamika Jones on the horn, calling for backup in her calm, on-air voice. That reassured everyone. They weren't alone. There was a whole coalition on this side of the rift, with resources that should be able to boogie out and help them with the trolls.

Someone in the platoon leaked a memory of watching trolls push aside the ruins of the Empire State Building and walk through the white dust clouds toward National Guard troops.

"Not helpful," Cale muttered.

They were ready to fight, but they'd all seen what trolls could do.

Rashad picked his way down the near slope of the gully, checking left and right like a good newbie. That first encounter with the trolls had rattled him, but he was also taking pride in having survived it, and having had the presence of mind all on his own to grab Marcel and drag him out of the kill zone.

LCpl Bradley Heath and Doc Dooley had a groaning Marcel on one of the squad's collapsible litters now, all bandaged up and hit with painkillers. They would have a tough time getting down the gully and back up the other side. HM3 Kaitlin Dooley was a PT nut, and so was Heath, but muscling Marcel up a hill would be a pain.

But they could see Rashad's steps, his route, and picked their own way down from what they'd seen through his eyes.

The sounds of the trolls still behind them somewhere spooked Rashad, and he nearly squeezed off a round into the rocky floor of the gully in panic. But the platoon steadied him again, reminded him that they were setting another ambush, and he pressed on.

Rashad crept across the gully floor, eyeing the sharp rise on the far side. Lady Wíela had graciously informed them of a dry streambed that rose more gradually out the other side. Rashad picked up her landmarks and started moving toward them. The directions took him down and west, closer toward that nightmare rift, where the draw emptied out.

He thought they could hear shrieks . . . or maybe it was just the wind whistling over those rock formations.

"A long way from Kansas," Rashad muttered.

"I thought you were from the Dakotas," LCpl Sheila Ysbarra said as she scurried down into the gully behind him. She spat at the ground and hefted her M27 Infantry Automatic Rifle, clearly taking comfort in the cold metal of the light machine gun in her hands.

"I am."

"What's Kansas gotta do with anything, then?" Ysbarra's eyes glinted in the artificial sight Rashad had been spelled with.

Rashad took a deep breath. "Nothing. Not going to explain it right now."

Ysbarra was casually familiar with the lore. More from the MMOs she played, where she was usually the tank. But there were some random gaps in her pop-culture familiarity that often tripped Rashad up.

"This place reminds me of upstate," Ysbarra muttered. "My parents would take me up to one of the last stops on the Metro North in the fall to go hiking, when I was a girl. Same weeds, same rock, same trees."

But the air smelled a little sweeter in the forest they had just come from, and a little fouler up ahead, where no one in the squad wanted to go.

CHAPTER THREE

IN THIS WORLD, the gully the squad was piling into was the kind that hid ogres and monsters that wanted to eat you, Cale thought, moodily looking into the dark and thinking about the Billy Goats Gruff.

No doubt the rest of the squad could give Cale a miserable list of things that were fey and would go bump in the night, ripped from the pages of their dog-eared books and monster manuals. As long as none of that shit showed up, they should be good to go for the next attempt at an ambush.

Hopefully there weren't any invisible caves, or crystal staircases, or anything else weird to stumble over, either.

It wasn't that Cale wanted to stop and fight the trolls, it was that he didn't have much choice. From here it was a straight shot back and little else but open ground between them and the relative safety of the Forward Operating Base. The trolls would run them down in the open ground.

A possibility was that the squad could drag the trolls all the way back to the Forward Operating Base along with them and hope the Marines there were up to the task, but Cale had a feeling his superiors would not appreciate that. And how likely were they to keep just ahead of the trolls all the way back to the FOB?

So, they could engage now and try to control the situation.

It was a bullshit buffet and they had to pick something to eat. Cale preferred the option that didn't endanger everyone asleep in their bunks back at the base.

"Wish we had a couple Gamgees with us," Corporal Barden muttered. She had taken off her helmet to adjust a strap, and her blond hair flashed in the night before she pulled it back on. She towered over the tiny Lady Wíela.

"What's a Gamgee?" Lady Wíela asked.

"SAMs," Cale explained. Then, realizing she wasn't following even that: "Surface-to-Air Missiles."

But the lady from the world on this side of the rifts was no less mystified.

"Think they'd even stop a troll?" LCpl Darleen Lomicka asked. She followed Ysbarra down into the gully.

Cale shrugged. "Couldn't hurt. . . ."

Barden snorted. She didn't fetishize heavy weaponry like some did, but she tended to insist on a full load-out and unit kit. Cale remembered teaching her in infantry training. She preferred firepower over speed when it was her call. But even she clearly thought they weren't going to be able to do much to a troll.

The squad followed Rashad down, keeping up their dispersion and trying to ignore the thudding troll footsteps in the distance. The trolls had gotten their shit together and were likely on their trail again. The sound of them certainly wasn't growing any fainter.

"Your weapons won't stop trolls," Lady Wíela said, agreeing with Barden. "We should keep running."

"If this doesn't work, half of us will stay back to harass and distract them while the rest bolt with you," Cale promised her. "Just bear with us a moment."

All those briefings about squad movement and local threat response theory had to count for something, right?

Rashad set up in overwatch once he had scrambled up the side and made his way back to a steep edge of the gully a little farther down. He perched on top just as the litter-bearers made it down the far slope with Marcel between them.

Sighting through the scope on his rifle, Rashad took in the landscape layout: the trees were thinning to nothing on the opposite side, and the treetops swayed as the trolls plodded through. Most of the platoon was up this side of the gully, now.

The squad started setting up on the lip while keeping a watch for the trolls through Rashad's eyes, measuring distance and time. It was easier, the second time, to pick out their flailing limbs and misshapen bodies, the thinning of the forest giving Rashad more space to see. Still, a fully glimpsed troll was just as terrifying as the half-glimpsed parts.

"Damn," he muttered. No matter how many times he would watch and rewatch the *Lord of the Rings* or the rift-breach documentaries, seeing a troll in real life was blood-chilling. Until now, they'd been a distant threat. And in that first encounter, he'd only had a few seconds to glimpse them before legging out.

Now they headed toward the gully with all the inevitability of a dinosaur-killing asteroid.

Rashad could only see two, which gave everyone hope that one of them had, indeed, panicked itself right off a cliff. They were preparing for three anyway, not that it made much difference: more than one stretched their resources to the breaking point. They had six kilos of C4, two collapsible anti-tank rockets, a dozen or so grenades, and a dwindling supply of regular ol' bullets.

"You are going to bait them into the ravine," Lady Wíela said to Cale, looking up at the platoon settling in on the lip.

Cale nodded at her. "Yes. We have explosives—"

She held up a hand to silence Cale. "I volunteer to be your bait."

"Oh, hell no," he said. "We're supposed to get you to the base, not dangle you in there like chum for trolls."

That was the exact *opposite* of the mission's goal. He could taste the court martial now.

"You have your Other World weapons," she pointed out. "Your leaders are determined to work more closely together, and my people want access to these weapons. Now I get to see with my own eyes if they're of any use. I can also see that if any of you steps away from your posts, it reduces our fighting power. I'm your best option. Besides, I'm faster than any of your men. If you are all killed, I'll slip back into the forest."

Jones was still on the horn calling for backup—air support, or advice from up the food chain. But there was only static in the air as an answer. Errant spells? Energy from the nearby rift? Who knew? The squad was on their own. And Jones's normally chill tone when on the mic sounded strained now.

Cale looked back down the ravine again. Lady Wíela *was* faster than the platoon. She'd run alongside him without even breaking a sweat. He had a faint premonition that she could run faster and lighter through the environment than anyone in his squad.

There was an argument for shucking all their gear and making a dash for it here, Cale thought again. But teams that had tried that against trolls usually lost people. You didn't need to be the fastest in a group of people running away from a troll, just faster than the others.

And that wasn't the Marine way. They weren't going to leave anyone behind.

Protocol said staggered engagements and controlled retreat. But that had clearly been drawn up by some asshole watching after-action video and drawing circles and arrows on paper. They didn't have to live through the shit.

So, another ambush, this one with bait.

The trolls would arrive at the lip, and she'd be down in the middle of the ravine. By the time they got down to her, the squad would pull her up on the other side, and the trolls would be trapped in the ravine, blundering through mines, claymore emplacements, and withering firepower from elevation on the side opposite to the one the Marines currently held.

There was no mistaking it now; the ground shuddered, the trees swayed, and there was no chance that it was a column of tanks rolling through to pick them up—the coalition still had problems stockpiling enough diesel on this side of the rifts to make it work.

"Okay," Cale said, grudgingly. "But you better be as fast as you say."

Rashad watched the last of the squad still on the gully floor hustle to improvise some claymores as Lady Wíela clambered back down to meet them, while LCpl Caiden Brust and Antoine set up with their anti-tank rockets.

Rashad kept looking from Lady Wíela to the tree line and

back again, feeling personally responsible for her safety, even though they had taken that on as a squad. His protective feelings toward the tiny, mysterious figure in the cloak leaked out everywhere and annoyed others. He could feel their impatience with him crackle around the Tactician's Weave, like little jolts of purple electricity. He still hadn't worked out how to handle his thoughts in the team-mind mode that came with Tactician's Weave. Keeping his thoughts bottled up properly would come with time and experience.

A lot of fantasy nerds got it in their heads that they were the next Aragorn—the movie Aragorn, no less—hacking their way through legions of orcs with a big fucking sword and a bad shave. Lotta assholes got killed that way, in and out of uniform. Rashad was determined not to be one of those assholes, and Cale all but smacked those fantasies out of everyone here. Staff Sergeant had no patience for *any* of that shit.

So, Rashad made sure he was a solid part of the team. He had been through the training, paid some dues. Now was time to see how it really got done on the ground.

But Rashad glanced at the Lady Wíela again. He tried not to let himself stare too obviously. No Cate Blanchett, but still. . . . It was hard to tell exactly what her features were, as the shadows kept falling *just so.*

Ysbarra's built up annoyance at the off-mission focus broke with a swift ruler-crack to Rashad's mental knuckles. *Save that shit for your bunk,* she thought at him.

Cheeks prickling, Rashad snapped back to the moment at hand.

When the trolls broke through the trees, Rashad was all business. He had eyes on them for the squad. Via Tactician's Weave, he estimated the ranges, and the squad read them right off the top of his mind. Too close. Far too close.

"Lady Wíela!" Cale shouted, and the Lady looked up at his pointed hand. The trolls were at the crest, near where the squad had come down, towering above them all.

Wíela shouted and waved, getting the trolls' attention, then turned to run. She looked impossibly small compared to the giant creatures.

If they reached her, Rashad knew they would stomp her into a stain. And for as quick as she was running, dodging odd-shaped boulders and spinning around the pillars of rock, the trolls were crossing the tortured ground even faster.

Cale made a decision and, on the other side of the gully, Brust pulled the trigger in response to his unvoiced command. An unguided rocket lanced out in a tight spiral. It blossomed orange just under the armpit of one of the trolls, which bellowed in rage through the fading explosion around it.

"He ain't too fucking happy about that," Cale said, allowing himself the luxury of a half grin.

From what Brust could see, they seemed to have finally injured one of the trolls—slightly.

"Nah," Rashad reported. "I think we just really, really pissed it off."

It bellowed again, and an answering roar came from down the ravine behind them all.

Fuck, Cale thought, spreading alarm out through everyone. Damnit, now he was leaking his thoughts all over the Tactician's Weave like a damn newb.

Barden and LCpl Heath scoped the end of the gully and saw the big, dark shape of the third troll lumbering up toward the squad. It must have fallen into the ravine as they had hoped, but had continued to follow them all. Now it had their flank. It was probably just a happy accident for the troll, but accident or not, everyone was in danger. And they'd put Lady Wíela right down there with it.

"We are supremely fucked," Antoine hissed.

The Lady was going to get run over if they didn't move quickly. And after that, the trolls were going to run over the rest of the platoon down there.

First things first.

"Wave her over and reel her up," Cale ordered Rashad.

They were not going to lose her.

Rashad grabbed the 550-pound–test cord loop from his gear and flung it over the edge of the gully, then hastily tied off one end to his vest. If she could get to that, she could climb up.

"Loop the end under your arms and tie it!" he shouted.

Meanwhile, Rashad was torn between firing at the trolls to drive them off or trying to make like a bump in the grass and hoping they got more excited about Brust and his spent rocket launcher.

He felt a tug on the rope and braced his feet.

Antoine fired on the other troll, hoping to draw them away. The distraction worked, though that meant all three trolls were now keying on Brust and Antoine. They were theoretically out of reach on the lip of the gully, but suddenly the walls didn't look so high.

And then the radio crackled.

Jones pumped her fist. Hope suddenly blossomed from Rashad and spread itself around the entire squad. It was a fuzzy and fractured human voice on the radio, but recognizable.

"Longshanks, Longshanks, this is Windlord, we are one mike out from your beacon, what's your sitch?"

They all somehow refrained from cheering.

Cale scrambled over to Jones and grabbed the handset from her.

"Windlord, this is Longshanks Actual," Cale shouted into the handset. "Three brutes, danger close, bring the thunder!"

"Thunder, aye. Hold on to your butts, Longshanks. Windlord out."

Rashad looked up and to the west. A flight of four sparks in the distance closed in, growing quickly. He pulled up on the cord and also moved to the lip of the gully, risking a glance down to where she was hanging, trying to scramble up to him as he reeled her in.

"Lady Wíela?"

"What are they?" She paused to look at the skies with the rest of them. "Dragons?"

"Even better," he shouted down at her. "Warthogs!"

She frowned—obviously not sure how a pig might be able to save their bacon right now—as the Warthogs arrived.

They were ugly and beautiful—almost-ancient jets made for a different war. Their huge rotary cannons, mounted under the cockpit, were designed to plow 30mm depleted uranium rounds into Soviet tanks and armored vehicles in support of ground troops. The planes themselves were actually armored, and as they dove on the gully, Rashad could see the cluster bombs and anti-armor rockets slung under the wings.

The trolls looked up just as four gouts of flame erupted from the planes, each stream of phosphorescent rounds looking like a laser beam. Two of the Warthogs loosed rockets, and explosions rocked the gully. The squad dropped flat and Rashad was thrown back as he came to an appreciation of what "danger close" *really* meant. The heat of the explosions washed over him, singeing the grass, reddening exposed skin, and the weight on the line went heavy.

The trolls bellowed, cried, and screamed, and it all mingled with the cacophony of the Warthogs' attack. The two trolls on the ridge across from the platoon turned to run toward the frontier with the dark lands. Two of the Warthogs overflew them while the other two circled back around and strafed them again to make the point.

As the smoke in the ravine cleared, the third troll lay unmoving in the middle of a crater.

"Fuck yeah!" someone said. Or maybe they all did. Hard to tell under the influence of Tactician's Weave sometimes.

Rashad grabbed hold and started hauling on the line again. Lady Wíela was still on it, but heavy, not assisting him. Fantasy nerds who had been through boot camp knew that their gaming stats had real world counterparts, and Rashad had gone in big on Strength and Constitution. Hand over hand, he pulled her up the side of the gully.

The squad picked themselves up, several limps and cuts and bruises, but nothing to keep them from hoofing the last few kilometers. They hurried over to where Rashad was pulling the Lady Wíela up over the lip of the gully.

Rashad was hoping she wasn't dead. Really, really hoping.

He saw her as he dragged her over the lip, and everyone relaxed slightly. She was unconscious, blood down the side of her face, but she took several deep breaths as they watched.

Doc Dooley got down to check her out and pronounced her alive, but started muttering, "This ain't right," over and over again.

And everyone near the Lady Wíela took a second look. Because now, instead of their gazes slipping past her face and leaving them an impression of haughty royalty, they could now *look* directly at her.

Rashad took in the state of her cloak and gown, torn and shredded by the trip up the rocky wall of the gully. Her skin was gray and mottled beneath, and that skin sure as hell didn't match the pale face and blond hair above her shoulders.

The Lady Wiela was clearly Not Human.

CHAPTER FOUR

THE LADY WÍELA's face and hands were covered in a glamour, Barden saw now, a magical disguise meant to fool them all. Now they saw the wood elf she really was.

Ysbarra drew her sidearm, ready to put two between Wíela's eyes, but Cale grabbed her wrist and pushed the weapon back. Staff Sergeant looked pissed.

Barden met Cale's eyes and inclined her head. *Go easy*, she tried to tell him. Ysbarra was just jumpy after putting her neck on the line against real-life trolls.

Cale seemed to get that; he relaxed slightly.

Rashad had moved to stop Ysbarra as well. They saw it clear in his mind over Tactician's Weave because he couldn't keep anything to his damn self. He was thinking back to Diaz's story about the two black Special Forces guys, riddled with bullets because the sentries had mistaken them for orcs.

He had a point, though, Barden knew. The lady's disguise was not going to survive a trip to Washington or any of the millimeter-wave airport security scanners she would pass through on the other side, so she must have known she would be unmasked long before she got anywhere the surprise might do her any good.

"I don't think she dangled herself out there as troll bait for nothing," Rashad said. "She's a friendly. And an important one."

"Could just be trying to get in good with us," Ysbarra said to him. "Lures us in, then hits us when we don't expect it."

"Ysbarra," Cale muttered. "Drop it."

Ysbarra grumbled, but did so.

"Our orders are to get her back safe and hand her over," Cale said. "Let's get it done."

After a moment, Diaz nodded and grabbed the second collapsible litter off Doc Dooley's back and unfolded it. They got Wíela on it and, as the Warthogs made one final strafing run along the gully, the squad started hoofing it for friendlier territory before anything else decided to crawl out of the gorge and come for them.

As the squad crested the rise at dawn on the back of a big Osh-Kosh truck, Cale could see the Seven Sisters Falls sparkle in the morning sun, pouring out from the sacred forest and into the river they all called "Binky" because none of the Marines could pronounce its real name. The Tolkien nerds gave it their best shot, but it turned out that the High Elven tongue had nothing at all to do with Finnish. Forward Operating Base Hammerhand perched on a bare sweep of rocky soil, just on the frontier of the High Elves' sacred forest.

As soon as they had stopped, Cale had Dooley haul Marcel off the back of the truck as two more corpsmen came running up. Together, they all hustled off to the Combat Support Hospital. An aircrew and some officer, meanwhile, came to fetch Lady Wíela.

The officer, at least, didn't look surprised at the mottled gray skin under her torn clothing.

"Fucking figures," Rashad said. And for once, the platoon didn't give him a hard time. That was hard-won knowledge—the fact that sometimes you're a mushroom: kept in the dark and fed orders.

Tactician's Weave was wearing off and they were all starting to fall fully back into their own heads, but they didn't really need it to make some decisions together. Dropping off the back of the truck, they hauled their weary bodies eastward, out to the end of the FOB that looked out over the forest and falls and the faint hint of golden spires away over the green and leafy canopy.

They shucked their gear, bodies steaming with sweat that evaporated in the cool morning air. As they settled in, a CH-53 Sea Stallion lifted off its pad at the western end of the base and formed up with two loitering Cobra gunships. They headed north at top speed and Cale wished them luck. Flying through the rifts back to the real world was nowhere near as easy as walking or driving.

There were two Ospreys parked in the center of the base. Those would be for the Lady Wíela, Cale assumed. Or maybe command would risk trucking her out by road to the portal back to Earth. Either way, it wasn't his concern now.

"It ain't D&D rules out here, that's for sure," Lomicka said, leaning back on her gear.

Next to her, like some salty vet, Rashad had already broken down his M27 and gotten out his cleaning kit, the pieces settled on his lap. Everyone followed suit, of course, even those who hadn't gotten off a shot.

"Yeah," Heath said, stretching his back and arms, oversized triceps clear through his sleeves. "I wish I could ignore encumbrance."

Everyone laughed. Most of the squad were nerds of some stripe or another, though Heath was newest to some of the nuances. He had studied up, though and picked his joke well, Cale figured. Most of his squad, it seemed, had rolled twelve-sided dice before taking the big chance and volunteering to go through the rift.

But reality, Cale knew, was not as simple as those worlds that had been conceived over kitchen tables and potato chips. All of those ancient stories game designers and wordsmiths had turned to, they'd been echoes of something real. Ancient memories of a world and time when the rifts had opened and the weird and scary and monstrous had poured out, populating nightmares and fairy tales for millennia.

"So did those elves sell us out?" Ysbarra leaned over her weapon to disassemble it.

"What do you think?" Diaz replied. "Those trolls were aimed right at us. They delivered their package, got paid, and then got paid for telling the other side where the package was."

"That's jacked up," Jones said. She wasn't as boot as Rashad, but still, she never cussed. It was curious.

"It's fucking complicated," Cale said wearily. "Just like the 'Stan, just like Iraq. I saw how fucked up it could be, even back there. No surprise it's the same here."

Everyone turned and looked over the sacred forest, the lands of humanity's allies. They didn't need Tactician's Weave to understand each other's thoughts. It wasn't a board game out there; it was a dangerous and hostile land.

"And no—no guarantees they can be trusted either," Cale said. "But if *we* trust each other and think things through, we'll be alright."

They all stared at him. Then Orley smirked, and someone else half-cracked a smile. Orley couldn't take anything seriously. It was maddening, Cale thought.

So, he stepped away. He'd done his leadership speech, made

sure the squad was doing what it was supposed to. Time to leave them all to decompress without him hovering around.

Cale headed back to his tent and shook off the last of the after-effects of Tactician's Weave. He saw to breakfast for the squad, then sent Corporal Barden to fetch ammo resupply for everyone and ordered the rest to the squad hooch for some "rack ops." He needed to sleep himself, but he knew it would be a while coming. Rest came harder and harder after every combat operation. Sleep, even exhausted sleep, could prove to be elusive.

Maybe some reading would help before he had to meet the CO.

His tent was a functional space, though he had brought a few touches along. A few pictures had been taped up on the support post opposite the opening of the tent—him and his squadmates from Charlie 1/1 playing football in the Iraqi desert, his best friend Tim Wright leaning against the hood of his beloved Mustang, him and Tim all geared up one night before patrol. They had been lance corporals then, fresh-faced and new to war. Tim would never believe what they were getting up to these days, what the "New Corps" was like.

He kicked a barbell weight at the edge of his cot and swore. Biting back more curses, he tossed his M27 onto his cot, then draped his vest and boonie hat on a wooden cross made of plywood. Stripping off his sweaty T-shirt, he draped it over a little makeshift clothesline across the back of the tent, then went to his footlocker. He opened it, and more of the past looked out at him from the lid. Taped up there were pictures from home—Mom and Dad, another one of Tim, his younger brother in football pads—the sort of stuff he desperately wanted to get back to. This was all too weird for him. As strange as Iraq and Afghanistan, and stranger still in a lot of ways.

A paperback copy of *The Hobbit* sat on his neatly folded pile of clean T-shirts. He hesitated, then picked it up and tossed it on his cot. He could read, and that would probably put him to sleep. The first page had done the trick a few times now, and he had yet to venture on to the second or third page. He pulled out a T-shirt and tugged it on just as someone shook on the canvas flap of his tent.

"Permission to enter, Staff Sergeant?" It was Heath, nervous and apologetic, like most junior Marines, at disturbing someone three steps above.

"Lance Corporal. Enter." Cale grabbed *The Hobbit* and tossed it back into the footlocker so that Heath wouldn't spot it. He dropped the lid as Heath pushed the flap aside and stepped in.

Cale settled back to sit. "Shouldn't you be racking out? I could swear I made that an order."

"Yes, Staff Sergeant, sorry, Staff Sergeant."

Cale waved away the apology with no little irritation. All that mattered to Cale was whether you changed course or addressed the issue. When he saw Heath stood there at attention, Cale pointed to a small three-legged camp stool in a corner of the tent. "Sit."

And, when Heath did, Cale asked: "What's on your mind, son?"

Only about ten years of difference separated them, but the Corps encouraged that sort of paternal relationship between leaders and subordinates. And . . . Cale found he fell easily into it.

Heath sighed and fidgeted a bit, looked around, then eventually stared up toward the top of Cale's tent. Cale snapped his fingers.

"It's weird, Staff Sergeant. It's not like they told us it would be in the Fleet," Heath said.

Cale snorted. "No, no I don't think it's anything like what they said it would be. When did you do Boot? A year or so ago?"

Heath nodded. "The rifts opened the day I reported to Infantry Training Battalion, Staff Sergeant."

"No one expected this. This isn't really the war anyone prepared for, or could prepare for." But then, armies were always ready for the last war they fought. Never the current, fucked-up-in-all-sorts-of-new-ways one.

"I get that, Staff Sergeant. I do. But I never read any of this stuff before the rifts opened. I didn't even play fantasy video games. My first platoon sergeant gave me a stack of books and suggested I cram like I was taking an exam. He figured it was the fastest way to promotion, given all the change. So, I buckled down."

"Smart man," Cale replied. His own CO had recommended the same thing once the dust had settled and the new reality had set in. Cale had not had the energy for it like Heath evidently had, and reading the first page of *The Hobbit* and watching the Peter Jackson movies was about as far as he had gotten. "And you got through them, sounds like. What's the problem?"

"That stuff is kind of just like learning some Arabic or whatever, if we were getting deployed to Iraq. But . . . it's the way they all talk to each other, Staff Sergeant," Heath said, and now Cale could hear the strain and confusion in his voice.

"Like how?"

"Lance Corporal Lomicka, she's a team leader, right, Staff Sergeant? And Ysbarra is in her team. But they were arguing about my encumbrance joke. And it seemed like Lance Corporal Lomicka is owed more respect, isn't she? Ysbarra shouldn't be arguing with her like that. Lomicka is a Senior Lance, and all. They've been arguing about optimal character stats since you walked off."

Cale thought about pointing out how there was no such rank as a "Senior Lance Corporal" but he had been in long enough to know there was a difference between the Official Book and how life in the Fleet really was, especially in the infantry. And now, especially deployed on this side of the rifts. But that seemed to be the source of Heath's consternation. And while the peculiarities of the rifts and this weird fantasy world were new, that was an old problem and one young Marines either dealt with, or didn't.

"Look, Heath," Cale said, running his hand over his bristly scalp. "It's like this. Do you always drive the speed limit when you're out in town?"

"Yes, Staff Sergeant." Heath actually stiffened, reacting like he was being tested.

"Really?" Cale shook his head softly with a faint aura of fatherly disappointment. He pointed to the picture of Tim and the Mustang. "Look, I don't. When I'm in that thing? I push down a little harder, especially when I need to blow off some steam. Let the engine rumble a bit, you know? That's all that's happening with Lomicka and Ysbarra."

"They're—"

"Blowing off steam. Those two will argue like a couple of barracks lawyers from here to sundown, but when we're out there, out in the shit," he said, pointing out past his tent flap. "Ysbarra knows her job, and she stays in her lane. Lomicka says 'jump,' and Ysbarra does it. I've got no worries. And you shouldn't either. You're a good Marine, Heath."

"Thank you, Staff Sergeant," Heath said, and looked off out the half-open tent flap himself. "It is just so weird."

Now they were back to the changes. Some people just had not been able to cope, in the service and out. It was just too crazy, too much like a movie, but happening right in front of them. 9/11 had been that way, to a certain extent. But for everyone who had said that terrorism had been an existential threat, the invasion of the dark forces from the rifts had woken everyone up to what a real existential threat looked like. Trolls sauntering into Manhattan out of thin air and levelling buildings reframed things for a lot of people.

So many people froze, but Cale hadn't. He had rallied his shitbird platoon in the worst of it and beat back a wave of orcs intent on rolling through a refugee camp. When the dust settled, he had been given a commendation and rewarded with more work. The Marine Corps, all of the services, were working to reconstitute units decimated by casualties. At least fifty percent of all casualties were mental breakdowns, worse than anything he had seen in Iraq or Afghanistan.

But long experience in combat had been his salvation. He knew that just when you got it figured out, everything fucking changed.

"It *is* weird," Cale agreed with Heath. "But it's a good lesson, too. A hard and true one. Shit changes. Catches you by surprise. You deal with it, or you don't. No one knew the universe had this kind of thing hiding in it. The only thing I've known is that everything changes. Sometimes little, sometimes a lot. This time, the universe went big on the changes, and you either adapt, or you don't."

"I don't know if I can." Heath looked suddenly small and miserable.

Cale checked his own frustration and did his best to buck the young man up. And he'd need to make a note to check up on Heath's state in the near future. "Fuck, son. You already have. You're here. Your brains aren't dripping out of your ears. You got this."

Heath responded as Cale hoped, straightening a little, looking a little more sure of himself.

"Now go get some rack time," Cale ordered, doing the thing

where his voice made it clear this was no suggestion. "We gotta be ready for things to change, right?"

"Right, Staff Sergeant."

"Good," he said. "Now get the fuck out." Heath had just eaten up all Cale's downtime and now Cale needed to wipe off, find something clean, and head over to the CO for his report. He understood why Heath had wandered over. Seeing Marcel get hit, things like that always shook people up. But there was always that chance someone in your squad would go down. Hell, they'd almost all gotten stomped like bugs by trolls. Eventually that would sink in and each of them would have to react to it somehow, even if in the far back of the mind. And, Cale knew, he would be seeing more "random" drop-ins over the next few days.

Heath stood and stepped to the flap. He flipped it open just as a gout of flame rose up from the direction of the front gate, followed by a rumbling boom and a fiery roar. Small arms and machine guns chattered out, a cacophony of fire.

Cale grabbed his body armor and his M27 and shouted out at Heath. "What is it?"

Heath stood transfixed for a second, and then, in a disbelieving, slow voice said, "Dragons, sir. It's dragons."

"Go!" Cale shouted, but Heath was already running back to the squad hooch.

CHAPTER FIVE

CORPORAL HEATHER BARDEN had just fallen asleep when the "whump" sound and smell of burning pitch woke her. She rolled out of her cot, jammed her feet into her boots, and scrambled to grab her M27 from where it had been slung on a stand next to her bed.

"Squad up!" she shouted, as other Marines stirred from sleep. All of them bunked together in a single tent near the center of the FOB. After coming in from the High-Value Target mission, they had eaten and cleaned weapons, then crashed for some shut-eye. She had been awake longer to see to everything else, including making sure LCpl Marcel was on the first chopper out, while SSgt Cale was getting ready for his debrief with the CO.

She laced up her boots, pulled on her flak jacket and helmet, then headed for the main flap of the tent. She wasn't sure if this was a bunch of green boots panicking about boggarts getting in past the walls and breaking a bunch of shit or something more serious that had gotten to the FOB. Always better to gear up, though.

She nearly collided with LCpl Heath as he came running

back in. She dodged him, then stepped outside into the light and ran smack into SSgt Cale as she blinked her eyes against the setting sun.

"Watch it, Barbie," he growled.

She glanced around to see if anyone was within earshot. Cale had given her the nickname half a lifetime ago and she endured it from him, but she wasn't ready to hear it from junior Marines. Their own nickname for her, "Corporal Mary Sue," was bad enough.

"Sorry, Staff Sergeant," she said crisply.

He hated apologies. To him they were unnecessary verbal clutter, and if he was calling her Barbie she'd wind him right back up while staying within protocol, which would annoy him even more.

But he didn't even notice her dig. "Is everyone moving?"

"Yes, Staff Sergeant," she replied.

"Good. Rally point Kit-Kat, thirty seconds. Keep an eye on the sky. Someone said something about dragons."

"Aye aye," she replied, and Cale hared off again, toward the Command Post.

Okay, *something* was going on. She scanned the sky and saw nothing but deep red hues and sunset clouds. There hadn't been any dragons south of the no-fly zone in a month.

Diaz and Lomicka piled out of the tent and nearly ran into her, most of the rest of the squad a few steps behind them. Barden turned to them and passed on Cale's urgency in her voice. "Kit-Kat, go!"

They nodded and ran past her, pulling their teams after them. Jones, Orley, and Rashad stacked up behind her, but Barden paused, hearing something strange.

She looked back at them. All three had their "war faces" on, though on Rashad it still looked a little comical. He looked like he was twelve. But then, she probably had, too, when she'd first run into Cale at the School of Infantry.

There it was again. A faint jingle.

"What the fuck was that noise?" Barden asked, sounding way too much like her own mother.

They all looked blankly at her. Another whump of fire went up from near the front gate. The whistles of high-velocity arrows came behind them and all four of them crouched down. As they did, Orley jingled. She was *sure* it was Orley.

"Orley?"

"Yes, Corporal?"

"Why are you jingling?"

Orley looked confused for a split second, then understanding spread across his squared face. "Oh, it's my local currency, Corporal. I've been trading MRE crap for them."

"What?" Despite the chaos behind them, Barden remained frozen in place to stare at Orley.

"Gotta collect them all, Corporal!"

"This isn't fucking Pokémon, Orley," she snarled. No one in her team was going to muster out with enough noise to alert everyone around them for kilometers. "Stuff a sock in that pocket or I'm going to make you eat every *single* one of those goddamn coins. Let's go."

"But I've got—"

"*Stuff it!*" Barden shouted the words over her shoulder as she ran to catch up with the rest of the squad. Rally point Kit-Kat was on the north side of the FOB's helipad, looking down on one long leg of the FOB's triangular, rammed-earth wall.

Darkness was falling as the sun dipped below the crest of the tall hills to the west. That way also lay the portal back to Earth, beyond the hills. An ancient dwarven tunnel connected the FOB with the valley the portal sat in. A road slashed across the valley, about a kilometer past the wall of the FOB, heading from the tunnel to Hilltown to the northeast.

Shapes moved in the broken ground to the north of the wall. Arrows zipped over the wall from closer in. Machine gun and M27 fire started up from a couple of the watchtowers along the wall. Tracers lit into the glowing darkness. For the moment, though, the squad was still and quiet, breathing heavily from their run, but otherwise without a mission or a target. The only immediate activity around them were two Ospreys spinning up from idle on the helipad.

"What are we doing here at Kit-Kat, Corporal?" LCpl Jones asked, the shorter woman nudging up against Barden's arm.

"Not sure yet," she muttered, taking a moment to check her gear one more time.

"We're Quick Reaction Force, Lance Corporal," Cale said. He walked toward them across the helipad. The Ospreys' enormous rotors started beating the air as he joined them. He had to shout to be heard now. "There's an attack in strength, moving against the FOB, supported by some kind of siege weaponry we can't place yet."

As he spoke, the squad clustered around him, junior Marines in front squatting down, team leaders Diaz and Lomicka in the back with Barden.

"They've never come at us this hard," Orley said.

Cale nodded. "Just talked to the CO. They're likely after the HVT."

"She's still here?" Cpl Diaz asked.

"Not for long," Cale replied, nodding back over at the Ospreys. "Docs wanted to make sure she was stable before they moved her over to our world. You know how the portal can mess with some people. They wanted to make sure she was one hundred percent."

That made sense to Barden. She'd been sick after crossing

over. LCpl Heath had thrown up for three hours, provoking jeers and heckling from others, until the hecklers all mysteriously ended up camped out in the Transition Base's porta potties.

"What about Marcel?" Barden asked. He had been mostly running her team while she assisted Cale. That was Jones, Orley, and Rashad. Now she had to run the team herself, and still take charge of the squad when Cale wasn't around, or when they had to split.

"Convoy took him back first thing. He'll be Stateside any moment now. When I hear something, you'll hear something."

That was a relief, and a small bit of tension eased in the group.

Cale glanced around the squad once, then looked back to the north.

"So, we hold the fort, make sure the Ospreys get out, then push back these chumps. As QRF, it's our job to move around to backstop any of the main defense points if they're getting hammered, got it?" Nods all around. "Good. Check weapons, check ammo, and spread the fuck out already."

Barden motioned for her team to follow her, and they shuffled west along the edge of the asphalt helipad. She put Rashad closest to the middle and Orley out at the far end.

Diaz's team was next to hers, Lomicka's on the far end. Cale prowled around behind them, waiting. Another cloud of arrows whined through the air as they settled in, and more skipped off the helipad.

The sound of the Ospreys' engines pitched up and Barden glanced behind her. Lady Wíela, or whoever she really was, walked between two intel officers up the back ramp of one of the birds. At a glance, she looked the same as she had when they'd first picked her up out in the woods, walking with an ethereal grace, wrapped in a dark cloak. Barden shook her head. So much bullshit for one VIP. Always seemed to work out that way.

Barden looked down to the wall again as more fire opened up from the Marines in the towers. Bursts of tracer fire converged here and there in the broken fields between them and the road. No one was trying to reach out beyond it, just yet. The Ospreys buttoned up and lurched into the air with a sudden ferocity that swept the squad with wind and grit, so they hunkered down. A storm of arrows greeted the Ospreys' flight, all of them falling short of the mark, but singing to the ground among the squad.

Ten meters or so to Barden's left, LCpl Jones shook her head. "I don't even know how they can get them things so far. What's the max effective range on a longbow? Three, four hundred meters? And they gotta know an arrow won't do shit against a plane."

Barden smiled to herself. Jones always focused on the engineering details, which meant that some days she could just not wrap her mind around the rules of this place. Even in the middle of a firefight.

Barden glanced left and saw Cale crouched down with Rashad. She crept a little closer to them, making sure she hadn't overlooked something with Rashad. Cale seemed to have taken the young Marine on as a project, more than she had seen him do before with any other boot.

"Get your sling clipped around this way, Private," Cale was saying. "That way it doesn't hang you up when you go to change magazines. Got it, son?"

"Yes, Staff Sergeant."

"Good man," Cale said and clapped him on the shoulder, then moved off toward Diaz's team. The Ospreys hovered higher now, a few hundred meters up, and slowly tilted forward. If they kept to pattern, they would fly north along the valley to turn around the far northern edge of the ridge, then back southwest along the adjacent valley to get to the portal. Up and down over the hills tended to be too steep of an approach to the portal, so they would have to go around. Why they hadn't sent actual helicopters, which didn't mind the steep approaches so much, she wasn't sure.

A fireball burst out of a cloud overhead. It cracked and burned as it fell toward them, and then splashed in the middle of the helipad. Molten asphalt shot up and out and the squad ate dirt. Barden felt it rain down, pattering and sizzling on her back. She picked her head up to see another blast of flame lick along the walls.

"Dragons!" LCpl Shane shouted, her voice oscillating between a scream and a squeak.

A shadow had passed over them after the explosion and risen once more toward the clouds. Barden's blood chilled. The last of the sun's light faded, and the night was only beaten back as far as the base's lights could push it.

Another shadow fell from the clouds and turned toward them.

"Jones!" Barden cried, turning to her left. But Jones was already moving. Like they had drilled, she flipped onto her back and pointed her M27 IAR skyward. Orley rushed over to her, flopping down beside her, and helped prop the weapon up with two hands; exactly like his own in every detail except for the bulky hundred-round magazine slung under it. As soon as he did, she fired, staccato six-round bursts clawing into the sky, not quite straight up, but aimed north just a hair so the rounds would fall outside the FOB's walls if they didn't get their target.

The first several bursts did not. Then high above, the dark shape coalesced out of the gloaming and Jones's rounds found their mark, sparking off the thick dragon hide. Three bursts on target, like they drilled, then Jones and Orley rolled away. Barden got up and hustled after them, pausing only to grab Rashad by the arm and pull him along. The other two teams had deployed the same way when the first fireball struck, and now they moved as a squad downhill toward the burning remains of one of the towers.

Doc Dooley ran ahead of them, her big medical kit bouncing on her back as she raced for the burning tower. A blast of fire raked the ground behind them, and everyone dropped. The gunners rolled on their backs again, assistants propping them up, and tracers sliced up into the dark sky. More sparks exploded like fireworks, and a chilling shriek of pain echoed off the walls. The squad rolled to their feet again and ran down toward the perimeter.

Just before they got there, fire lanced through the sky. It wasn't aimed at the ground anymore, but something in the air.

"They're attacking the Ospreys!" someone yelled, and Barden couldn't tell who amidst the rest of the shouts and general din. Machine gun fire spit out from the bellies of the big tilt rotors, but then they saw fire engulf an engine and the ungainly Osprey tipped toward the ground.

The other one circled back to pepper the dragon with machine gun fire, but then it too was engulfed in flames. Both Ospreys spiraled toward the ground, then plowed into the ridge to the northeast.

Finally, it seemed, the LAAD gunners got their shit together and opened up on the dragon. But maybe only twenty seconds or so had passed from the first fireball hitting the ground to the Ospreys going down. And the anti-aircraft guys had to make sure they weren't shooting at the friendlies.

When they did open up, though, it took Barden's breath away. Two sets of paired .50-cal machine guns opened up from the backs of the Humvees they were mounted on. The guns thudded rounds out at the cyclic rate, chewing into the sky and raking across the wounded dragon. Then, with a hiss and a roar, two, three, four AIM-9X Sidewinder missiles leapt out of their launchers.

Barden laughed a little, in joy and relief, as she watched the missiles streak through the darkened sky, twisting and adjusting to track the dragon. Three found their target in rapid succession, explosions rocking the dragon and sending it tumbling out of the sky away to the northwest.

"Barden!" Cale was shouting and she looked back at him. "Get on the berm and call for fire!"

The dragons were just one part of the attack. There were still forces outside on the ground.

"Aye aye!" She scrambled the rest of the way down to the big rammed-earth wall. Inner steps had been carved in the hard-packed dirt here and there, and she hustled up one set of them, not far from where a guard tower still burned. Unpleasant smells of every variety washed over her from the blaze and she fought to keep her breakfast down. Flopping on her belly on the top of the wall didn't help much.

Her team followed her up and dropped down on either side of her. Jones headed right for a M240G medium machine gun that had been abandoned by the wall defense, and opened up at once. Orley and Rashad followed, sending tracer fire licking out into the dark, dead space ahead of them. Arrows whistled out of the darkness in return, but each time an archer stood, concentrated fire met them.

Barden dialed up the fire support channel on her personal radio and pressed a hand to her right ear.

"Grond, Grond, this is Longshanks-One."

"Longshanks-One, this is Grond, go."

"Fire for Effect. Shift target point Paladin, drop one hundred. Danger close. At my command, over."

"Copy, Longshanks-One. FFE, Paladin, minus one buck, danger close, over."

"Fire."

For a moment there was nothing, just a series of hollow thumps in the distance behind them; then the space between the wall and the road lit orange and black like the deeps of Hell. Individual explosions of 60mm mortars blended together into a single thunderous roar. Only ten rounds fell, but it was enough for a moment to turn twilight into daylight, obliterating everything near the wall in a hundred-meter swath.

Marines cheered around them, but then the huge, dark shadow of a hill-troll loomed through the bright orange maelstrom, crushing flames underfoot. Tracers lanced out from all along the northern wall, and Jones went cyclic on the medium machine gun, holding down the trigger until a belt ran dry and Orley fed her another one. The machine gun's barrel glowed cherry red.

"Grond, Longhsanks-One, Repeat!" Barden shouted. She didn't want to see what would happen if a hill-troll made it to the wall.

Or worse, got inside the FOB.

"Repeat, aye."

More hollow thumps, and just as the figure of the huge hill-troll reached the center of the swath of destruction, a new hell rained down on it. High-Explosive rounds pelted a hundred-meter circle and tore the thing to pieces.

Sporadic machine gun and M27 fire continued to reach out into the darkness around the impact zone of the mortars, but soon calls for "check fire" were going up and down the line. The attack had been halted, at least for now.

But with the Ospreys down, Barden had to wonder if it had succeeded, all the same. Those arrows and the troll had been there to keep them occupied. The real attack had been the drag-ons versus Ospreys.

And on that front, the Marines had certainly lost the en-counter.

CHAPTER SIX

THE LULL FELL in a sort of sonic valley after the last mortar round exploded. Into it fell the wet splat of a few pieces of the troll dropping to the ground. Cale grimaced at the sound, but otherwise did not flinch.

Barden had her team up on the wall. Diaz was backing her up, and Lomicka had moved her team to reinforce the north gate, a few hundred meters from Diaz. Cale stood back and up-hill just far enough to see the squad all in one glance.

Fire echoed from the west side of the FOB, but there didn't seem to be much of anything happening here by him just now. In any event, the other positions were not his responsibility, not just yet. He had to stay focused on his area of operations. Running around like a panicky boot outside of his AO was the sort of thing that got people killed.

"Sit tight, Longshanks," he shouted. "Don't take your eye off the ball."

Barden gave him a thumbs-up, as did Lomicka. Diaz seemed to be in his own world, at least for the moment. Probably busy trying to figure out what kind of troll that had been.

Cale shook his head. Some people needed to get their heads

out of the books and into the moment, Diaz most of all. At least Barden didn't bog down in that shit, though she could hold her own with any of them on trivia night.

Shit. He paused as he remembered bumping into her. Had he called her *Barbie* outside the tent? He was going to have to find a moment and apologize. He'd been way too deep in his own world as well.

"Staff Sergeant Cale?" a voice called.

"Ma'am?" he asked, half-turning. Captain Hobbs had approached with her radio operator on her heel and taken position in a fallback hole a few meters uphill of Cale. He trotted back up to her and Dooley followed, keeping her eye out for anything to do. But no one was getting wounded anymore, not around here.

"Everything under control here, Ray?"

"Yeah, yeah, we're good, ma'am. Plugged the gap and got the bad guys down on this side," he said.

"Good. I think we've got the situation handled here. Attack broken, and everyone is roused, finally. Gonna have Second Platoon reinforce this side," she said, and met his gaze squarely with a meaningfully raised eyebrow.

"Which means my people have work to do." It wasn't a guess. He hadn't been working with her long, but he'd gotten a sense for what was plain on her face to be read.

"Yeah," she replied. "You saw the birds go down."

"I did."

"We need to get to them. You're QRF, so it's going to be on you."

Figured. He was going to have to take the squad back out beyond the walls.

"Any vehicles?" The last hump-out had required a lot of running around, and Barden had griped about being restricted to only what they could carry.

"Not that are going to do you any good," Hobbs said, then took a map from her radio operator and laid it out on the sandbag wall.

The map had been pieced together from drone flights, and rumor had it they'd be putting up dirigibles soon, super high-altitude, supposedly out of the range of dragons, to give them more observation, as well as comms and ad hoc GPS coverage. Just not yet, of course.

The map was crude, but better than the Middle Earth map Diaz had pinned up over his bunk. FOB Hammerhand was situated at the south end of a long, wide valley that tapered off to the north into a single line of hills, just under the eaves of the elves' forest. The ridge to their west would have cut them off from the portal were it not for the ancient dwarf tunnel. The ridge to the northeast blocked them from direct access to the forest, and made for a roundabout trip toward the nearest village, Hilltown.

"We spotted the Ospreys down here." She tapped her finger halfway up one of the northeastern ridges. "Good news is they came down pretty close to each other. Bad news is it's pretty rough country, and the Humvees we still have won't get up there."

"Fantastic." Cale sighed. "What do we do if we find anyone alive up there?"

"If they're ambulatory, extract them," she said. "But I don't have high hopes. Stretcher cases, get Doc to stabilize them as best she can and we'll try to ring up some casevac in the morning. If you need to fortify, call home and we'll launch another squad to your pos so you can dig in properly, maybe bring an extra corpsman or two out to help Dooley."

Cale hated to ask the next question: "And if none of the above?"

"Stack the bodies and mark the spot, then get your butts back here. Slag any crypto on the Ospreys that survived, and bring back dog tags."

Cale looked down at the map, not showing anything on his face but thinking that this was a cold business, sometimes. "Alright, ma'am, we'll get it done."

"One more thing, Ray," she said, and her voice hardened just a fraction.

"Ma'am?"

"Lady Wíela."

"What about her?"

"If she's alive, we need her back. If she's dead, you need to make sure. If she's wounded and Doc can't stabilize her, or you plain old can't get her back here, put a bullet in her."

Cale's eyes widened. "Ma'am?"

"Don't make me say it again," she said, eyes hardening a little more. He knew that look, he'd used it himself. Eyebrows as a shield against one's own misgivings. "She comes back here, with you, or she doesn't leave that ridge alive."

"Alright, ma'am." Cale took a deep breath and resolved to do it himself if necessary. No sense passing that kind of shit any farther down the chain than it needed to go. "What's the story with her? We got fuck-all in terms of background when we went out to walk her in."

And if they were being asked to kill her, that was some next-level espionage shit. Spy stuff, not Marine stuff.

Hobbs sighed and rubbed the back of her neck, between her helmet and the collar of her flak jacket. "Word from On High is that Wíela is a Big Deal with the wood elves. Word is, if she's playing for the right team, we can swing the balance of the whole war. But on the wrong team. . . ."

"Fuck if I haven't heard that before." Cale shook his head. Afghanistan and Iraq, both. Warlord—or king of this group of magical creatures—it was the same thinking.

"I know, Ray. But we're going to need to do something. If the Corrupted One up in the north subverts them, then we could lose control of this portal altogether. And that could make Central Park a really exciting place to be, more than it is now."

No one in New York liked having their prestige green space turned into a fortified military base and staging area for trips through the portal. But if they lost this side, the fortification and build-up would only get more intense on the other side. Out of necessity.

Some politicians were already promising that this portal would become yet another gateway to America, that it would make New York a port city in a whole new way. But that depended utterly on what happened on this side in the war. For now, everyone holding a weapon on this side knew the foothold was still tenuous.

"Alright, ma'am, we'll get it done."

"I know it's a shit sandwich, Ray. But I wouldn't be asking you to eat it—"

"—if I didn't know how to get it done, I know, ma'am. Your confidence in me is the warm blanket I sleep under every night."

Captain Hobbs slapped the top of his helmet as she stood. "Nice try, Ray. I'm not going to bust you for insubordination just yet."

"Worth a try, ma'am," he said.

"One last thing," she said, before walking away.

"What's that, ma'am?"

"No Tactician's Weave."

"Why not?" Getting tapped with a wand and being able to control the entire platoon with thoughts was, well he didn't want to say magical, but it was at least damned convenient.

"I'm not punishing you. The equipment was blown up in the attack. We lost our arcane tables and incantation stores."

"We'll make do," Cale said. Marines had made do in worse situations. He turned to head back down the hill and gather up his squad. As he headed down, he saw elements of Second Platoon hustling around to the northern wall.

"Hey, Welborn!" he shouted as he saw a familiar face trot past. "Send my squad back this way."

"Aye aye, Staff Sergeant," the junior Marine replied, not breaking stride.

As he waited for the relief to take their place, Cale sat down on the slope of the hill, just a few meters below the fallback position, and faced the northeast gate. All quiet out there right now, but then he'd have to go out in it. Again.

He didn't dread the patrols themselves, just the weird shit they would run across. The trolls that morning hadn't even been the craziest he had seen, and he was only a few months this side of the portal.

The Battle of Manhattan had been one thing, of course. That had been his first real taste of fairy tales coming to life to kill you. The goblin hunt through the sewers of Flatbush had been a thing of nightmares. But there, at least the territory was familiar, solid things he could touch and knew how they worked. This place . . . this place had its own rules, and nothing was familiar. Even out in the countryside, which should have been at least somewhat familiar to his upbringing in Northern Michigan, was stranger than Manhattan had been.

So much stranger.

"School circle!" he shouted as his squad approached. Those who had been meandering slowly toward him picked up the pace a little, and twelve Marines formed a tight semicircle around him, standing a bit downhill so that their heads were level with his as he sat.

"What's the good word, Staff Sergeant?" Barden asked.

"Another exciting opportunity to show the Captain our true fighting spirit and quality," Cale snapped. Barden's eyes widened as she saw that he wasn't too thrilled. Her mouth tightened.

"The very highest," Hassel said in his crap Sean Astin impersonation, completely not reading Cale's mood.

Lomicka smacked him upside the back of his head. Like Barden, she could tell Cale's expression meant something seriously un-fun was coming. As squad leader, she was also looking slightly embarrassed at Hassel's general dumbassery in the moment.

"Ow," Hassel muttered.

"What exactly is the mission, Staff Sergeant?" Lomicka asked, shooting a glare at Hassel.

Hassel would have been a handful on anyone's team, even Cale's. And yet, LCpl Darleen Lomicka knew when to slap him upside the back of the head and when to let it ride, making a somewhat messy Marine come through when it counted.

Hassel had his own reasons for being on this side of the portals, and no one begrudged him those. But he could be a pain in the ass when it came to unit cohesion.

"TRAP mission, Lomicka," Cale replied. Tactical Recovery of Aircraft and Personnel, not that they stood a snowball's chance of actually recovering the aircraft in question, but they could destroy anything useful in them.

"On the Ospreys that went down?" LCpl Diaz asked.

"You got it in one, Diaz. Our friend from this morning was aboard one of those birds, and we need to find her, dead or alive, before anyone else does."

Grumbles sounded around the semicircle. The mission that morning had been a clusterfuck, and their only consolation was that it had been over.

Well, this was the fucking Marines, and they would have to live with it. Just as he had to live with their grumbling. Cale gave it thirty seconds, then slowly scanned the squad, meeting each Marine's gaze one at a time.

"Everyone got that out of their system? Good," he said, not waiting for an actual answer. "One satchel of C4 each, patrol packs, all the ammo you've got, whatever else you think might be actually useful. But keep it light, we've got some rough terrain ahead. Assemble at the northeast gate in fifteen minutes."

With a ragged chorus of "aye aye," the squad hustled off up the hill toward the billowing fabric walls of the hooch. Cale followed at a more leisurely pace, his tent being closer to the northeast gate. His patrol pack was set and ready to go inside. He reached in, grabbed it, and slung it. Then he headed back. Three minutes, maybe, and he was shuffling downhill toward the gate. As he stood there, he heard Second Platoon popping off a couple rounds.

Things weren't all *that* quiet yet. Leaving the FOB might be a little exciting.

With two minutes to spare, the squad came running back, Barden driving them toward the gate from the rear. All twelve fetched up in good order, and Doc Dooley wandered out of whatever shadow she had melted into previously. Navy Corpsmen, Cale figured, had been practitioners of black magic long before any portals opened up.

"Alright, patrol order, let's go. Barden's team, then Lomicka, then Diaz." They sorted themselves out at his order, moving on toward the gate. Rashad was on point, with Barden right behind him, then Jones and Orley. Cale stepped into place behind Orley, and the other teams followed.

When Rashad reached the gate, he sprinted across twenty meters of open ground, then disappeared down a small slope into a narrow draw. Barden followed, almost on his heels.

Machine gun fire lanced out from the towers as they hustled

out the gate, raking the ground ahead of them first, then along either flank. An arrow whistled by from somewhere in the dark. Cale lifted his M27 to his shoulder and fired a quick burst in the direction he figured it had come from.

In less than a minute, the whole squad cleared the gate and advanced northeast down the draw.

FOB Hammerhand perched on a small hill south of the big road running from the tunnel to Hilltown. The draw led them down to the base of the hill and near to the edge of the road, mostly unobserved, though they were still somewhat exposed due north and across the road. Nothing moved in that direction, and no more arrows came at them from out there. Still, Cale felt relief when they came down off the hill and into the broken ground on either side of the road.

Diaz's team rushed ahead then and took up positions on the road while everyone crossed. Once Lomicka indicated she had passed, Diaz gathered up his team and moved to the north side. Strung out in a long file again, they made for the northern ridge and the burning smudge on its slope.

The broken ground proved perfect cover for this kind of stealthy movement, but it forced them to stay closer than Cale would have liked. Still, it wasn't like the bad guys had grenades or mortars, so sticking closer was only marginally more dangerous. Less, in fact, if they counted the threat of stealthy wood elves leaping out from cover to slit throats. But they were all on guard for that, and Cale had never seen more Marines actually wearing the Kevlar gorgets that came with their flak vests. Likewise the so-called "nut plates" that dangled down in the front to cover other sensitive areas.

They covered the distance to the first wreckage in under an hour and without incident. Only when they got close, where they could make out the flames still leaping up off the wreckage, did they see tall and graceful shapes, armed with bows and curved swords, moving back and forth in the firelight.

Cale clicked the talk button on his personal radio and whispered into the mic: "Barden, assault. Lomicka, base of fire. Diaz, watch our six."

"Check." Three whispered answers came at once over his headphones. Barden moved her team out off to the right, a little uphill, while Lomicka got hers settled in just to the left.

Cale fished a folded card out of the slash pocket on his right sleeve and opened it up. Scanning quickly by firelight, he found the right phrase.

"Desist now, for the clan of these fallen warriors comes to claim their bodies and their war gear!" Cale shouted.

The silhouetted elves whipped around, and several immediately put arrows to string to shoot at Cale. Lomicka's team fired as soon as the first arrow flew, and Barden rushed her team forward. Cale dove to the ground, rolled to the side, and came up kneeling, his M27 up and searching for targets. Movement and silhouettes drew bullets.

"Shift left, shift left," Barden called over the radio. Lomicka's team immediately twisted, their concentrated fire sweeping left and down the hill. Cale fired three times in that direction, then stood and hustled toward the wreckage.

Barden stood near the burning fuselage, waving them in. Cale got to her first, and she glanced down toward his crotch.

"Any lower, Staff Sergeant, and you'd be singing Katy Perry tunes at karaoke," she said.

Cale looked down. An arrow had stuck in the Kevlar pad. It waved about as he walked up.

Shane, coming up with Diaz's team, heard her. "Could have been to the knee, Staff Sergeant. Then your adventuring days would be over."

"Shut up and set a perimeter," Cale growled at Shane. He yanked the arrow out and tossed it away. They had serious business here.

He understood the impulse to joke at death; for many of his people, humor was the ultimate blunt weapon. But Cale wasn't in the mood for it. Not when they were going to be sorting through the wreckage for Marines' bodies.

Not when he might have to put a bullet between someone's eyes.

Even if it was an order.

CHAPTER SEVEN

BARDEN GLANCED AT THE EXCHANGE and sighed. When Cale had snapped at Shane, she'd looked as though someone had kicked her puppy, and she'd frozen for a second. The rest of her team pressed on, moving at Cale's terse directions to start inspecting and clearing the wreckage. Barden's own team had taken up positions near the nose of the downed Osprey and Jones looked to be poking at one of the dead elves, maybe to make sure the bogey didn't get up again.

Dooley picked up a fire extinguisher and aimed it at some smoldering bit of wreckage. Automated fire suppression had kept the whole thing from going up in a kerosene blaze, but still bits and pieces flickered with dancing flames.

Barden started downhill a little, toward her team where they clustered at the wrecked nose. A flashlight flickered through the busted windshield, no doubt Cale or Diaz checking on the flight crew. Probably a lost cause, as the Osprey looked like it had been smoked thoroughly by dragon fire outside before getting crushed like a beer can when it dropped.

"Come on, get in a perimeter and stop poking at the elves," Barden told Jones. "They die just like anything else."

"Well, not like *just* anything . . ." Orley muttered from nearby.

"Yeah, yeah, they've gone off to the undying lands, whatever." Barden pointed as she talked and her team moved, taking up their positions. When she looked back up, Shane still looked stricken, though thankfully she had at least taken a knee and was aiming her rifle at . . . the darkness.

"Shane!" The Marine's head snapped around at Barden's call. "Get your combat cam out and get some snaps of the bad guys. Let me know what we got here."

Barden gestured at the elf corpse at her feet. To her credit, Shane snapped out of her funk and hurried downhill.

"Aye, Corporal," Shane said as she got closer, fumbling with one of the pouches on her vest. Thankfully she didn't see the look Diaz gave them both, which said to Barden "better you than me."

Barden stifled a sigh. Between Rashad and Shane, she was starting to become the caretaker for the wayward souls of the squad. Rashad was a boot, but Shane had been in over eighteen months now and still seemed lost at times. She loved her MMORPG games, and someone figured that had made her a good candidate for field intelligence training. But that had only taken her away from the squad while they were doing crucial work-ups for deployment through the rift. Sometimes the lack of unit cohesion showed. Nothing soured a unit on an individual Marine like the impression that they had skated out of essential training, or shared hardship.

That Shane had put in the extra hours to get her Marine Corps Martial Arts Program black belt was lost on . . . just about everyone. Even Cale, it seemed, though he should know the squad top to bottom. Though it could just be that the two of them didn't gel, and that could happen in any unit with any two people. Barden waved her down, and Shane skidded to her knees right next to the corpse of an elf. She had her ruggedized combat camera out and started snapping pictures.

"Wood elf, for sure," Shane said conversationally. Barden knew she was trying to impress her. *Look at me, Corporal!* Barden had rank, and she'd been inside Staff Sergeant's circle of confidence. And that was a damn tough place to get to. "Clan of the High Leith, by the tabard."

Shane tucked the camera away again, glancing once at Barden for her reaction, and tugged a bit at the tabard. It had been pocked with two neat holes from someone's M27. The garment usually hung like a tiny poncho over the elf's torso, with a silvery crest on the front backed in brown to show off clan affiliation. The tabards were not good for much else, especially stopping bullets.

"Good eye," Barden said, and Shane glanced over, working to hide a pleased smile. "You've been studying."

"Not hard, Corporal," Shane muttered. The Marine looked to be fighting down some kind of reaction to handling the dead body, but Barden couldn't blame her. Most Marines wanted nothing to do with the dead up close. They preferred to shoot and scoot. "They have crests and colors, both make them stand out from each other."

"The rest look like this one."

"Sure. So, one clan, at least this group. Not surprising." Shane finished tugging the tabard off the dead elf, then started to fold it neatly.

"What are you doing?"

"Physical intel. Pictures aren't usually enough." She tucked the tabard away in another pouch, and looked up at Barden. "Now, if I could gather up nine more of these, I'd be able to turn them in at Company HQ for some gold and experience."

Barden was about to reply, but Cale loomed up from the darkness behind Shane: "Goddamnit, stop nerding out here. We have work to do. Shane, get up with your team, you're on point up to the other wreck. The Lady Wíela isn't in this one."

Shane nodded and hurried off, struggling to put her camera back away as she ran. Barden got her team up and falling in behind Team Two, with Lomicka and Team Three bringing up the rear. Cale fell in step beside her as they hustled farther up the ridge toward the second wreck.

"A little hard on Shane, Staff Sergeant?"

"Maybe." Cale growled the word out and Barden refrained, just barely, from rolling her eyes. He looked back along the line, likely checking to make sure they were dispersing properly, or just to check to see if anyone was within easy earshot.

"Maybe?" She pushed back at him.

"Maybe." He sighed and rolled his shoulders, hitching his gear up a little, then fumbling to tighten a strap. "Maybe I'm just sick of all the nerd shit. I get that that's why we need them—you—through the rift. They're not as spooked by the elves and dwarves and trolls as the average knucklehead is."

"Just about everyone else was becoming a mental casualty within days of getting here." She nudged him in the upper arm with her elbow. "You and Marines like Heath are the exceptions."

"Not because of our exceptional resilience, I'm sure."

"Then what?"

"Colossal stupidity?" He waved off the words almost as soon as he spoke them, forestalling any response. She looked away and concealed a sigh. Something weighed on him, something he did not want to talk about. She figured it had to do with Wíela, but if he wasn't volunteering anything, dragging it out of him would take longer than they had, and more words than they should probably be speaking while trying to move a patrol up a ridge in the dark with possibly hostile elves around.

"Maintain dispersion," he said when she didn't offer any

other insight, and stretched out his legs to chew up some ground toward the other Osprey. She fell back in line a little, nodding to Jones to keep her team moving.

Drifting back, she let Brust pass her, then Ysbarra, until she fetched up near Lomicka. Hassel came along in the rear. He turned back every ten paces, sighted through his scope on the Osprey they'd left behind them, then hustled up to catch up to the squad. Lomicka walked with one eye over her shoulder to make sure he got back in line each time.

"Any movement?" Barden asked when he trailed a bit longer and had to double-time to catch back up.

"Some, creeping on the downed bird."

"Alright, call it in to Cale."

Hassel nodded and a moment later his voice came to Barden through the air and over the squad radio hooked into her right ear at the same time.

"Six, this is Slack. We've got bogeys moving in on the downed bird."

"Roger that," came Cale's reply. "Light it up."

"Light it up, aye."

On the order, the squad ahead slowed their pace while Hassel swung his rifle around onto his back. Out of a vest pocket he drew a remote detonator that looked a lot like a rather stubby stapler. He flicked a switch on the end, a little light burned red, and he jammed the detonator closed repeatedly with both hands. A second later, the Osprey dissolved in a bright orange ball, ripped apart by scuttling charges and denying the scavenging elves of anything useful, they hoped.

Barden had read that intel suspected some powered beings in this world could work a lot of magic from a scrap of flesh or clothing, or even circuit boards. The bodies of the fallen had been tucked away for safe retrieval later and the scuttling charges would hopefully reduce the rest to uselessness for any magical purposes. They'd probably send some combat engineers out later to scrape up everything they could find anyway, just in case.

Screams and shrieks wafted to them in the wake of the explosive boom, evidence that they had caught some of the scavengers in the blast as well. Hopefully that would knock them back from pursuit, and keep them from coming too close to any of their stuff again.

Not likely, but one could hope.

Before the echoes faded, the squad was moving again, hustling faster up the ridge.

"Contact left!"

Cale heard the initial call over the squad radio, and then its echo traveling down the line. They were strung out along the ridge, two or three meters below its peak. The Osprey smoldered on the broken slope a few hundred meters ahead of the point team and maybe a little downhill. The bird had spiraled down, its tilt-rotors up, as though the pilot had been hoping to make a somewhat controlled vertical landing, rather than plowing it into the flat badlands below. But the effort had been futile, and the big bird lay on its side, wings and rotors mostly smashed, belly pointed downhill, and nose away from their approach.

An arrow whined out of the darkness as Cale hit the dirt, scrabbling for cover behind a rock. He dropped his night-vision goggles down and flipped them on, searching for targets. To his left and right, he heard the muted "clack" of suppressed M27s firing single shots and short bursts downhill. Rather than firing himself, he scanned the slope below them. Movement drew his gaze along their intended path of travel.

"Diaz," he said, tapping his radio button. "Movement. Looks like runners."

"Got it."

Cale kept his eyes on the movement in that direction as more arrows whined through the air and skipped off stone. Three elf-in shapes suddenly jerked, flailing, falling. A fourth ran on for another few paces before imitating the others. Elfin chattering broke out below them, maybe two or three hundred meters away.

He shook his head again at the marvel of the elves being able to shoot bows with any kind of accuracy at that range.

Shapes rose out of the ground to run, either toward or away, but then they went down. The stream of arrows had stopped and the muted check-in of Marines rippled up and down his line.

"Casualty check," he breathed into the mic.

"None."

"Zero."

"Nada."

"Alright, up and move. Diaz, assault through the wreck, let's go." As a squad they scrambled to their feet and Cale quickly found himself the head of a new, shorter column of Marines as Diaz took his team and double-timed across the remaining distance. Cale trotted along and Barden brought her team up on-line with him, spreading out downslope to cover that side of the crashed aircraft.

"Objective secure," Diaz said over the radios.

"Roger that. On my way." He glanced back at Dooley, who had stayed a few meters behind him the whole time, including during his conversation with Barden. With a gesture, the two of them hustled up toward the wreck as Barden and Lomicka took their teams to create a perimeter.

He arrived to find Antoine and Shane working through the wreckage at the rear of the Osprey. They had already found the body of the crew chief and set her aside a few meters back from the wreck.

"Really wish objectives in the real world glowed a little, or had some sparkle effects around them or some shit," Shane said as she tossed aside a busted-off section of jump seats.

"Not a fucking MMO, Shane," Antoine replied.

Thinking of his prior conversation with Barden, Cale bit down on a reply and swallowed it. She was right, as much as he hated to admit it, that he was being too hard on them. They were bitching and bantering like any two Marines would, just . . . in another frame of reference.

"Questing in the real world just sucks sometimes, you know?" Shane tossed a chunk of twisted fuselage skin into the pile with the seats.

Antoine, right by her side, hefted the twisted remains of a 50-cal machine gun and cast it aside. "We need a real quest. An epic journey to set the world in order. Not one of those fetch-and-carry things in your video games."

"Yeah, yeah." Shane grumbled and shook her head. Cale stepped away around the uphill side of the wreck to see Diaz and Heath at work near the cockpit. "I'm happy to gather some lumber, or kill ten orcs, or find someone's lost heirloom. Just don't ask me to walk a thousand miles and chuck a ring in a volcano."

Antoine snorted, and they worked together to lift a twisted section of the tail ramp. Someone found a fire extinguisher and started dousing pockets of burning fuel.

"What is that compared to Hegli's quest to woo the Valkyrie Sigrún, or Sigurd slaying Fafnir?" he asked.

Cale shook his head. Shane had it right, to some extent. Their part was never to be the storybook heroes like that. That was just the reality of life at the grunt level, where they had to do all the little things that combined with other units' little work to make big work. In the real world, taking out a single big threat almost never made that big of a difference to what was happening on the ground. The work was all small and grubby and tedious, when it wasn't life-threatening.

And even sometimes then.

"Corpsman up!" Shane and Antoine shouted, interrupting his musings. "Corpsman up!"

"Here!" Dooley shouted from the other end of the wreckage.

From where he had been listening and doing his own ruminating, Cale trotted back around to the tail of the downed Osprey. Shane looked up at him in surprise as she crouched over the form of Lady Wíela.

Whatever glamour had been on her when they'd first picked her up in the southern woods, down near the Escarpment, had now fallen completely away. In place of the blond magazine model lay a dirty and blotchy elf. A whole elf, happily for them, and Shane took off her gloves and pressed two fingers to Wíela's neck to check for a pulse.

Rather than the impossibly fair beings of the movies, these elves, wood elves at least, had brown and grey mottled skin, which sometimes looked a little like the blue face paint Mel Gibson had worn in *Braveheart*. Her ears were long and pointed, swept back and obvious, and her hair was dark, pulled up in a ponytail. She had a long face and eyes that would blaze violet, if she was anything like the other elves they had encountered.

Dooley rushed in, sliding to her knees beside Shane and pushing her out of the way.

"Trying to make friends?" Dooley asked, not looking up.

"Just checking for a pulse, Doc."

"That's my job, nerd," she said. Her hands moved—quick, precise and confident—assessing heart rate, respiration, checking for bleeding wounds and spinal damage.

"Well, she's alive," Dooley said, looking up at Cale. "But out cold. No idea when she might regain consciousness."

"We don't need her awake, at least not yet. We just need her safe. Safer," Cale replied. He sagged with relief, then straightened again, hoping no one noticed. But a glance toward Shane said she had. "Get some photos of her, Shane, and the rest of the wreck, while you're at it. Maybe the anti-dragon researchers can make something of the damage."

Shane popped to her feet and nodded. "Aye, Staff Sergeant."

Again, her ruggedized camera came out of the pouch on her vest and she started shooting pictures, first of Wíela, then of everything else of interest.

Cale reached over to Antoine and unclipped the collapsible litter that he carried strapped to his patrol pack. He unfolded it with a quick snap, and laid it on the ground beside Wíela. He and Dooley then lifted her limp body onto it, just as Diaz came running up with Heath.

"Any other survivors, Corporal?" he asked, glancing up at Diaz.

"No, Staff Sergeant. We got the pilot and co-pilot out and laid them out away from the wreck. Found another body downhill a bit near Barden's perimeter, probably tossed out in the crash. Looked to be an Air Force officer or something."

"Makes sense. Escort." Cale nodded as he spoke, then sighed. "Where's Hassel?"

"Placing charges now, Staff Sergeant," Diaz said.

"Alright. Antoine and Heath, you've got litter duty to start. We'll step off as soon as Hassel's done."

Orders given, he stepped a few meters away from the wreckage and looked over toward the FOB, now a halogen glow below them and three or four kilometers away.

"Truesilver, Truesilver, this is Longshanks Actual, over," Cale said, holding the main radio handset up to his ear, over the earpiece of his squad radio.

"Go ahead, Longshanks." Hobbs's own voice came crackling over the encrypted channel.

"We are Underhill, over," he said, passing along the name of the first planned operation to pick up Wíela, to indicate they had recovered her.

"Roger that. Get your butts back here. Things are getting squirrelly again. I'll send Stormcrow out to meet you as soon as I can spare them."

"Roger, Truesilver. We're Oscar Mike in two."

Hobbs signed off and Cale started everyone in motion, checking with Hassel to make sure he was ready to blow the second wreck. Cale got a thumbs up, then got the squad into marching order. Barden would take her team back on point with Lomicka's team again in the slack position. Diaz and his team's burden would enjoy the dubious safety of the middle of the line.

As they set off, something rumbled low, growing in intensity. In the distance, the lights of the FOB flickered, then seemed to be obscured in the night by a growing cloud, rising up from the ground.

"Barden, Barden what's going on?" He struggled to keep his voice even over the squad radio, though a disaster seemed obvious. She acknowledged, then the link went silent for a moment. They continued to move downhill, straining ankles over the uneven terrain.

"Hammerhand's been undermined." Barden's voice came over the comms, a minute later. "Some nightmare shit crawling up out of the ground."

"Circle back. Let's hold up and sort this out." He clicked off and growled as the line stuttered to a halt, and the leading and trailing teams curled in toward him.

Cale just stood for a long moment and stared out toward the FOB, seeing shadows and flashes and little else off in the distance. Their beacon of safety, their castle in the wilderness, the FOB burned in the night.

CHAPTER EIGHT

CALE FOUND HIS BINOS and watched the chaos around the base as the others moved in toward him. Unable to watch any more, he shoved his binos into LCpl Shane's hands. "Shane, keep an eye on the FOB."

Shane looked a little shaken and Cale bit his lip. He let too much of his impatience slip, and it didn't help.

Barden, Diaz, and Lomicka gathered around him, and all four of them knelt down.

"The FOB is under attack again," he said, looking each of them in the eye. "Looks like someone was digging under it, collapsed a huge section. We might have to sit tight until they get shit under control. Set up a perim—"

"Cave spiders!" Shane interrupted with a shout. "Jesus!"

"Cave spiders?" Heath asked. "What are those?" Cale glanced his way and saw the young Marine pull what looked like a field guide out of his right cargo pocket and flip through it by penlight. A second glance later and Cale realized that it wasn't an actual field guide, but one that Heath must have put together himself out of a D&D Monster Manual.

"Kill that light," Cale snapped, making Heath jump. "Report, Shane."

"The spiders are all over the base, Staff Sergeant. Looks like our people are bugging out the other side of the walls and falling back to the dwarven tunnel."

Cale swore, then his big radio crackled. The handset for it was clipped to his helmet strap near his right ear; Cale tugged it free.

"*Longshanks, Longshanks, this is Truesilver.*" Captain Hobbs' voice squeaked a little over the radio as something interfered with the signal.

"Longshanks Actual, go ahead, Captain."

"*We're bugging out through the tunnel, Longshanks. How are your people?*"

"Present and accounted for, ma'am."

"Fan-fucking-tastic. A small piece of good news in a shit situation. I've called down some thunder. Adjust them as needed after their first run. They'll be on channel eighteen. If they can pulverize those spiders, we'll try to regroup on the FOB. Your primary role is to protect the package, and we'll link up as soon as these bastards are toast."

"Aye aye, ma'am."

"Good man. Hammerhand out."

Cale clipped the handset back on his helmet strap, then dug the big brick-sized radio out and flipped it over to channel eighteen.

The Marines' hold here was still tenuous enough that a large enough force could—and had, clearly—make them abandon a FOB and boogie back to the portal. Once there, with some reinforcements coming through from the fortress that was Central Park these days, they could hope to retake the FOB again with a larger force. That back-and-forth had already happened at least once with the portal in London.

Cale would have to hope Hobbs could hold the portal long enough for all of Cale's people to get there, too. It was a long hike and they were on the wrong side of the valley, with elves pressing from the north and creepy-crawly monsters tunneling around underneath.

"Hobbs is bugging out, getting our people back to the tunnel at least, and waiting for air support," Cale said to his team leaders. "The FOB looks like it might be lost altogether, though she thinks we can retake it later."

"Shouldn't we be bugging out too, Staff Sergeant?" Diaz asked.

"No," Cale said. "We're going to call in any adjustments on the air support needed to maximize their effectiveness. That's our best chance of retaking the FOB."

Lady Wíela stirred, and Cale glanced over.

"And covering the balance of the company in a retreat," Barden said, acid in her voice.

"That too," Cale replied.

"What about Wíela?" Dooley knelt beside the litter to check her over again as she showed signs of coming to.

"We keep her safe."

The elf propped herself up on her elbows and blinked into the darkness as she looked around. She grimaced, then looked beyond them, off toward the FOB.

"What is . . . have . . . happen to me?" she asked, her broken words slurred.

Barden moved over to their VIP.

"You were shot out of the sky." Barden laid a hand on the elf's arm. "A dragon attacked your flight. We came out to find you, to bring you back."

"Back where?"

"To the base."

Wíela's eyes widened and she looked toward the remains of the FOB. Dirt still churned there as spiders crawled out of the ground and tried to chase down any cut-off troops.

"No, you must run . . . or the worm will kill you all. . . ."

"The worm?" Cale asked.

"The worm will destroy your defenses. Nothing can stand against it. It destroyed my guard, killed my attendants. We were powerless before it."

"Is she talking like sandworms from Arrakis?" LCpl Jones asked from farther downhill, in the dark. "Because that would—"

"Quit eavesdropping and watch the fucking perimeter," Cale snapped.

"Worm is the right word, I think . . ." Wíela said, then slumped back on the stretcher and closed her eyes.

The growing rumble of approaching Warthogs filled the air, the sound a balm to any grunt's soul. It hadn't been twenty-four hours since a flight of them had saved their bacon with those three huge trolls.

"She probably has a TBI," Cale said. Traumatic Brain Injuries were no joke, but they also could render her utterly useless for anything other than being a deadweight.

"Yeah, I dunno about that, Staff Sergeant," Dooley shouted back as she pried Wíela's eyelids open and flashed a penlight at her. "She's not showing any other signs."

"She's talking gibberish." Cale grabbed his binoculars back from Shane to observe the first strike.

"To be fair, between the translation wards laid on us and English not being her first language, anything could get lost on the way to our ears," Dooley pointed out. At least they still had the translation wards at all—unlike Tactician's Weave, those took months to wear off.

The roar of Warthogs rose in pitch and they flashed into the valley, sweeping around the far ridge and bearing down on Hammerhand. Their big chin guns spun up and actinic fire sliced into the churned ground that had been the FOB, lighting it up like day for a moment. Cale could see pieces of giant spiders being tossed into the air.

"Damn." He smiled. Cale keyed the handset to call out to the flight and give them information for the next pass. But before he could even open his mouth, a white streak lanced into the air.

He pulled the binoculars away and looked out into the night. From the opposite ridge, a bright line lanced out again and smashed into the leading 'Hog. Fire bloomed and the plane staggered to the right, reeling like a drunk man.

The pilot tried to correct, but spun the plane into the ground. A bright fireball rose into the air that lit up the ragged ground across from the platoon.

More shrieking lines of light jumped up toward the other three planes. Two jinked away, one took a hit and kept flying, now racing away from the ridge rather than getting ready to circle back for more.

"What the fuck was that?" Heath called out. "Magic missile? Fireball?"

"It's a fucking Stinger," Barden snapped.

Another rocket leapt into the air, but useless now as the Warthogs thundered away, limping back toward the portal.

"How the hell did locals get Stingers?" Lomicka demanded, looking stunned.

"Someone will figure it out later, and there will be fucking hell to pay." Or maybe there wouldn't, Cale thought. The arms industry had been supplying both sides of conflicts since forever. They shouldn't have been surprised that a dealer got over here somehow with Stingers.

That meant soon they'd all be facing orcs with RPGs instead of swords. That stab of light in the dark now meant the entire war would be changing, and fast.

"Right now," Cale continued as the situation clarified itself to him, "our air support is gone and getting the FOB back is not an option."

The whole squad collapsed in around him, most looking out toward the action, but all of them at least glancing in toward him. Looking for leadership.

"What next, Staff Sergeant?" Diaz asked.

Cale glanced at Wíela again. "We can cut straight across the valley, hump it over the far ridge, then down the other side and across several klicks of open ground to the portal."

Which might be held in defense, and might not. On the far side was Central Park and far more than a band of wood elves would want to deal with, but it was all useless to him and his squad if they couldn't get there.

The next-nearest friendly and fortified space was the stone forts along the Escarpment, but he hated the thought of going there. Otherwise, there was FOB Vimes, about five hundred kilometers away to the northeast. Assuming that hadn't fallen as well. But Vimes, it was much deeper into friendly territory.

Much friendlier.

"The Central Park portal is closer," Cale said, looking around at them, every pair of eyes on him now as he made a call. He could only hope it was the right one. "The Captain has enough firepower on her to hold it until we can get there."

"Alright, you heard him. Patrol order," Barden snapped. "Rashad, you take point."

"Aye aye, Corporal," the young PFC said, and stepped out away from the group. The cluster of Marines unspooled downhill. Heath and Antoine snatched up the litter and started hustling down as fast as they dared. Cale fell in just behind them, then looked back over his shoulder.

"Hassel?"

"Yes, Staff Sergeant?"

"Blow the second Osprey."

"Aye aye, Staff Sergeant," he said.

Cale looked back down to the floor of the valley as he heard the remote clicking repeatedly in Hassel's hand. A moment later, the bloom of a fireball leapt up behind them and cast the side of the ridge in daylight for a moment, sending the Marines' shadows running out ahead of them into the night.

CHAPTER NINE

RASHAD PICKED HIS WAY carefully down the ridge and tried not to flinch when the charges went off to obliterate the downed Osprey. He mumbled a quick prayer to Allah for the men and women who had died up there, and hoped fervently not to join them too soon. The valley floor rose to meet him abruptly, leveling out like a tabletop. His feet crunched in the mix of dry scrub and drier sediments.

"Was that a prayer?" LCpl Jones asked from five meters or so behind him.

"Yeah," he muttered, not turning to look back at her. He changed his footing a little, stepping to come down with the whole sole of his foot at once to try and make less noise. He pulled the night-vision goggles down and activated them to pick his way through the dark. "Best I can do in the circumstance."

"Not home anymore, that's for sure."

Someone had told Rashad that Jones was pretty devout, always camped out with the base minister. People like that often meant flack for Rashad, but Jones had been cool.

"Yeah," Rashad agreed.

"Where's home for you?" Jones asked, conversationally, though a little too casually. She'd been curious, but not pushy. He was on her team, and while Corporal Barden had been professionally curious about him, it had been in the way a leader was about knowing who she'd been placed in charge of. And Orley's interest in Rashad had waned when he realized Rashad hadn't smuggled anything interesting through the portal.

"Watford City, North Dakota," Rashad said.

"The fuck?"

"Mom was a geologist. Worked for oil companies. The land out there wasn't all that different than this stuff."

Rashad had spent most of his childhood in Grassy Butte, but that just spawned more jokes than anything else. So, Watford City, where he had gone to high school, got the prime place for his "Where are you from?" answer.

He could almost hear Jones struggling with the "But where are you *really* from?" follow-up.

To her credit, she swallowed it, for the moment.

"But where are you *really* from?" was a complicated question. His mother had been a geologist from Murray, Kentucky, who met Rashad's father, an extraction engineer, while working oil fields in Saudi Arabia. She had told him that was when she'd converted, they married, and gone on the Hajj. When she became pregnant, they decided on the US to raise him. They had moved closer to some of Dad's family in Michigan. But before he was two, Mom quit her job teaching geology and they headed out to North Dakota for the big oil boom there.

Oil, the Midwest, and moving near family. It wasn't much more American than that.

But it was always "where are you *really* from?" because Rashad was mixed race and carried a prayer mat.

He needed to sit down and talk to Diaz some time, based on the stuff Diaz had shared when they were all in Tactician's

Weave. But Diaz was a corporal, leader of another team, and the company high shooter.

Rashad was utterly intimidated by Diaz.

"Rashad." He glanced back. Barden waved him around to the left of his current path. A low hill, maybe only fifteen meters high, rose slowly out of the scrubby valley in the still-flickering light of the distant, burning Osprey, and she wanted him to angle around to the south. He gave her a thumbs-up. With his rifle stock in his shoulder, he swept left and right in a slow arc, trying to pick out all of the natural formations from anything that might be a bad guy.

"So this is like the Badlands?" Jones picked up conversation again.

"A lot like it, yeah. Deposited and eroded sediments all over, thin regolith layers. . . ."

"Now, I thought those were only found in arid climates," she interrupted. "It seems too wet for that around here."

He shrugged. "My mom's the geologist, we should ask her."

"Been reading what I can since we got here. The land here makes no sense," Jones muttered. "Geologically speaking."

"Well, neither do trolls that turn to stone in the sunlight." You had to roll with it a bit.

Rashad swept around the southernmost finger of the hill, which rose right out of the flat ground like a blister. To the south and west, the ground got more broken, undulating here and there with channels. The ridge to the west crept higher as they approached, looking so very steep. He let his gaze wander away from his area of responsibility as he tried to pick out a likely path for scaling it.

"Know why they always put newbies on point?" Jones asked a minute later, a whisper just loud enough for him to hear.

"We're expendable?" Rashad guessed.

She laughed a little. "Nah. You all so jumpy. Hard for the bad guys to get the drop on you."

He liked that explanation, and certainly preferred it to being expendable.

The remains of the FOB lay off to their left now, two or three kilometers away to the south, down in the middle of the valley as it opened wide onto the plain that ran down to the Escarpment. The ground between them and the ridge flattened out and opened up. He felt more exposed, but all the same, a little safer here.

Rashad found a winding route up the ridge behind the FOB that looked promising without being too obvious. He swept left and right to check for movement, but nothing popped up.

Within another couple of minutes, they were at the base of the ridge, and he started up into the narrow cleft he had picked out from on the open ground. It looked a little more daunting close up, but he figured the experience scrambling around Grassy Butte back home had to be worth something. He felt, rather than saw, the marching order shifting around behind him as Barden moved up into Jones's spot and forced the other two members of her team to fall back.

"Good work all around, Rashad." She crunched up behind him in the cleft. "This morning, too."

"Thanks, Corporal." He didn't turn his head, but he appreciated the pep talk. He had to keep one hand free to move up the narrow slot. His other hand gripped his M27, and his eyes didn't move off the next step.

"You've got a good head. You'll do okay as long as you remember the fundamentals."

"Doesn't always feel that way, Corporal," he said in a moment of honesty, thinking back to all the shit he'd been given in the last twenty-four hours.

"Me and Staff Sergeant see it, Rashad, and that's all you have to worry about."

"He seems grumpy with me, for thinking I'll do well, Corporal. And he's constantly showing me what I did wrong."

Rashad had clambered up now almost forty meters above the floor of the valley. He glanced back, first out to see what looked like Ysbarra and Brust in a little defensive position at the bottom of the ridge, and the green-tinged night-vision goggle figures of everyone else working their way up. Their VIP was still on a stretcher being handled slowly up the path by Shane and Antoine. Barden was less than a meter behind him, scanning up the slope with her weapon in one hand, the other steadying herself on the weathered sediment layers.

"That attention he's showing you is practically a date, Private. And Staff Sergeant's always kind of grumpy," Barden said. "As long as I've known him, anyway, and that's been five-plus years."

"Must be hard to tell when he's upset with you, then," Rashad said as he continued to climb. He tried holding his M27 up to his shoulder one-handed, the way Barden was doing, but it made his arm tremble. A new respect for the blond NCO's strength blossomed in him.

"No," Barden said flatly. "It's actually very, very easy to tell when he's pissed at you."

"Copy that, Corporal," Rashad muttered.

They climbed on in relative silence, a few whispers from below drifting up over the light crunch of combat boots on dried and flaky rock strata. Sweating, he pulled himself up and stopped to take a drink from his Camelbak.

"Are we in the middle of the fucking Endless Stair?" Hassel complained from farther back down with his team.

"No, dumbass," Antoine's voice came from behind a boulder. "These aren't stairs, for starters."

"Shut up," Diaz said over the radio, voice level. "Keep discipline."

A hundred meters up, the fissure leveled off more, and the slabs of sediment reared up well over their heads for fifty or so meters. The cleft angled down to meet the crack in the cliff that they had climbed up. Two hands on his weapon, Rashad hustled forward a little faster, crouching down a bit as the ridge crest approached. Soon he'd be able to glimpse the portal, and the way home.

"Careful," Barden whispered behind him.

Rashad nodded, and kept moving forward in a crouch. He scanned the upper reaches of the ridge, but nothing stirred. No one had bothered to get up here, at least not this far north. The Stingers that had chased off the Warthogs had been fired from this ridge, but way down to the south, nearer to the tunnel.

More confident now, he hustled to the crest, which actually reared up from the slope like a parapet wall at this point, the topmost meter or so a single thick layer of compressed and hardened sediment.

Hitting it, Rashad took up a good, low silhouette position. Far off to the southwest, in the center of the wide valley that lay between this ridge and the next one, stood the huge rent in spacetime that had brought them here. Swirling with blue and white energy, crackling at spots with purple lightning, it towered over the plain.

Fires dotted the open ground between the crest and the portal. Huge, hulking shapes moved here and there in the dark. More scuttling and scurrying figures moved among them: dark elves perhaps and orcs, working their way around the gargantuan trolls.

The ground teemed with the enemy, Rashad realized, stunned. He wondered if the rest of the base had gotten through the tunnel and to the portal, or if they'd been trapped. The horror of thinking about everyone he'd just gotten to know at the FOB—outside the squad dying down there—overwhelmed him, and he stood up to get a better view as his rifle drooped by his side.

Sporadic fire started up on the eastern side, and red tracers lit up the darkness as Rashad watched. Some kind of ordered defense remained, but even as he stood there, Rashad could see it diminishing as it collapsed back toward the portal.

Then he tumbled backward, grabbed by a strong hand that yanked on his gear hard enough to make his knees buckle.

"Get down, goddamnit," Barden snarled.

"We're fucked," Rashad mumbled, still in shock. "They've got the portal."

They were utterly cut off from Earth.

CHAPTER TEN

Barden looked up as Lomicka crouched near her and Diaz. Everyone else was strung out down the cleft, where they had the most concealment. Barden thought Lomicka looked a bit frazzled.

"Yeah, we're fucked," Lomicka muttered.

The team leaders were putting their own eyes on the situation, along with Staff Sergeant.

Barden had already gotten her own turn putting eyes on the bad news around the portal.

"Will you quit saying that?" Diaz replied. "It's not good for morale."

"Fifty trolls and an army of dark elves and orcs aren't doing my morale any damn favors," Lomicka said.

"If we're gonna—"

"Shut up, both of you," Cale said, wiggling back from the crest. He handed his binoculars to Barden, who tucked them into the pouch on her vest. After the fifth time he lost them, they had just agreed she would hang on to them all the time. The man was the quintessential Marine in so many ways, but everyone had their weakness, and when it came to keeping track of specialty equipment, Cale still had a little boot in him somewhere—something Barden had discovered, to equal parts amusement and dismay, about nearly every Marine she had run across, no matter how senior.

"Staff Sergeant?" Lomicka scrabbled down after him.

"It looks like the balance of the company made it through to Central Park." Cale brushed off his pants, clearly using the gesture to buy time to think. "But First Division will have their work cut out for them, retaking this side of the portal."

"*If* they take it back," Lomicka replied.

"They have to." Barden shot the junior team leader a sharp glance. "For the same reason we came through in the first place. Controlling the portals from both ends is the only way to guarantee safety for the people at home."

"And keep them from going mad at the sight of trolls stampeding through Manhattan," Diaz said.

"Alright, you bunch of generals. Let's keep our focus local for a minute, okay?" Cale fished about in his right cargo pocket and pulled out a laminated map made from the overhead photos the drones captured. "We're here," he said, and poked a spot on the map marked Greyjoy Ridge. "And the Ospreys crashed over here, on Stark Ridge."

"Why did they name these ridges after people from *Game of Thrones*, anyway?" Lomicka muttered.

Barden answered. "Because they're brutal and bleak."

Cale ruffled the map. "South, we have the Escarpment and Shitsburg. Nothing good comes of heading that way. North is the Elves' Wood, and that's fucked, too. No idea who they're siding with, if anyone. West is super-fucked with the small army encamped over the other side of Greyjoy. East is. . . ."

"Five hundred klicks to FOB Vimes," Barden said, and got a puzzled look from Diaz. "British Army and Royal Marines."

"Ohhh."

"Any luck on comms, Staff Sergeant?" Barden asked.

"No," he said, reaching to his shoulder and fiddling with the long-range radio's handset. The olive-drab box of the JTRS radio on his vest had a stubby little rubberized antenna and a coiled cord to the handset. In theory, it could reach out and talk to any military radio within forty kilometers, which should have easily gotten them in touch with Central Park Command. "They still haven't figured these new radios out. The portals fuck with them too badly. Fine for talking to the FOB or aircraft loitering overhead, but everything else is shit."

Barden knew that as bad as Cale could be about losing his binoculars, he knew radios pretty well, and he had taken to the JTRS when it replaced the old Vietnam-legacy SINCGARS radios. If he thought it was shit, it was almost certainly shit.

"What's our move, then, Staff Sergeant?" Lomicka asked.

"Stay here and ride it out, right?" Diaz piped up. "We got good position, firepower, all that shit."

"But we haven't got much in the way of rations or water," Cale said. "Our ammo is limited, and if we get surrounded, we're completely out of options unless we get rescued. On top of that, we have Lady Wíela with us, and I was expressly ordered not to let her fall into the hands of the enemy. Remind me how sitting here is better?"

"We won't get as tired, Staff Sergeant?" Diaz was hoping to defuse Cale with a bit of humor. Barden wished he'd stop misreading Cale's disposition.

Cale shook his head and looked back down at the map. "To the northeast we're relatively clear. We've got Hilltown out there past Stark Ridge a ways, and then there's Mount Grunt—"

"Did a Marine name that?" Diaz leaned closer to the map.

"No, that's the local name for it," Barden replied.

Cale kept tracing a line to the northeast. "Up here we get FOB Vimes. If we can get up onto Mount Grunt, we might just get enough range on the PRC"—which he pronounced "prick" as every good Marine did since time immemorial—"and maybe raise Vimes, and the Brits can come to our rescue. If we push through, we can hop through the portal to Salisbury Plain and bring the Lady with us in time for high tea."

"Wasn't that a Peter Gabriel song from the eighties?" Lomicka asked, then began to hum a bit of the guitar intro.

"Try seventies." Cale sighed. They were all a little scared and leaning hard on chatter to break the nervousness, Barden realized.

"That's 'Solsbury Hill,' Lomicka," Diaz said. "Totally different place."

Lomicka frowned. "I thought that's where that big portal in the UK was. Solsbury Hill, where the Battle of Badon was fought. King Arthur?"

"No, their portal's on Salisbury Plain, right by Stonehenge. Right, Barb"—Diaz swallowed the last consonant—"den?"

Barden glared daggers at Diaz, while Cale shook his head at Diaz.

Diaz shrank back a bit under dual disapproval. Barden could see that he knew arguing with Cale about hunkering down versus moving out had been a bad idea, and everything he'd said since had only made Staff Sergeant angrier. Now Barden was pissed at him, too.

Lomicka was very clearly not saying or doing anything, her body language suggesting she was just an innocent bystander.

"We're a Marine rifle squad," Cale moved on. Barden wanted to keep glaring at Diaz a moment longer, but they weren't hashing out differences back at the FOB. They were in the field and Cale had rank. It was time to button up and pay attention. "We're in the business of fire and maneuver. And that's what we're going to do. Not sit tight and hope we get rescued in time, not while we have other viable plans."

"Yes, Staff Sergeant," Diaz said, one-hundred percent attentive and nothing but serious.

"Get with your teams and get a count on rations and ammo. Pass the word to conserve water as best we can right now. We're going to step off in twenty minutes. Move over Stark and lay up through the morning on the far side. Looks like we might catch a stream or two on the way to Hilltown, so we can fill canteens and Camelbaks, then keep pushing. Everyone got it?"

"Got it, Staff Sergeant," they said as one. Some things, they didn't need Tactician's Weave for.

"Okay, move."

Barden crawled back over to her team: Jones, Orley, and Rashad, strung out along the top of the ridge with weapons pointed west down at the valley of enemies below. She liked to think of it as a target-rich environment, but one that outnumbered them ten, maybe twenty to one. If they could achieve the fabled "one shot, one kill" for each of them down there, they could fight their way through. But that was a complete and utter fantasy, more so than golden dragons and fair elves and any major first-person shooter ever dropped on a platform.

"Okay, we've got movement in twenty minutes." Barden gathered them in close enough they could all hear her. "How are you all fixed for ammo and food?"

"Two MREs, and five mags," Orley said. "Plus two drums for Jones."

"Two drums of my own, four mags, and three rat-fucked MREs," Jones said.

"Four MREs, I think. And six mags," Rashad said. "Plus some loose rounds in the bottom of my patrol pack, Corporal."

"Fucking boots," Orley muttered.

"We going to assault the portal?" Jones asked.

"I wouldn't be asking you about rations if we were," Barden replied. "Because we'd either be in Central Park by chow time, or we'd wind up troll chow ourselves."

"So, where we going?" Jones asked.

"Back over Stark Ridge and on to Hilltown. Then, if our luck holds and we can beg, borrow, or steal some food there, move on to FOB Vimes and through there to the UK."

"Always wanted to see Stonehenge." Orley grinned.

"You're thinking of Solsbury Hill," Jones said.

Jesus, we need access to Wikipedia, Barden thought.

"Can we really get that far, Corporal?" Rashad fidgeted with his M27, but kept his gaze mostly toward the far valley.

"If we knew the terrain, and didn't have to step too lightly, we could make it in a couple of days, easy," Barden told the young private. "Before you even got *really* hungry. But it'll take us longer, since we need to be careful. Otherwise, there's no reason why we can't."

"Okay, Corporal."

That was the nice thing about boots. They didn't take quite as much convincing as saltier, more jaded Marines. She still needed a lot of convincing herself. She'd been focused on Cale, providing another somber senior leader's face to Diaz's bravado and joking about, and Lomicka's worried questions. Now that she had time to roll the order around in the back of her head, she realized it made her nervous. It was a lot of ground to cover by themselves with no support. They said an army was only as good as its supply chain, and they'd just lost theirs.

A lot could go wrong.

"Why don't we just head for the Escarpment forts, Corporal?" Jones asked.

"Because they're sixty kilometers in the wrong direction. With the FOB gone we don't have radio contact with them." The war out there was far more active. It was a goddamn front, with dragons and mages and trenches and death.

Barden rubbed her face. Fatigue was setting in, but it would be a few hours yet before they could put another ridge between them and the bad guys, and maybe get some shut-eye.

"Any other questions?" she asked.

"Squad, form up," Cale said over the radio. All four of them stiffened up, then began to move.

"Rashad, you've got point," Barden said. "Back the way we came, Private."

"Aye aye, Corporal."

Moving slowly, as much out of exhaustion as effort at stealth, they took their positions. They trudged back toward the narrow cleft that had brought them up the steep sides of the ridge.

Cale moved up and down the line, taking a quick count while Dooley knelt beside the litter and checked on Lady Wíela. When Cale stopped at Dooley she just shrugged, then gave a thumbs-up. Barden did not envy Doc that job.

"Okay," Cale whispered over the radio. "Let's roll."

And they were off into the dark, and a mostly unknown, magical land.

CHAPTER ELEVEN

DAWN BROKE ON THE SQUAD in a small, grassy hollow about a kilometer from the eastern foot of Stark Ridge. They had been there an hour or so, the first round of sleepers crashed out on the ground, curled up in poncho liners and lying tightly together. Barden and Cale took first watch, then woke Diaz and Lomicka an hour after dawn. By midday, they had all gotten at least five or six hours of sleep, and Cale ordered the march to resume.

Rashad took point again, with Jones and Orley behind him. Barden brought up the rear of her team, just ahead of Shane and Antoine, again lugging an unconscious Lady Wíela between them. They had traded off with Dooley and Hassel for the march from the crest of Greyjoy Ridge to their morning halt position, and would probably do so again later in the day.

For now, though, it seemed to Barden they were all in good spirits and chattering behind her about dark elves.

"You think that's what she is?" Antoine asked, shifting his grip on the stretcher and looking down at Lady Wíela.

"I dunno," Shane replied. "Could be. I mean, her skin isn't all black like a drow or anything."

Antoine shook his head. He had been studying for a minor in some sort of folklore degree, Diaz had told Barden. He had wanted to go for a doctorate after grad school, but left school with all that unfinished after the battle of Central Park. "That's just an invention of Gary Gygax and *Dungeons & Dragons*. At best, most of the dark elves of mythology were described as swarthy. She's more like that. And we have to be careful about ascribing that stuff to skin color; it's all mixed up with light and dark imagery that comes out of some mythology that often gets hijacked by more recent colorism. Just because she's a dark-skinned elf, that doesn't mean she's one of the 'dark elves,' see what I'm seeing?"

"Yeah, and I dunno if I would even call that swarthy," Shane said. She glanced back at the unconscious woman over her shoulder. "More like . . . mottled. I think she's an orc."

"The orcs you're thinking of are just Tolkien's invention." Barden could hear frustration in Antoine's voice as he responded. "Nothing at all like the legends that came before. His world was all hand-crafted out of the chaotic literature that came before it. He needed an antithesis to the elves, so he made the orcs. And blamed it on Melkor or Morgoth. The orcs of mythology were nothing of the sort."

"He had to be on to something," Shane disagreed. "Those orcs that came through into Central Park looked pretty familiar. I mean, they were evil enough, just taking out joggers like that with those swords that looked like they came out of *Guild Wars 2*."

"Never played it," Antoine said.

"Look up Nightmare Greatswords when we get back across. You can't judge someone by their weapons, but they looked dark-elf evil, you know?"

"But," Antoine seized on that point, "dark elves weren't any more evil than the light ones were good. They just were supposed to embody different characteristics of nature, you know? Light and dark, sky and ground."

"So, we don't get color-coded lightsabers."

"*Star Wars* got it from the same places Tolkien did. Good and evil being immutable forces." Antoine trudged along. "I just think that dark elves represented something else, in the original mythology. By the time it gets to a big book, and then a movie, it gets simplified."

"It's like any other conflict," Barden said, glancing back at them, then hanging back to come alongside the litter they bore. She was loath to call attention to their burden, since they hadn't complained about *that* for the last two hours, at least. She figured their back-and-forth was to keep their mind off the load. "You have to figure it out on the ground, once you're there, who you can trust and who you can't."

"I just want to be able to trust *someone*," Shane said, glancing back and down at Lady Wíela, still out cold on the litter. "And if not her, then who are we supposed to trust?"

Barden didn't have anything to add to the conversation. She drifted back through the column slowly enough that no one paid attention to her shifting her position until she walked just in front of the pair bringing up the rear.

"You think we'll need to start foraging?" Hassel glanced to either side of their path, no doubt seeing, as she did, nothing but low, rolling hills with vegetation that was barely more than scrub. The squad wound their way among the hills, trying not to climb too much, but also trying to stay relatively close to the road. "That could be bad."

Barden shook her head at the idea of foraging.

Brust shrugged. "Maybe. How far is this Hilltown supposed to be?"

"Hundred kilometers, I guess?"

"We'll probably be alright, I think," he said and shrugged again, then fished in one of the spare magazine pouches on his chest for smokes and a lighter. Cale had been back with them a couple times through the march, but now he was up talking to Doc. Perfect time for a smoke.

"Yeah, I guess. Shouldn't take us a couple days, and we all did the Crucible on one MRE each, right?"

"Fuckin' Hollywood Marine." Brust gave Hassel some side-eye. "You got a whole MRE? At Parris Island we got some Charms, a spoon, and a tube of peanut butter to share per squad."

"Fuck you." Hassel laughed. "And fuck that 'Old Corps' stuff." He sobered for a moment, fingers twanging at the taut sling on his M27. "My older brother, the one who died in the troll attack on Seattle, he went to Parris Island. Said it wasn't any different. Just less hills."

"And more sand fleas." Brust took a long, glorious drag on the cigarette and held the smoke for a moment, then breathed out slowly. The blue-gray curls of smoke whipped away in the breeze. "I'd like to forget about them. That was ages ago."

"How long have you been in?"

"Too long," he said. "Long enough to know it's going to suck marching in strange country on short chow, and long enough to know that one wrong turn could leave us pretty fucked. Almost done with my four." He took another drag on his smoke.

"Why are you here, then? You had to volunteer to come through."

"And you volunteered 'cause your brother bought it, right? Gotta get some?" Brust laughed, though it had a bitter edge. "Life in the rear sucks more than it does in the field sometimes. And I knew a few things about all this"—he waved his arms around—"or thought I did. We really don't know shit about this place, other than what we think we know, and that can be dangerous."

"Strangers in a strange land," Hassel said.

Brust shot him a glance. "*Bible* or Heinlein?"

"Huh? No, I just mean we're strange to them, and this place is strange to us."

Brust sighed. "Never mind."

They spent some time circling around until they settled on complaining about their load-out and what they *would* have taken with them out of the FOB if they'd known everything would have turned to shit.

Barden picked up her pace to catch up to Ysbarra and Lomicka.

". . . .let me get this straight." Ysbarra glanced back at LCpl Lomicka trailing about five meters behind her. "If my folks had drawn up a lease agreement and we had all signed it, then the Corps could be paying me an extra grand a month basic housing allowance?"

"Yeah." Lomicka chewed on the end of her MRE spoon. "You were lucky that way, 'cuz your folks live within fifty miles of Camp Pendleton. If you'd requested command permission to live off-base just before we deployed, then set up the lease deal, you could be drawing BAH the whole time we're out here. Wouldn't have worked, though, if your folks lived in Tennessee or some shit. Too far away to be a legit legal residence while you're stationed at Pendleton."

"That's bullshit. No way."

Lomicka shrugged. "The radio nerd in the COC"—they gave the requisite chuckle as she pronounced the acronym for Company Operation Center—"is a reservist from Missouri. He told me that all reservists have that kind of deal when they get activated. So long as they've got a legit mortgage or lease, they can still draw BAH even though they're deployed. Doesn't matter if you're living in some crappy apartment block in Temecula or Ma and Pa's basement: as long as it's a legit lease, the Corps pays out."

"Fuck. Wish I'd known that before we deployed."

"Those dragons *have* to be armored up like tanks!" Rashad said, and kicked a clump of dirt out of the peaty soil, spraying a small shower of soil and ripped-up grass in front of him.

"No, look, the physics don't work," Jones said, the strain in her voice telling now as the debate ramped up. "Plate armor, it's just a hunk of steel. It can't be that thick on an elder dragon because the damn things make so little sense aerodynamically. Those plates can't possibly be real armor. And if they were armor plate, the AMRAAM missile they fire from the F-35 would chew right through it or slice into the gaps. And yet, they survive the hits. The scales aren't armor."

"I don't know . . ." Rashad said.

"Well, I do, Private," Jones replied, not giving him a chance to counter.

Rashad smiled. He didn't *mean* to get under Jones's skin, but she was so often upset about the world they were in, there was little he could say about it that did not offend her sense of order. He mostly found it fascinating.

"Mom would love to see all this." He said it to himself, but it caught Jones's ear.

"The geologist, right?"

"Yeah."

Jones looked around. "If I was her, this place would drive me nuts. I mean, look back there, back at the ridge."

He glanced back, as instructed.

"That's badlands, right? But aren't badlands supposed to be, like, sunken? In gullies and canyons and stuff?"

"Sure."

"Then what's all this?" Jones gestured around them. "We came down off that ridge onto something like foothills, or a rolling plain. Stark Ridge was over a hundred meters high, and these hills are barely ten. And they been going down toward a plain. How does that make any sense? There should be another ridge, leading *up* to plains, right? Otherwise, where's the other bank of the river that eroded that ridge?"

"Well, maybe it's not like badlands, you know, Lance Corporal?"

"No no no, don't give me that," Jones said. "You said it, and I see it. Layers of sediment deposited on some giant seabed a million years ago, then all dried up, and some rivers come running through, eroding it all down. *Down.* Not up. That wasn't thrust up by seismic anything."

"Yeah, that's why Mom would enjoy it so much," Rashad said. "It would be a mystery for her to solve, something new and cool to discover."

"I suppose so." Jones looked somewhat deflated for a moment.

"I mean, either we're all hallucinating, or we have to accept that this is real." Rashad stomped on the ground. "Feels real, feels solid. And if it's real, then we need to figure out how it works, like all those physicists are trying to do with the portals, to see if we can open and close them at will and use them to travel to the stars. Assuming we're not there already."

Rashad looked up. The sky was still blue and clear, but night would come eventually and show them, again, the wonder of a completely strange and alien starscape.

"Alright, Neil deGrasse Tyson," Barden snapped at them. "You made your point. Keep your eyes forward."

But Rashad spotted something in the far-off distance. He stopped and pulled out his field glasses.

"What is it?" Barden asked, startling Rashad. He hadn't realized she'd moved up so close next to him.

It was hard to tell even through the binoculars; there was a lot of landscape in the way. "Ruins," Rashad guessed.

They were supposed to stay away from anything that might get them noticed until they reached Hilltown. But Cale had told him to be on the lookout. And with the way Cale rode his ass, Rashad didn't want to get yelled at later for leading the squad right up to something Cale wasn't expecting.

Barden squinted into the distance. She clearly wasn't even seeing the interruption in the edge of the horizon. But she trusted him enough to halt the squad and call for Cale. All the conversations died out around them.

CHAPTER TWELVE

CALE HUSTLED UP ALONG the line to PFC Rashad. The young Marine knelt in the lee of a very small hill that looked out over a wide plain. Cale dropped to a knee beside him.

They'd been trudging their way around, far from any roads, over hills and badlands and scrub, for half the day. Heath and Hassel had been given Lady Wiela's litter and they were pretty fresh. They'd all be faster if she would wake up and walk on her own damn feet. The squad had started to mostly fall silent, except from the usual chatter of youngest Marines.

The sun was getting much lower behind them and Cale wanted to find shelter before full dark came on. He could smell the rain in the air, and hated the idea of being caught in the open.

The wind started to whip up out of the south.

"Whaddaya got, son?" Cale asked, coming up to the point man.

"Ruins, Staff Sergeant."

Cale had to use the binoculars to make out a crumbling pile of stone, vaguely arrayed in a square shape, with the remains of towers on the corners. It was all tumbledown and hopelessly old, but what had survived this long appeared to be pretty stout.

"Barden?" he asked.

"The lee of the wall would be enough protection against this building storm," she said, looking up at the distant clouds.

"Yeah," Cale agreed. "I like our chances better with some stone around us."

"Agreed." Barden looked weary, Cale thought, but cautiously optimistic. They were making decisions that could have an impact on whether they made it through all this, and they both had the time to dwell on it. This wasn't like combat, where you had to make a snap decision and ride it. Doubt had time to creep in.

"Alright, take us in, but tread carefully. No telling who might have had the same idea." At least it was far from any of the roads on the map.

"Aye aye, Staff Sergeant."

They started the careful trudge toward the horizon.

The wall and castle looked to be the remnants of some ancient fortress or fortified town, but there was fuck-all to show for it at this point. Whatever had been here, apart from this, had sunken into the grassy turf. Nothing left but an idyllic meadow and some crumbling stone. Heath, now on point because Cale wanted someone with a bit more experience and some fresh eyes, brought them into the shadow of it quickly and carefully, just as the rain started to patter down.

"Barden," Cale called back along the line. "Recon the structure."

She grunted an acknowledgment, then trotted forward with her team. They ducked through a gap in the nearest wall. She stepped back out seven tense minutes later and waved him forward.

"Not much shelter up here." She jerked a thumb at the interior of the castle, calling attention to the lack of roof, and the water gathering and cascading down through the collapsed towers. "But Rashad found a cellar entrance of some kind. Seems dry enough down there."

"Alright, it'll do," Cale said, relieved. "Let's get some shut-eye in the dry, and move on when the rain eases."

"Roger that."

Rashad had marked the entrance to the cellar with a green ChemLight, giving it a bit of an eerie glow as they approached. He guided the squad down, pausing with Doc Dooley to strap Lady Wíela to the litter. The way into the cellar was steep and unforgiving, and the last thing they needed was to drop her on her neck after all their trouble to keep her safe.

"Lomicka, your team has first watch at the stairs," Cale said as they settled into the dim underground space.

The cellar was wide and dry, with a little pile of debris in one corner. A couple of flashlights came out, as well as two more chemlights. Barden walked over to a dark arch on the far side of the space, waved her flashlight around into the gloom beyond, then retreated.

The rain drummed hard on the stone floor over their heads.

"Not a bad find by the kid," Barden nodded over at Rashad, who was finding a place to sit down with Orley and Jones.

"He's doing okay," Cale allowed.

Everyone settled in on the dry, hard floor and started in on weapon maintenance. Somewhere, water dripped and echoed around the walls, somehow sounding louder than the rain beating down outside.

"He thinks you're riding him, Staff Sergeant," Barden said, using her flashlight to look over the parts she'd quickly and smoothly pulled apart and set on cloth in front of her.

"You know as well as anyone I'm not riding him," Cale said. "*You* think I'm giving him special treatment?"

"You're focused on him enough that Lomicka and Diaz are starting to pick up on it." Barden blew out some dirt. "I told them you're an equal-opportunity asshole of a Staff Sergeant, and they believe me. For now. But . . . what's going on, sir? He's on my team. I've been putting this off as long as I can, but we're out in the shit and it's starting to bug me."

Cale realized she'd see through any denial. He paused.

"The 'Stan," he finally said. "There was a kid. A whole family. Back when they were shifting to more community-oriented policing. Get to know the locals, help them out. Wrong people found out how friendly we were."

"Shit. I'm sorry."

Cale resumed cleaning and ignored that. "Rashad looked like this kid's brother. Not just because he was another brown kid, but, in the way that you run into someone and the way they hold themselves, talk, just remind you of someone? It fucked me up a little."

"You talk to anyone?" Barden asked, sounding way too casual. Cale could tell there was concern behind it, though.

"I don't want anyone here getting hurt, Barden," Cale said wearily. "But, if I don't make sure Rashad's up to speed and something happens to him, it'll stick to me. That's all it is."

"But have you talked to someone, sir?" Barden finished re-assembling and sat with her rifle on her lap, looking directly at him.

"I'm talking to you," Cale said. "And if this is jamming him up, I'll back off. It'll be on you."

Barden's lips tightened. "He's one of my team. It's always been on me."

Cale saw right then that part of this was some pride. He was stepping all over her and micromanaging things, wasn't he?

"Okay, Corporal," he said. "It's on you."

He felt a little odd sharing it, and even stranger handing it over to Barden. But, even stranger, he felt like he'd shucked a vest.

Cale hugged his M27 against his chest, and leaned back against the wall. Lady Wíela lay on her litter beside him, with Doc hunched against the wall on the opposite side. Some Marines grabbed a little snack, others started going through their patrol packs for the first time since leaving the FOB hours before.

He should order them to sleep. They'd covered twenty-five or so kilometers of nasty terrain, but some of the younger Marines were all keyed up, whispering to each other as they re-sorted and re-packed everything. The last forty-eight hours had been intense.

But that was the job. Days and days of utter boredom followed by moments of sheer terror, and often a lot of sweaty hiking while keeping an eye out for someone who might, but not necessarily, want to kill you.

Cale started to doze, nodding a bit, when a prickling cold sensation made him shiver. It felt like ice water had run down his back, but when he shifted, he realized he was dry.

A green flicker near the arch on the other side of the cellar caught his eye. At first Cale dismissed it as someone cracking a new chemlight. Then he opened his eyes all the way as a whisper of voices broke out into shouts.

Cale clutched at his M27 as the green glow oozed out of the void toward them with what he instinctively felt had to be menacing intent.

"Everybody up!" He twisted around onto one knee, and brought his weapon up to his shoulder.

Lady Wíela surprised them all by sitting up, looking at the green light, and shouting in an alien tongue. The terror in it made Cale's stomach shrivel. She'd been calm when staring down the prospect of getting smashed into toothpaste by trolls, but whatever that green light was freaked her the hell out.

Shots popped off into the green-tinted darkness.

"What the fuck is it?" Heath shouted across the cellar.

"*Wights*!" Orley replied from closer to the arch. "More coming down the stairs."

An animated skeleton shambled into Cale's line of sight, looking both more fake and more horribly real than any Harryhausen flick. Shots peppered it and he saw the thing's femur shatter, but it kept moving, undeterred. The pieces of a broken arm swung a rusted sword, the green, glowing power that held the undead remains together utterly unfazed by the squad's bullets.

"Out, out, everyone out!" Cale shouted. "Lomicka, secure topside!"

"Why did you bring me here?" Wíela shouted.

"Doc! Get her out of here!" Cale got to his feet and moved two steps forward, closing toward two new shambling wights that had now gotten within ten meters of the nearest Marine.

"Keep back!" Orley shouted. "Don't let them touch you!"

"Why not?" Jones shouted back.

"Fuck if I know, it just seems like a bad idea." Orley lit off a quick three-round burst, then scampered up the stairs. Just as his feet disappeared from view: "*Damnit*! I dropped my pack!"

Sure enough, two or three patrol packs were on the ground, now close to the feet of the advancing wights.

"No time. Move." Cale fired another three rounds at the wights, then just snarled and hurried toward the stairs.

He and Jones were left at the bottom as the wights advanced. Jones scampered up, pausing halfway to fire a burst from her automatic rifle. Cale followed as she did, then they both ran up into the pouring rain.

As they cleared the steps, the heavy wooden door slammed down on the opening and the green glow oozed out around the edges of the planks. Cale stared for a second, then looked over at Heath, who had clearly just dropped it back in place.

They all backed away, weapons aimed at it.

"Staff Sergeant!"

Cale whipped his head and weapon around as one, looking for the threat, but instead all he saw was Lady Wíela stalking off into the rainy darkness. Doc paced along beside her, trying to get the woman to stop moving, but not having much luck.

"Oh, *now* she fucking walks," Jones muttered.

Diaz, who had called him, was trying to form some kind of perimeter around Wíela with his team.

"Barden, take rearguard, make sure that shit doesn't follow us." Cale snapped the order off, then trotted after Wíela. "And don't stop moving!"

Her acknowledgment was lost in the thrum of the rain, but he saw her moving her team. He hurried up and caught the robed figure of Lady Wíela—elf, orc, whatever—just as she crossed the crumbled boundary of the broken keep. He put a hand on her shoulder, but she shrugged it off with a strength that didn't seem possible to Cale.

"Are you trying to rend my soul from my body?" she hissed. "Can't you tell this place is cursed just by its very nature?"

She didn't look back at him, just spat as she stalked through the rain. The hood of her robe was in tatters from the various ordeals of the past few days, and did nothing to ward off the wet. He was pleased to see she was getting just as drenched as he was.

"It seemed like a cozy place to hole up for the night."

"Your ignorance is deadly. It was a mistake to seek you people out. I should have just delivered myself to the Corrupted One's forces and been done with it."

"Now hold up," Cale shouted at her. "We're not just blundering about in the dark because we *like* it. If you would share some of your knowledge with us, we might have a fighting chance here."

"You have no chance. You are too far out of your depth."

"*You* came to *us*."

"You don't even know what I am facing. How will you even know to help? You're a peon, muscle, no more."

"Then tell us how to help." Cale wanted to shout at her, to dig deep into that drill-instructor voice he was all too good at dragging from his chest. But this wasn't some private first class that needed the stupid scoured out of them with some good yelling and the judicious assignment of shitty working parties. So, he kept his voice calm, cool, and professional. Cale the fucking diplomat.

"There is no point. You are too in love with your ignorance. You'll all die out here from general stupidity."

This was going nowhere. Cale stopped walking for a beat or two and let her carry on. Doc stopped with him.

"What do you want to do?" Dooley asked as they started walking again, a few paces behind her. Diaz had assembled some rough formation in front of Wiela, but for the moment, all he was doing was keeping pace.

"Keep walking," Cale said, and turned to step backward a few paces. Two, four, six, eight. All accounted for, though Orley was dragging ass enough to be mistaken for a shambling wight in MARPAT camouflage. "She's at least headed in the right fucking direction, as of now. We'll see if we can nudge her onto the correct path, assuming we can find it ourselves. Maybe she'll even help us when she cools down."

"And if she doesn't cool down?"

"We'll blow up that culvert when we come to it," Cale muttered.

But he couldn't deny that she had spooked him a bit. She was local. She knew the ground. She had to know why enough trolls had shown up to send a whole FOB scurrying back through a portal.

It dawned on Cale that the entire attack on their base had been for her, and that they were now de facto bodyguards for a player important enough to prompt that level of response.

If so, he didn't want to imagine what else might track his squad down.

Cale suspected it might end up being a hell of a lot scarier than just some shambling skeletons surrounded by green light.

CHAPTER THIRTEEN

BARDEN WAS STARTING to rethink her preference for preparation as she shifted her pack to better sit on her hips. All the gear seemed to be getting heavier and heavier. They had been on the move almost two full days now—one night of little rest once they had crossed Stark Ridge, then a day across the plains to the ruined fort. Then another incomplete night of sleep, followed by a hard march toward Hilltown, hearts still hammering from their escape from the wights.

There were no breaks; they were keeping pace with the elfin figure of Lady Wíela.

And Barden could tell, as the sun hung high overhead and beat down on them, that by late afternoon they were all well past exhausted. She knew that because the Marines had stopped chattering.

She ignored blisters, ignored that metallic taste in the back of her throat, and focused on step after step while trying to keep situational awareness. This was basic training, doing the ruck march, covering your afternoon's twenty klicks with a full load.

The Romans did thirty, and she knew Cale would tell them that fact if anyone complained. And if anyone complained,

Barden also had a lecture loaded and ready to go: An army marched. Troops marched. It was just what they did.

"We should talk water, Corporal." Dooley paced alongside Barden in the bright sunlight.

Rashad was on point, now, and Lady Wíela had graciously allowed herself to fall back into the middle of the squad order. Dooley had started the day pacing along beside her, making sure their VIP wasn't going to fall over again, but a few hours of that had gotten tiresome and the red-headed corpsman quickened her pace to join Barden's team.

"My Camelbak is about empty," Barden said. "I told Orley and Rashad to keep an eye out for water. The grass has gotten a lot greener."

"Doesn't mean too much, though," Jones said. "Could just mean it gets shit on a lot."

"Well, then it has something in common with Marines," Barden said, then glanced over at Dooley, a bit mortified. She didn't let slip things like that, unless she was drunk.

Dooley rolled her eyes. "Don't worry, Corporal. I won't tell Cale you have a sense of humor."

It wasn't that. Barden just had to keep a certain level of Cale-like hard-ass going in order to be taken seriously, and then some more. Most of the men assumed she'd studied folklore history and mythology to get a promotion and a team. And she'd caught several of them trying to explain some seriously basic-ass squad tactics to her. Sure, screaming "there's a *Corporal* in front of my name, *boot!*" put them on the right path.

But no one did that shit to Cale.

"Eventually we have to run into water somewhere," Barden said.

"We can keep walking maybe two days once we run out," Dooley said.

As much water as had been falling on them back at the Haunted Ruins—which was what everyone was calling the place, complete with audible capital letters—they hadn't been able to catch much of it, or find any pooled usefully anywhere.

When Lady Wíela finally agreed to stop for the night, deeming a section of a rocky meadow to be safe enough, Barden collapsed gratefully to the ground with the rest of her team.

It had been a long time since Basic, and the interrupted sleep the night before had left her feeling off her game.

Barden sipped sparingly at the water, and accepted a mint from Jones, who conversationally complained, "I'm missing my shea butter. It's right next to the cot where I left it, and now I'm already getting ashy as fuck."

"Hold on." Barden dug around in her pack, and came up with a small tin of off-brand moisturizer.

"Goddamn, Corporal, you really do carry *everything* when you head out."

By the next midday, canteens and Camelbaks were dry and Barden noticed that her Marines looked flushed.

Cale directed them back south of the road where the land sloped down a bit, hoping to find a river valley or something. But it turned into just more of the gently rolling plains, undulating barely enough to keep them from getting a good look around. Trees and hills, and even the hint of mountains, loomed in the distance, but that was about as good as it got.

Barden didn't like that they had lost track of the road. They had been heading generally northeast, and they could kind of pick out their general position from the overhead photo-maps, but they were already skirting the edges of those maps, and landmarks had gotten really hard to come by since leaving the Haunted Ruins. They could go another day or maybe two as Doc said, on really limited water rations. Then they would have to spend at least a day trying to figure out how make water vapor condense usefully for them to extract survival amounts of it.

And Barden was worried that they might be getting farther from Hilltown, rather than closer.

"Corporal!" Rashad shouted. "I hear water!"

"Where?" Jones asked. "There's no streambed around here."

Rashad trotted forward, up a long, shallow rise. He reached the top, then beckoned to the rest of the squad and headed down the other side. Barden hustled, trying to catch up with him, and she could hear the rest of the squad coming up behind. A glance back revealed even Lady Wíela was double-timing as much as her dignity would allow.

"Oh yes, there's water here!"

Barden ran smack into the back of her team, who'd stopped and bunched together like a bunch of dumb boots. But the automatic reprimand died on her lips, and she felt the rest of the squad pile up behind her, as they all stared down the gentle slope at the scene.

A glade spread out before them, with slender and supple trees that swayed gently in the softest of breezes. Magenta and yellow flowers dotted the grass around the glade, peeking from between vibrant green blades, looking as if they could advertise lawn products. The very air seemed to have a pastel hue to it, so soft and pleasant it made the sunshine earlier seem harsh and scorching, though it had been much like any pleasant summer day. Glittering sparkles that reminded Barden of iridescent insects flashed in the light and weaved through the air.

The water that Rashad had heard came from a burbling

spring framed by a small, natural cairn. The water tumbled gracefully down into the glade, first forming a narrow stream, then spreading into a wide, shallow pool, surrounded by the thickest patches of white lilies and lilacs.

And nymphs.

There were at least a half dozen naked nymphs that frolicked in the pool, cooing and singing to the beautiful air.

"Holy shit, they're naked as porn stars," Orley said. "Only better."

They were beauty itself, sublime and transcendent, somehow both beyond mere sex and yet embodying it.

Rashad stood still, transfixed, and the squad started to stumble around him, their thirst forgotten in the wonder of the glade. Barden hooked her arm in under Rashad's shoulder and dragged him along toward the pool. She inhaled lilac perfume, so gentle and inviting.

Diaz shed his gear at the edge of the pool and waded in, maybe twenty meters from the nymphs who, having caught sight of them all, giggled and beckoned them on.

"This isn't right." Heath stood, rooted in place, just a few meters from the edge of the pool. His whole body strained against something, concentration writ across his face. His M27 was up on his shoulder and he had it pointed somewhat in the direction of the nymphs as sweat started to drip down his chin. Barden reached up as she and Rashad approached, and made sure the weapon's selector switch had been flipped to SAFE.

Dooley now pushed past Diaz, wading up to her waist in the pool. The susurrus of nymph voices and dancing lights in the air weaved all around them, drawing them all closer. It even finally broke Heath, who dropped his weapon to dangle on the sling. He took a jerking step forward.

"It's. Fucking. Beautiful."

The metallic taste of thirst had faded. All Barden could think about was—

—the bleating of a herd of sheep eviscerated Barden's newly found serenity. Just as Dooley reached out for one of the closest nymphs, who studied her with a sudden, deep interest, a shaggy shepherd waved a long crook through the air at the pool.

"*Fria ga surika ka fria!*" the shepherd shouted.

He swung his long crook in another arc, smacking one of the nymphs on her bare bottom. Shrieking, she sprang out of the water and traipsed off along the stream, then vanished into the pastel air.

"What's he saying?" Barden shouted. "I can't understand him!"

"Should I engage?" Diaz asked.

"He's saying: get back, damn you!" Lady Wíela shook herself. "Those are nymphs!"

The man was hairy, nearly as wide as he was tall, but clearly packing very little fat on his stout frame. Beard and hair were unkempt, and Barden felt sure if he smiled there would be gaps in his teeth wide enough to march through. He wore a dark woolen vest that seemed to blend with the hair on his chest, shoulders, and arms, and his leather pants were well-worn and shiny. A huge brass cowbell dangled from a strap around his neck.

"He says get the fuck out of the water!" Lady Wíela shouted.

Barden looked around as the fog behind her eyes faded. "Why can't we understand him?"

"It's the Midlands dialect," Lady Wíela said, annoyed. "Even with your translation spells, he's barely intelligible. I can hardly understand the man myself."

The shepherd jabbed his crook through the air again, scattering the rest of the nymphs, who all evaporated into the sparkly air. The shepherd swung irritably at a few of the sparks, too, and they hustled away from him.

Dooley had just stopped, waist deep in the water, arms outstretched, until the spell she was under faded into personal horror as she started to look around and shake her head. She was hardly alone, though. Lady Wíela, whom Barden assumed should have known about this sort of thing, had been right behind her, until she'd stopped to translate, and half the squad were behind the two of them.

"The flowers . . ." Brust sobbed, on his knees, hands on his head.

Some of the hundred or so sheep in the flock had splashed across the little stream and now were on the near side, munching at the numinous flowers scattered through the glade. Other sheep were head down, drinking from the stream and pool contentedly and bleating happily.

"The damn flowers will grow back tomorrow," Lady Wíela translated for the shepherd wading through his flock to approach the squad. "You all should be careful, messing around with magical springs and the spirits of the waters."

Cale, who'd been bringing up the rear, looked a bit dazed. He'd escaped the indignity of running into the pool, but he was pulling his gear back on, somehow giving off a rueful air with his slow and deliberate movements. "Magical springs?"

"You need to make a lot of noise before you come in the glade, to startle them off." The Lady continued to translate as the shepherd spoke. He lifted the bell around his neck and gave it a couple swings, the harsh clanging drowning out the bleating of the sheep for a moment. "Otherwise, you end up addled."

Dooley splashed back up out of the pool, soaked from the chest down.

"Hey, Doc," Barden started, and got the sort of glare that could kill goats from a hundred meters. "The water okay to drink after all that?"

Dooley woodenly nodded. "Just add the tablets."

"Okay, fill your canteens." Barden shook herself off and glanced around at the rest of the Marines, who seemed to be slowly coming back to themselves. It was time to give them something to do and focus on. "Let's go!"

Rashad filled his own canteens and Camelbak, then helped others to do the same. Jones tried to deadlift Brust off his knees, but was struggling.

The shepherd still eyed them all suspiciously as Barden walked over to him and held out her hand.

"We're Americans." She didn't bother saying which ones, if, as Cale had told her he suspected, with other forces out looking for them, there was no reason to advertise.

"He says he's never heard of them," Lady Wíela said. "But, these are dark times and he hears tell all manner of foreign folk traveling about. And evil armies descend upon the land like locusts. He says someone just stole his grandmother's favorite robe from her clothesline last night. He's using a lot of profanity to indicate that they are animals."

The old man shook his head sadly, as if he'd never seen such horrors in all his life.

Barden smiled at the shepherd a little and looked around. "It's lucky that we happened across this place. We've been days without seeing any fresh water. We weren't sure if we would find any more between here and Hilltown."

The shepherd cocked his head, bushy beard and all, as Lady Wíela spoke to him.

"No bad luck then, you're on the right track," Lady Wíela said. "Cross three or four more regular streams, all running next to each other, between here and Hilltown. Can't miss, he says."

Jones gave up on trying to get Brust to his feet and just pushed him down on his face in the remains of some glittering lilac blossoms. "Rivers don't work like that. They don't run parallel. Find me a map on Earth where there are three rivers running parallel, Corporal, and I'll give you everything in my savings account when we get home."

She turned to the shepherd, fixing him with a skeptical eye. Behind her, Brust groaned and struggled to stand.

The shepherd spread his arms and glanced to the sky. Lady Wíela said, as he babbled on, "Do you know a fellow by the name of Araulo?"

"No," Barden said.

The shepherd narrowed his eyes after being told the answer, then nodded.

"He says if you're heading to Hilltown, he can show you the best ways of it." Lady Wíela wrung her cloak out. "He's taking his sheep to market."

"We'd really appreciate that," Cale said, coming forward to shake his hand.

As Barden went to fill up on water herself, she heard Jones mutter: "It's not even the right season for taking sheep to market."

"So, you're a farmer now, Jones?" Orley asked.

"No, just educated," Jones snapped back.

Barden put a stop to the disagreement by ordering Jones to double-check that everyone had put their water purification tablets in their canteens or Camelbaks.

After the sheep ate and drank their fill, the shepherd shouted at them to move on. A bedraggled sheepdog meandered out of the hill to snap at the sheep, and soon the squad was sidestepping sheep droppings as they hiked up out of the now muddied, sheep-trampled glade.

They followed the herd and its shepherd up and out into the land beyond. To Jones's disgust, the sheep eventually forded four shallow rivers, splashing across merrily as the laconic dog urged them on.

At one of numerous stops, where the shepherd pulled out a pipe and sat there smoking what to Barden seemed like a suspiciously calming substance with a sweet smell, he would chatter at them.

Sometimes Lady Wíela would translate. Most of the time she just ignored the shepherd.

She'd been even grumpier than usual since the glade. Barden assumed it was because the great Lady, who seemed to have come from some sort of royalty, thought that getting trapped by the nymphs, in similar fashion to the squad, had been a slight to her station.

After a night around the shepherd's fire and some sleep, they approached the foothills and spotted the smoke fires and tips of chimneys of a small town nestled in the clefts ahead.

"That Hilltown?" Jones asked the shepherd.

"It's near hills," someone added.

The hairy man babbled on for a moment at them and waved at the land around them, leaving no one the wiser as to the answer.

"It's an outlying village," Lady Wíela snapped, and stalked on by. "Hilltown is not much farther ahead. Clearly. You can see the smoke from its fires just over there. If you cared to look."

Wíela's disagreeable nature only intensified from there.

Barden tried to drop back, but Cale motioned her to leave her team and remain next to him and Lady Wíela. He wanted Barden to know everything he did. Or maybe he just wanted someone else to share in Lady Wíela's annoyance.

"I *had* hoped, with the help of your people, to change a great injustice," she said, apparently edging toward giving them the information she'd been holding close to her chest up until now. "But if my people were attacking your base, then the die has been cast. It's too late for you to help me. I should leave."

The squad wasn't strung out cleanly anymore; they were all tired, and they had started to take on the now-unmistakable odor of sheep shit. Tagging along with the shepherd, or drover, or whatever he was, had not been without its drawbacks.

Cale kept trying to argue with the Lady, and that was fine with Barden. He had command. This was his shit duty, not hers. "While we're on our feet, at least, nothing is out of our reach."

Ooh-rah! Barden thought, half with a smile, and half seriously. Sometimes it was both at once, wasn't it?

"You are all dead men walking with a huge target on you. I need to see my kingdom returned to rights, and it's not going to happen battling through the countryside with a bunch of losers and . . . nerds."

She had learned that word from *someone*, and in her tone, gave it twice the insult it ever implied.

For a while they focused on getting up a steep dirt road into the little village in the gap ahead. The shepherd sent the bleating mess of livestock scurrying toward a pen at the edge of town, and Cale's own herd shuffled off through the village.

"Yeah, not a town. Definitely a village," Orley said. There couldn't have been more than fifty buildings clutching to what little dirt remained on the cut in the land.

Evening was creeping along, and they were all tired and hungry. Barden could smell meat sizzling away, the scent heavy on the wind. Her mouth watered.

"You know, we're tougher and better than you think," Cale said to Wíela as they passed through the gate among a crowd of Marines, starting his argument up again. "We got you out of that wreck, after all, didn't we? That's what we can do when motivated."

"So, that was your best," Lady Wíela said flatly. She appeared to mull that over as they walked through the village, while a few people in cloaks looked at them with curiosity. A few faces peeked out from behind shutters that slammed shut when Marines looked back up at them.

Lady Wíela shimmered, and her face twisted in front of Barden's eyes. Before anyone could react, she drifted aside through the gap between Antoine and Shane. And just like that, she was gone, blended instantly with the tiny village's crowd.

"Fuck," Cale muttered.

At least half of them had seen Wíela slip away, but no one could agree which way she went.

The Marines paused halfway through the village, trying to find her, but it quickly became obvious she was gone. After ten fruitless minutes, a clearly annoyed Cale called the search off.

"Too much attention," he growled, pointing at the villagers staring at them. "Let's get to Hilltown and regroup."

"Regroup," Barden knew, being Cale code for "figure out what the hell to do next."

CHAPTER FOURTEEN

GODDAMNIT if Cale wasn't tired.

They all were.

Now their VIP had run off.

His orders were to get her back to the portal and to the US. He hadn't been able to do that. His alternative orders were to put a bullet in her so that the opposition couldn't get access to her.

He definitely had failed to do that.

But at least they'd found Hilltown.

Cale twisted his foot in the umpteenth gopher hole since leaving the village behind them two hours before and stifled a curse, again. They were all staggering through the pock-marked landscape where grass grew long enough to make it all look deceptively even.

Behind enemy lines and low on food, with potential hostiles in the countryside looking for both his Marines and Lady Wíela, no doubt.

First things first.

Cale had ordered his Marines to skirt around Hilltown. They'd crossed a northbound dirt track out of the town, then sludged around between there and the northeast road that ran parallel to the Escarpment and off toward FOB Vimes. So now Cale called a halt at the base of the hill he had spotted from their last stop. A clear position, with line of sight to the town.

"Whatever chow you can all divvy up, and water, clean weapons," he said, shucking his daypack and laying it in the grass with satisfaction. "Leaders recon to the top of the hill, let's go."

Dropping the fifteen pounds in the pack made him feel lighter, so the climb up the hill wasn't quite entirely torture. Barden moved up beside him, while Diaz and Lomicka fell in behind them. Short of the crest of the hill, they dropped down to the ground and crawled four abreast to the very top.

"Alright," Cale said. "Tell me what you see. Lomicka."

Hilltown sprawled out below them, accessed by the northbound road on their right, and the one going northeast to their left. Directly across the town from them, the southwest road ran down eventually to what was left of FOB Hammerhand, the tunnel, and the portal home to Central Park.

"Gates across the road, but no towers," Lomicka said. She lay propped on her elbows, small collapsible binoculars pressed to her eyes. "Ditch filled with brambles, looks like maybe they can, or have, flooded it in the past. Short hedge above the ditch, but no fortifications."

"Good." Cale shifted, annoyed at a stick worrying at his inner thigh. "Diaz?"

"Two market areas, one on each of the big roads going into the town on the northeast and southwest. Public square almost directly in front of us. Lot of residences clustered in the southeast corner, by the look of the clotheslines and such. Bell tower, some ropes off behind it."

"Well spotted." He nudged Barden with his elbow. "How about you?"

"Two guards at the near gate, I think we can assume two at

each of the others. Two at the big building on the east side of the square, that's got to be a local government building. At least two more on foot patrol in the town. There's three paths through the brambles, which look to connect to cutouts in the hedges, so avoiding them shouldn't be too hard, if we feel we need to." She dropped her chin onto her fists, stacked one on top of the other in the grass to keep her head up just enough to see.

Cale took another glance over the town. Something poked at the back of his brain like a stone in his boot, but he was too tired and hungry to figure out exactly what it was. He had seen all the same things his people had, even before his team leaders mentioned them.

He drew out the map and spread it in front of them, putting the sector that showed Hilltown right in front of him.

"Good reads. Looks like the map-makers highlighted the government building for us, right where you said it was." He nodded in Barden's direction, and she shrugged up one shoulder in acknowledgment.

He reached into the slash pocket on his right sleeve and drew out his notepad and pen, flipped the pad open, and jotted down some of those observations. Then he looked behind him, estimating the distance the sun had to go to the horizon—not far enough—and flipped back through the notepad.

"Okay, intel suggests that the open markets down there wrap up business just after sundown. Gives us about two hours." He glanced down the line, each face turned toward him, but their gazes strayed back to the town, tracking movement. "Diaz, go get your team together and recon those paths through the ditch. Use the most promising one to get up into the market and see what you can buy."

"What should I use for currency, Staff Sergeant?"

"These." Cale dug into one of his pouches and came up with a roll of gold dollar coins. He passed it off to Barden, who passed it on to Diaz. "S-3 says they're good to go in town here for limited trades. Don't go trying to buy a house or nothing, but ten to twenty of those coins should be able to get us some provisions."

"What will I be looking for?" Diaz shifted and tucked the paper roll of coins into a pocket.

Barden jumped in with the answer, saving Cale the trouble. "Stuff that will travel well. Salted meat, dry bread or biscuits, that kind of thing. Nothing with too much moisture. Jerky, dried fruit, good shit like that."

Truth was, Cale just hoped for anything. But travel food would be good too.

"Got that?" Cale asked, and Diaz nodded. "Good. Get a move on now. I'll take Doc, Lomicka, and her team down to the ditch to wait in case you have trouble in town. Barden will sit up here on overwatch with her team."

Diaz slithered back from the top of the hill, then turned and hustled down the backside.

"I'd like a taller vantage than this, Staff Sergeant." Barden glanced left and right, as if hoping to find a taller hill just popping up out of the grass.

"Yeah, and I'd like a bunch of drones, the rest of Second Platoon, and a couple of seven-ton trucks, but this is what we got, Corporal."

"Aye, Staff Sergeant."

Cale looked down the hill at the rest of the Marines and thought for a moment. "I want Rashad to head down to market with Diaz. I'll leave you Shane for now to make up for it."

"Can I ask why, Staff Sergeant?" Barden's grip on her binoculars tightened and she pressed them hard to her face as she resumed scanning the town below. Cale clenched his jaw. He'd had far more of a heart-to-heart about Rashad with Barden then he'd wanted. He could tell she suspected this decision had some-thing to do with that. Cale didn't like getting second-guessed, but he saw where she was coming from.

"He's talented," Cale explained. "I see him defuse problems, even if he is just a boot and causing his own share of them half the time."

Really, though, it was instinct about who to give what respon-sibilities to more than anything, though that had gone wrong for him at least once or twice since this clusterfuck kicked off.

Barden shook her head. "Not 'Why Rashad,' Staff Sergeant. But why pull Shane? She's our intel specialist. Shouldn't she be down there in the mix and not left behind?"

"Maybe." Cale looked down the hill. The truth? He didn't want to voice his concern that a woman on the foray into town might cause problems. S-3 hadn't really gotten a read on gender relations or politics in the town, only noting at this point that all of the dignitaries they had met with on previous trips had been men. On a normal patrol with FOB in place and support easy to call in, he wouldn't have been worried. But this afternoon? "Shane's carrying a lot of valuable intel on her, and we have no way of copying it or securing it. We need to make sure that stuff makes it back to the rear."

"Makes sense," Barden said.

Cale had the gut feeling that she didn't believe him for a sec-ond. Bad decisions and shit decisions: his choice.

"Good. I'll let her know. Who do you want up here with you?"

"Send me Shane, if she's going to stay behind, Staff Sergeant. If she's not going down into the town, I want her up here to observe, maybe snap some pictures."

"Keep your eyes peeled and radio if anything changes."

"Roger that."

Cale slithered back himself and moved down the hill. Diaz's team was ready to move, though Shane looked like her puppy had been kicked to the moon, disappointed at missing a chance to go into town and get a close look around.

Rashad, to his credit, wasn't kicking up any fuss about being separated from his team, just moved quickly and joined Diaz as Shane sulked her way up the hill past Cale on his way down.

Right before Diaz and his team headed off, Cale announced that Antoine and Brust would swap, too. Brust was the most senior first-term Marine in the squad. He had almost lost rank twice and would never pick up corporal, but he was tough, and had some street smarts about him. Better to have him charging around the medieval town on the other side of a portal in hostile ground if Diaz needed help.

Antoine looked similarly disappointed to be left out.

Too fucking bad.

Cale felt better about the make-up of the teams now.

Lomicka lead her modified team off thirty seconds behind Diaz, following in that team's single-file footsteps until they reached the edge of the ditch. The lane that Diaz chose through the ditch and hedge started at a relatively sheltered spot. A couple of trees grew up to cast some shade and give them a hint of concealment.

Nothing much appeared to happen beyond the path, not even sheep grazing or anything like that. A nice way for them to fade their way into the town.

Satisfied with the position, Cale let Lomicka set up to cover and secure Diaz's exit and took a shady spot for himself near the base of one of the trees. From there, he could keep both the hedge and the road in view with a single glance.

Cale watched as the town swallowed Diaz and his team.

Once they had supplies, he could think about what to do

next. Track down the Lady Wíela, or focus on getting his people back to a base.

Rashad grunted as Diaz announced "Boot on point" as they regrouped on the far side of the hedge. Of course. He moved up among the team to where the gap in the deceptively thick growth deposited them in a tight little alley between two stone walls, with an even narrower gap ahead of them that led into the street.

Though the walls looked ancient, Rashad could imagine some bickering or "neighborly" squabble that had inspired two people to wall off their yards on their own, rather than building a common wall together. Twice as much effort and no discernible purpose, but it gave them the opening the team needed to slip into town unobserved.

He wondered if it might have been better to go through the main gates and skip worrying that they might not be welcome once spotted, but Cale was experienced, and no doubt knew what he was doing.

Rashad crouch-walked along the narrow alley, then turned sideways to ease himself through the gap at the end. Heath muttered a curse behind him as he slipped through behind Rashad. They took up positions crouching on either side of the opening, watching. The area they were in seemed quiet, and no foot traffic passed across the opening between the two stone houses on either side of them.

They straightened up at the very corner, and Rashad peered around. First to his left, toward the northeast gate, then to the right and the center of town. He glanced back in and nodded at Diaz, who then moved up to stand beside him. Despite the thumbs-up from Rashad, Diaz did his own inspection of their immediate area, then nodded to the other Marines.

"Okay, sling weapons and let's go for a nonthreatening look." Diaz unclamped his helmet and hung it by the strap from a magazine pouch on his waist.

Rashad and the others followed suit, and Rashad ran a gloved hand through his hair. Such a greasy mess, and getting way too long, at least by infantry Marine standards, which meant it was approaching two whole inches in length on top.

They stepped out two by two and headed down to the market. The deserted street gave way to a slowly growing crowd as they got closer to the actual vendors, then a moderate throng milling about the various stalls and blankets laid out on the cobblestones. Voices shouted back and forth in the local tongue, which the translation spells set on them months ago still delivered to them in their chosen language. If Rashad concentrated hard, he could make the translation come out in Arabic, but that tended to cause him headaches.

"Salted beef?" Diaz held out a fistful of coins. "Bread?"

No one would sell to them. They'd just stare for a moment, then slowly shake their heads.

"Is it language?" Diaz shook the coins. "Or am I just doing this wrong?"

Rashad's mother could talk a used car salesman into buying a heater in the middle of summer. Looking at the grim faces at the market here, he shook his head. "I think they understand us, Corporal. I just don't think they're going to sell us anything."

After one quick and fruitless circuit of the market to confirm, Diaz gestured them toward the front of one of the buildings facing on the plaza.

"Let's step inside the tavern and regroup for a sec," he whispered when they were all close. "Something's wrong. I wasn't expecting this to be the PX, but Jesus."

"Radio in and figure out what the hell is going on?" Rashad asked. Diaz shot him a look, and Rashad understood. Who wanted to be the one to have to admit to the Staff Sergeant that they couldn't get a basic task done?

"What *is* going on?" Heath asked as they stepped into the cool and dim interior of the tavern. The crowd inside was a middle-of-a-workday modest gathering. Not a lot of people with time to drink while there was hay to be made, or something.

"Fuck if I know." Brust ran his fingers through his own ragged hair. His pushed regulation lengths in garrison, with access to a barber, and he was starting to look absolutely shaggy.

"Maybe we stink too bad," Diaz said. "Like any week in the field, we lose sight of how rank we are after about three days."

"The shepherd didn't help," Rashad observed.

"Has it been a week yet?" Heath asked. He surreptitiously raised an arm and sniffed.

"Getting close." Rashad fidgeted with his weapon and glanced around. Everyone inside was doing that thing where they tried hard to look over at them by the door while also trying to act is if they weren't. "But I don't think that's it. They all looked wary. Almost like they didn't want to be seen talking to us."

"Yeah, I saw that." Diaz said.

"You gonna radio in, Corporal?" Heath asked.

Diaz nodded, and Rashad could see annoyance radiating off him. The corporal wanted to prove himself, show Cale he could handle a detached mission like this on his own. None of them wanted to go back to the squad empty-handed. But, short of theft, good choices were scarce.

"Yeah, alright—" Diaz got as far as reaching up to squeeze the talk button clipped to his chest when the tavern door burst open and everything went to shit almost faster than Rashad could process it. Four really, really big farmhand-looking men with boulders for hands rushed them as they hollered incoherent insults.

"Pig mother in your ear!"

"Hardscrabble garlic wind!"

Some things, the translation spells did not do very well at.

"Diaz?" Rashad wanted to ask how to respond. But the men coming at them weren't armed, and so he knew the answer.

A proportional response to the threat.

Rashad side-stepped one and kicked him in the back of the knee as he went by, and the incoherent tough guy stumbled to the tavern floor. Heath jammed one in the gut with the butt of his rifle, and another got a punch in on Diaz, square in the chest, then yelped back with a squeal and broken fingers, thanks to the ceramic strike plate.

Diaz staggered back though, not at all immune to the momentum, and another of the goons rushed him. Brust jumped on that guy's back, trying to drag him down, but got dragged along instead.

Pandemonium ensued. Others rushed in, coming in either from outside or from among the tavern patrons, Rashad couldn't tell. He swung the butt of his rifle around like he'd been taught in boot camp. Several went down, but he got kicked and punched for his efforts. Most of them got him in the body armor, a pain for any attacker, but the intensity of the fight still took its toll.

The only thing that really saved Rashad from a serious beating was Heath at his back and the close press of locals. It kept anyone on either side of the brawl from really being able to wind up and land a proper blow.

Glass broke and excited shouts worked their way up from the back of the mob. They melted away like teens at a busted keg party, leaving the Marines battered and swaying on their feet in the middle of the tavern's common room.

And facing four town guards in shiny armor with drawn swords.

CHAPTER FIFTEEN

BARDEN PRESSED the field glasses tighter to her face, shifting this way and that, trying to spot faces and clothing on the bodies streaming out of the front door of the tavern. Nothing. No Marines, just a lot of chaos.

Not good.

The exodus from the tavern wrapped up after what seemed to her like a thousand people had rushed out into the market plaza, but still no Marines.

Sunlight glinted off the polished armor of a town guard exiting the tavern. And then another. Behind them, Diaz's team filed out and fell in smartly behind the two guards.

Two more guards exited the tavern with drawn swords, and they all stepped off.

"Fuck," she muttered, then let one hand drop from her field glasses to key the mic on her radio. "Cale, this is Overwatch."

"Go, Overwatch."

"I think Corporal Diaz and his team just got busted."

"Fuck."

"My sentiments exactly. They're being marched southeast toward the center of town."

"Alright. We're through the hedge but we popped into someone's back yard or something. We're split up on either side of a wall right now, trying to get into the street."

"Roger that."

"No chance that was just an escort?"

"Diaz would have radioed if they had acquired an honor guard."

"Yeah." Cale's voice sounded heavy, even through the radio channel.

A quite deliberate twig snapped behind Barden, and then a soft, almost melodious baritone in an accent that did not belong to anyone she knew said, "That is no honor guard, and your people are in quite a bit of danger."

Barden twisted around from prone to her back in an instant. Her right hand went to her hip where she had an M17 handgun holstered. She drew it and flicked off the safety in one motion to draw a quick bead on the man standing just below the crest of the hill, maybe just a *fucking meter* or so from the soles of her boots.

"Who the fuck are you?"

"A friend, to you and your people." The man raised his hands to show he was unarmed. He did wear a sword at his belt and she spotted at least two "hidden" knives peeping from under his travel-stained clothing.

Shane, by this point, had finally gotten swung around with her rifle, after getting tangled up in the sling trying to whip around like Barden had.

At least Shane was paying attention.

"Jones! Orley! Where the fuck is my rear security?" Barden looked down the hill, past the sudden stranger, for the rest of her team, fearing the worst, but kept her sidearm pointed firmly in his direction and her finger tensed on the trigger.

Two startled squawks from farther down the hill gave her an answer. The visitor had evidently snuck past them, which was some relief. She had worried for a second that they were dead, and she eased the pressure on the trigger ever so slightly. He probably didn't mean harm to them, then.

Probably.

"Do not blame your soldiers—"

"Marines," Barden said, and cursed the reflex.

"—but few there are in any realm or land who can mark me when I mean to go undetected."

"Fantastic." A creeper, *and* an arrogant one at that. "What do you know about what's happened to our people down there?"

"Hilltown is not the friendly oasis you might hope for it to be in these days."

"Our commanders visited a month ago and met with the town elders, said it was a potential safe haven at need." She lowered her weapon a fraction, then glanced over at Shane. If he had wanted them dead, so the cliché went, they already would have been. As much as it annoyed her. But now that she could see him, well, she thought her chances against a sword were pretty good. "Scope our people."

Shane nodded and rolled back over, taking her weapon off the interloper.

"Your leaders were not deceived," the stranger said, and took a half-step closer, leaning forward with his forearm against his knee. The muzzle of her sidearm remained close to his face, but Barden didn't move it, just yet. "But the good people of this town were suborned, perhaps by servants of the Dark Lord himself. They were turned against you, not from fickleness or greed, but fear of what evil those servants might bring."

His accent wavered all over the place, and that was distracting enough. Piercing blue eyes and a smell like he'd been in the field for a year were also distracting, albeit for entirely different reasons.

She dug her heels in and scooted a little farther from him, trying to slide sideways a bit on the crest of the hill.

"Yeah, okay, that's cool and all. But who the hell are you?"

With a laugh, he dropped down and folded himself into a neat little lotus position, his sword angled out behind him.

"I am a friend, of course. I am known to your forces along the Escarpment, and among many of your camps." He smiled and threw his head back, shaking greasy, lank locks of hair. "You may call me Peridot, as others of your ilk do. I am a Ranger."

He let that hang in the air for a moment, and Barden just greeted the silence with a shrug.

"That means nothing to you?" Peridot looked just *slightly* wounded.

"Nope."

"So, my renown has not spread quite as far as I had feared, then," he mused. "Perhaps this is for the best."

Barden finally lowered her weapon, though she didn't holster it or safe it yet. "What are you doing here?"

"Trying to help. I had heard the land tell tales of your flight from the disaster near the Silvene Forest, and hoped to aid you in your quest. You are traveling with the Lady Wíela. I would lend my sword to you, if your quest is to protect the True Silvene Heir."

Barden jerked her head back toward the town. "Our quest? We need to know more about this danger our people are in, for starters. But I think Cale would love to talk to you about Wíela. She took off on us."

"Cale?"

"He's in charge—"

"Corporal, they got them to the town square," Shane interrupted. "They're putting the whole team in the stocks. But there's a gibbet next to them that looks like it gets a lot of use."

"Cale won't be letting any of our Marines hang from a gibbet," Barden said.

And neither would she, that was for damn sure.

Damn it, Peridot had disappeared from sight in the moment she'd just slightly turned back to Shane and the town. Barden grabbed her mic to update everyone about the situation in Hilltown.

And about their mysterious new guest Ranger.

"This *sucks*." Rashad lifted his head for the tenth time and hit himself with the thick wood plank clamped down over his wrists and neck.

"Shut up, boot." Brust, next to him, squirmed in the wooden bonds.

"Shut up, both of you." Diaz stooped over next to Brust, with Heath on the other side of him.

"What are we going to do?" Heath's voice edged high and a little twitchy, even as he struggled to keep it even. Heath seemed to be having a worse day than Rashad.

"Sit tight and chill," Diaz said through gritted teeth. "Corporal Barden saw us, no doubt, and Staff Sergeant is going to be making some plans. He's not going to leave us here all day."

But after an hour, Rashad had his doubts. The sun beat down on them and the half-bent position they had been standing in to stay in the stocks killed his back. Of the four of them, only Brust could get close enough to kneeling without choking himself. But even then, it seemed little more comfortable than standing.

"This reminds me of Haiti," Brust said. Rashad lifted his head and smacked the back of it on the thick plank yet again.

"Haiti?" Diaz looked over. "You were locked up like this in Haiti?"

"No, no," Brust said.

Two of the town gendarmes guarded them, polished swords drawn and cuirasses burnished to a high shine. Occasionally they flashed the sun into Rashad's eyes.

At least the sun was going down. Just another hour to go.

"If we came back to the ship drunk," Brust said. "Or Shore Patrol had to drag us back, they'd throw us in these cages right there on the dock until we sobered up. Fucking Shore Patrol. Mocked us the whole time. Like they'd never been drunk in port."

A man stepped over the bright white line three meters in front of the stocks. The general public were meant to stay outside that line. To keep from aiding the prisoners, Rashad figured. The guy was dressed well, fine materials in his clothes, a flash of gold or precious stones here or there, but nothing overboard.

"Excuse me, who is in charge?" the man asked the bent-over Marines.

"What?" Rashad looked up as best he could.

"I would speak to your leader?"

Diaz raised his hand as best he could. "Yeah, that's me."

"Ah, right, excellent." The man adjusted his collar and regarded them all. "You look like strong and capable people."

They all looked sideways, then back to the man in front of them.

"I can pay your disturbance fine and have you released. If you would do me a favor."

"What . . . kind of favor?" Brust asked.

"Ah, well, as I was traveling from my home in Deorana, I was waylaid by terrible thieves who stole something *very* precious to me: a portrait of my mother that I was bringing to my brother in his ducal seat in Parazia. They took it and taunted me, you see? They said it would look good over the fireplace in their filthy hideout. Can you imagine? If you could help me get it back, I would be most grateful. I could give you each some gold as well, when you return the painting to me. I'm also a trader, so I can offer you some sturdy leather pants, if you need."

"Sorry, Chief," Diaz said, politely. "We're kind of busy here."

"I dunno," Brust said. "Sounds like a solid side quest to me. We should accept it. Gain some loot. Upgrade our weapons."

"We stay on the mission." Diaz looked at the nobleman. "Thanks, but no thanks. Maybe later, when we're done, but I think we're supposed to stay put, or our Staff Sergeant would have said something."

The man moved off and the four of them watched him go.

"We're gonna be stuck here forever."

"Shut up, Brust."

"Yeah, shut up, Brust," Cale said.

They all snapped their heads up and smacked them in one single coordinated *clunk* against the stocks' planks.

"Staff Sergeant!" Diaz blurted out.

Cale stood in front of them. He had a long, brown cloak draped over his shoulders, almost reaching down to the ground, and a shapeless, goofy hat. The suppressor on his M27 just slightly poked out of the cloak's folds.

Cale put a finger to his lips. "You Marines holding up okay? Just nod, leave the customs-and-courtesies bullshit in the rear."

They all nodded, and Rashad managed to keep from hitting the back of his head against the stocks this time.

"Okay. Looks like they didn't ratfuck your gear, which is good." Cale glanced left and right at the two gendarmes. "And I'm working out how to get you out of this. I don't want to smash-and-grab, but we will if it looks like it's going to get bad for you."

"This sucks," Brust grumbled.

"Yeah, we heard you, Brust." Cale said. "The Crucible sucked too, but you all made it through that, and that was sixty hours of misery. We've got some overwatch on you. We'll pop anyone who looks like they're going to try to fuck with you."

They all nodded carefully again.

"Okay. Good work keeping the team together, Diaz, and all of you, good work staying not-dead. Now, I apologize for what comes next." Cale reached under his cloak.

"Staff—"

Cale threw a chunk of rotten tomato at Brust. It exploded against the wooden stock between Rashad and Brust and sprayed them both with juicy pulp and seeds.

By the time Rashad spit and shook it off his face, Cale had slipped off into the small crowd that mingled in the square, moving among them with barely a ripple.

Cale flipped his cloak's hood back up over the funky hat he'd stolen as he headed into the crowd, concealing the earpiece as he fit it back in.

"How's Rashad?" Barden asked over the radio.

"He'll live."

"That's encouraging."

"They're all fine," Cale said. "It's the worst combat-conditioning stint they've ever done, but it's not going to kill them."

"Probably." Barden's own sigh came through loud and clear.

"Lomicka and Ysbarra have overwatch. They'll take out whoever they have to, if it comes to that."

"I hope it doesn't. That's going to make everything a hundred times more complicated."

"More like a thousand, or a million," he said.

"Roger that."

"Did you get the coins off Orley?" Cale asked.

"He made me give him a damn receipt." Apparently Orley had been carrying around local currency this whole time. Barden requisitioned it so they could make a second go at trying to get supplies.

"Good luck, keep me apprised. Going back to squad channel." He didn't wait for a response, just tapped the channel button twice on his squad radio. He pressed the talk key again, "Antoine, Hassel, what's the status on our new friend Peridot and his hunt?"

"He did what he promised on the tin. Tracked Lady Wíela due north of town, Staff Sergeant." Antoine's voice crackled in his ear. "About a klick north of our observation hill. We've got eyes on her."

"Okay, I'm Oscar Mike. Be there in fifteen. Try to keep her from wandering off any farther."

"We'll do what we can."

Cale made his way out the northeast gate, thankful again for the cloaks that this Peridot character had scrounged for them. In fact, they fit like they had been tailored to drape over his weapons and gear, so he had to wonder exactly where the stranger *had* gotten them. They certainly seemed to carry some kind of enchantment that made people look away. And Cale thought it suspicious that Peridot had brought enough for the entire squad, including the four in the stocks. But at the moment, he'd take any lifeline offered if it wasn't too obviously a snake; the mission and the welfare of his squad took priority.

Once out of sight of the northeast gate, Cale broke into a trot and angled off the road to take his bearings on the hills that bordered the north side of the town and gave it its name. He let

Antoine guide him in, and before long he dropped from a trot into a fast and agitated walk to fall in beside the still-fuming Lady Wíela.

"Lady Wíela!" Cale shouted after her as she climbed a grassy rise just outside of town on the northeast side. Trees dotted the landscape in the distance, thickening toward forest as the hills crept to the foot of Mount Grunt in the distance.

"Lady Wíela, stop!" He knew she could damn well hear him. She waved back at them, clearly annoyed, and carried on.

Shit.

Cale couldn't blame her. He'd be annoyed with himself at this point, too. But, she *was* his mission, one way or another.

"Lady, please stop, now!" He surged forward at his own shout and broke into a trot with Antoine and Hassel tight behind him. He gripped his M27, resisting the urge to click it off SAFE. It would be an easy shot, and in keeping with one of Captain Hobbs's last orders to him, but he wasn't quite ready—

An arrow smacked into the turf at Wíela's feet, and she yelped. She turned fully around. "*What* do you think you're doing?"

She wasn't looking at Cale, but right at Peridot, a few meters off to Cale's left, casually nocking another arrow.

"Hey, hey, hey," Cale said, spreading his arms out and letting his rifle dangle from its sling. He moved between the Ranger and the forest elf. "No threats, just . . . let's talk, okay?"

"I just wanted to get her attention," Peridot said.

"Oh yes, *now* you want my attention, hmm?" Wíela yanked the arrow out of the ground and stalked back toward the Ranger. Something about her tone and posture said an old argument was about to be rekindled.

"Let's calm down," Cale said.

"Did you join with this . . . *itinerant wanderer* to track me down and help him plight his troth?" Wíela snapped.

Plight his troth?

What the fuck did that even mean?

Cale groped around for a response. He glanced back at Antoine, who was absolutely no fucking help.

Peridot slung his bow over his shoulder. "If I, trained by the elves of Morrimar, can track you so *easily*, how do you know your own kind will not find you just as easily, and kill you?"

"At least it's a chance." The sneer twisted Wíela's beautiful, mottled face into something almost demonic. No wonder they had thought her an enemy the first time the glamour wore off. "If I'm with these bumbling fools, I will die twice as fast!"

"Have you even told them who you are and what you seek?" Peridot pointed at the Marines. "Surely they have a right to know what they are caught up in?"

As usual, someone trying to make contact in order to help with intelligence didn't just want to help, they had an axe to grind or an agenda of their own. Same as in Iraq, Afghanistan, or just about everywhere: a painful lesson learned and relearned in every war. But the necessity of trusting *someone* when isolated and alone on foreign soil also never changed, and so the cycle went ever on. He just had to hope he had trusted the right person, and that he could gracefully undo the inevitable complications.

"So, what are you after?" Cale dropped his voice, exuding calm as best he could. Peridot's threats might have gotten her attention, but they wouldn't keep her around.

And he needed to keep her with the group.

"My birthright!" She turned away, dramatically twirling her cloak as she did so. She stared off toward Mount Grunt, arms crossed.

"And what is your birthright?" Cale glanced over at Peridot. But the Ranger just glared at Wíela like a disapproving parent urging a wayward child to confess their sins.

"With the death of Queen Thahuarlein in battle with the Corrupted One, the Fiend of the North, there were seventeen claimants to the Silvene Citadel's throne. After the Great Treachery and the orc raids on your people through the portals, as well as our lands, there are now three claims. I have the strongest of them."

"Ah, right," Cale said.

"But that's not all." Lady Wíela's voice dropped and became hollow. Sorrow creased her dappled features. She'd be hella hard to spot in a forest, Cale thought. "The Tree of Divine Power was uprooted from its sacred glade and hidden deep in the Citadel by a worm of hideous strength. Now, the upstart Chouro controls it, though he's not in *any* line of succession. The elves follow him, for they have no other choice. He controls the Tree."

Peridot moved beside Cale until an inch or two of space separated the Ranger's chest and the Marine's shoulder. Cale sighed and nudged him back with his elbow.

"It is vital that Lady Wíela has your aid, and the aid of your people," he said. "She, at least, is a legitimate ruler of the wood elves. She will be forever grateful for your help. Once she touches the tree, all of them will have no choice but to obey her, even the traitor Chouro."

"Just like that?" Cale raised a dubious eyebrow.

"Well, some may resist, but it would be difficult for them," Peridot said.

"And the rightful ruler will smite them with the power of the Tree," Wíela said, steel in her voice.

"And that's what this has all been about?"

"The Silvene Citadel would be a powerful ally on this side of the rift," Peridot explained.

Cale tried to get to the summary sentence in the report. "You want to enlist the full might of the US military to steal back a *tree?*"

"Strange powers of the Corrupted One were at work in the original theft." Wíela's voice wavered, at once hard and mistrusting, then afraid and despairing. "The Tree was uprooted like a sapling."

"And with the Tree in Chouro's possession," Peridot continued, "the Lady finds few allies among her own people who she can trust. Chouro, though not the rightful ruler, when touching the Tree can read the thoughts and designs of all ordinary wood elves. Only Wíela and the other two claimants can withstand his probing and control."

"And that was what you were flying off to do, ask for help getting a tree?" Cale asked.

Peridot looked offended. "A most powerful, Divine—"

"Alright, got it, but it's still just a tree. You know where it is?"

Ranger and wood elf looked at each other. "Yes."

"So, it's a retrieval mission. We do this kind of thing as squad-level operations all the time."

It would be better to have the whole company for something like this. Overwhelming firepower and all that. But as long as Wíela knew for sure where the tree was being kept, a squad that still had most of its ammo would be enough for that kind of op. Especially if it was primarily infiltration. They weren't Force Recon by any means, but they were a solid-enough squad they could make it work.

But at what cost? Their technological superiority was not the force multiplier it would have been in a less magical, vaguely late Iron Age environment. They could still get overwhelmed or outmaneuvered, as the fall of FOB Hammerhand showed. He would be leading them farther away from any known portal, not to mention resupply or safety. No one at home would have the foggiest clue where to even look for them if the portal was retaken.

FOB Vimes still seemed like the safest bet, and they could drag Wiela with them, then return here to help her with some real force.

A way forward began to form for Cale.

"Our squad, or a whole division, once we can get that many through the portal at Vimes, can help. But I need you to help me." Cale held up his finger as Wiela started to say something. "I need to see if I can raise the next-nearest base on the radio, by getting to the top of a hill. I need instructions on how to proceed, and if possible, reinforcements and resupply."

He couldn't really promise to run a mission just for her. But he could give enough to get them to help him get them all to safety and deliver his Marines to the people who could make the call.

And they probably would. Cale would write a hell of a convincing report, now that he knew all the angles. Maybe it would keep her from getting the intelligence guys to spirit her away if he told a base commander "time was of the essence" and that the Divine potted plant would be moved again if they didn't act right away.

"I can help you," Cale promised, even more firmly now. "If you help me first."

Neither Peridot nor Lady Wiela looked completely sold. So, Cale did something that he knew would catch shit for, but hoped would nudge this over to him. It was a moment of inspiration, he thought.

He unslung his M27 and held it out in the air before them all, conscious of the other Marines' eyes on him. He'd once seen something like this in a dumb movie with knights, and princesses with handkerchiefs.

Sometimes, you just had to suck it up and do what the mission called for. At the very least, this would keep her nearby.

Cale carefully lowered to his knees, incredibly aware of how silly it looked, and even more aware of how the story would be told and retold and embellished if they got out of this and back to a base.

"I promise you my steel, Lady. My weapon is yours," Cale said formally.

Peridot and Wíela looked at each other for a long moment, then nodded. She gracefully tapped the M27's barrel with a finger.

"The true heir to the Silvene Citadel accepts your help."

Cale refused to look back behind him as he stood and re-slung his weapon.

"The nearest ridge is this way," Peridot said.

"Okay," Cale snarled. "Move out!"

He stared at every Marine who walked by, daring them to say anything.

No one met his gaze.

CHAPTER SIXTEEN

BARDEN SLIPPED TOWARD THE PLAZA she'd been studying through binoculars, while tugging her earpiece out and tucking it into her collar. With the volume turned up she could still hear if someone squawked loudly at her, but it let her keep her cloak's hood down.

"Okay, second time's a charm, right?"

"Sounds good to me, Corporal."

They had magic cloaks from the Ranger this time. More of a read on the situation. It was getting really close to sunset and time to shutter the market, so hopefully the sellers would be more willing to make some coin quick before packing up.

And Barden had an extra sneaky add-on to the plan.

Jones joined her as they approached a little girl sitting forlornly on the curb. An empty wooden bowl that the merchants had all ignored sat at her bare and dirty feet.

Barden dropped one of Orley's collected coins—wrenched from him with great pains and threat of extra duty, not to mention the receipt with a list of all the coinage that Barden had to sign—into the bowl.

"Thank you, nice lady," the little beggar girl said. Her smudged face wasn't *really* that dirty, Barden thought. More . . . artistically daubed. Well, if she was just playing the begging game, she wouldn't object to making some coin with a little more acting.

Barden crouched down to meet the girl's eyes on her level, while using her own body to conceal the conversation.

"Hi sweetie, I'm wondering if you can help me out a little." Barden smiled and held out another coin, same as the first one. "I'm new to town—"

"I could tell," the beggar girl said matter-of-factly, the faltering, grateful voice gone and replaced with a plain confidence that didn't fit Barden's expectations.

Barden stopped, caught off guard as her planned spiel faltered. "Was it my accent?"

"Your boots." The girl nodded down at the buff suede boots visible under Barden's cloak. "Only portal travelers have boots like that."

"You've seen a lot of us around?"

The little girl shrugged. "Here and there."

"So. . . ." Barden faltered for a second, wondering if they had run into the same problem Diaz and his team had. "Does that mean you won't help us out?"

"Help you?" She giggled, but the sound was light and, well, twee. It eased Barden's mind somewhat. The little girl made the second coin disappear from Barden's fingers with a sly smile. "What is it you need from a child like me, Traveler Between Worlds?"

Barden looked around. "None of these merchants seemed to want to help me and my friends when we were in our regular clothes. I was hoping you could help me pretend we're from this side of the portals. None of our people bring children with them—"

The girl cut her off with another delighted little giggle. "Oh, I see. Yes, that'll be a fun game!"

"That's very nice of you," Barden said. "What's your name?"

"You can call me Salia, Milady. And what's *your* name?"

"To you, I'm Heather, though you might hear my friends call me other names. Titles, I guess you'd say." Barden nodded toward where Jones, Orley, Dooley, and Shane stood waiting. "But they're going to hang back there while you and I go talk to a couple of the vendors, okay?"

"Sure thing!"

The girl bounced to her feet and scooped up her begging bowl in one hand. She tucked it, and her coins, away into what must have been inner pockets in her tattered dress.

The day was wearing on and the merchants didn't have the same volume and selection of goods as they had earlier. The crowd was smaller, too. Barden took Salia by the hand and led her down an outer lane of the market, trying to move as though she hadn't already decided on her target. She perused the goods, and got a few encouraging words from the vendors, which seemed like a good sign.

Barden stopped in front of a stall selling sausages and dried meat. Good travel rations. They kept well and packed a lot of protein.

"My family and I are looking for provision for a long trek," Barden said casually. "What will you take for ten of these?"

Barden pointed at the sausages. The woman behind the burdened counter started to answer, then snapped her mouth shut when she looked down at the tiny bit of Barden's digi-cammie peeking past the edge of the cloak's sleeve.

"No, I'm sorry, not for sale," the woman said in a pinched whisper as she looked back up.

"I will pay your price." Barden held up Orley's hard-won local coins and let them glint in the late sun. She could see greed kindle in the woman's eyes, and then die.

The merchant slumped and shook her head. "No."

"Why?" The single word could have dropped out of the air onto the stall table between them, it was so heavy with Barden's annoyance.

"It's no good anymore. Bad meat, not for you, sorry." The woman's words, after an initial stutter, came out in a rush.

Salia slipped under the front of the stall and grabbed something.

"Hey!" the merchant hissed.

Salia ducked back outside the stall before the woman could grab her.

"Look, it's a likeness of you!" Salia said brightly. The little beggar girl held a piece of plastic up in the air, which the merchant made a grab for. Barden snagged and inspected it.

It was a picture of her.

Well. Not Barden specifically. It was an official drawing done of various Marines in the desert and forest MARPAT "digi-cammies," done back in 2003 when the uniforms were issued. They were intended as an artsy-yet-simple guide for dummies (read: Marines) on how to wear the uniform appropriately.

It looked like it had been printed on some kind of color printer, then laminated.

And distributed.

To merchants.

In Hilltown.

Red X's crossed out each Marine's face.

"What the fuck is this?" Barden hissed. The merchant woman gestured at her to ward off hexes and the evil eye and who knew what the hell else.

"All the merchants have them." Salia snatched the picture back from Barden and tossed it at the merchant, who dropped to her knees behind the counter in fear.

Salia grabbed Barden's hand and dragged her away.

"Hey," Barden said. She wasn't done with the merchant.

"I thought you were trying to play the game," Salia said woodenly. "But now you're spoiling it, and *everyone* is staring at you. Let me help you."

Salia tugged Barden off through the anonymity of the town's square, and Barden's Marines followed her deeper into town. The little beggar girl wound them down back alleys, skirting the square, then she cut across the handful of big streets that sectioned off the town.

"Those pictures," Barden said. She wanted to stop and talk, and she realized that the child was guiding her. Somehow Salia had slipped into taking charge. Barden wanted to put a stop to that in a second: the kid could be leading them anywhere, even into a trap. Yet . . . she had given them some of the best local intel from the town yet, so Barden wanted to keep tugging at this string for a little while longer.

"Every merchant in town has those pictures." Salia glanced up and down a narrow street, then hurried Barden across it. The others followed one by one after checking the street themselves. "They know not talk to your kind."

"Who gave them the pictures?"

"Town guards. But who knows where those shiny guards got them."

"Fuck." Barden said softly. Diaz and the others hadn't just been locked up for brawling. They were probably being held for something, or someone. "Where are you taking us?"

Salia stopped and rolled her eyes as dramatically as a child could, and then included a theatrical sigh for further effect. "If you want to keep playing your game, traveler, you'll go to the farms, where you can get good food for good prices and they've never been threatened by the guards."

"But you let me talk to the merchants, knowing they were looking for us?"

"I didn't know they were looking for *you* specifically until I saw her make that funny face," Salia grinned. "Big people are weird. I mean, sometimes you all go out and get in trouble on purpose. Like when I was really little and Mama would sneak out at the strangest hours to meet with the king at night."

A thousand questions crowded Barden's mouth as Salia leapt back into action and walked them out through a tiny, unguarded gate on the town's west side, which then led onto a narrow farm track.

"Okay, what king?" Barden asked, a kilometer or so down the road. The hills around the north and west side of the town tailed off in a slender crescent and low pass between two hills where open farmland then stretched out beyond, well-hidden from the town itself.

"I don't know," Salia said lightly. "He was always just 'the King' to me. Mama disappeared when I was five, and then I had to leave quickly, so I didn't learn a lot about where I once lived. It was big and shiny, and I always had fine clothes with gold embroidery. Oh, and hot food. And sugar cakes. The cooks always had sweets for me."

Salia explained her history nonchalantly, as if every kid ever had royal secrets in their past to talk about.

"How did you get here to Hilltown?"

"A friend of Mama's came to take me away before the King locked me up." Salia started jumping from paving stone to paving stone, laughing when she missed and hit mud. "We traveled a while and he gave me to other friends, who gave me to others, and so on. Then I traveled alone for a while."

Her tone suggested that this was totally normal, and Barden supposed that for Salia it was, even if it did sound like half her life had been spent on the move. If she was telling the truth. Though Salia's mannerisms suggested sincerity, even despite that slight aura of mischief around her.

She ran up ahead, and Barden slowed to let Jones catch up.

"Something odd about that girl." Jones hitched up her day-pack on her shoulders. Drums of ammo for her M27 jangled inside. "You get that feeling?"

"Definitely something sketchy going on in the market," Barden said. "And she kept us out of that."

"Good point, Corporal."

"That's why they pay me the big bucks." Barden laughed, then lowered her voice. "Keep your fingers limber in case she's walking us toward something. Jotun. Pass it down."

"Got it, Corporal."

Another few kilometers down the dirt road, they reached a pair of walled farm compounds, one on either side of the track. A few huts dotted the hills in the farther distance, and Barden figured this constituted a village.

"Hayward's Hope," Salia said, though Barden hadn't asked about the name.

Salia directed them in what to buy from which farms, and even set to work on convincing the farmers to accept the US gold dollars Barden had tucked away in her small pack instead of Orley's local coin collection. She managed to get them a couple of sturdy rucksacks from the farmer that sold salted meat and cheese, the sort of sturdy leather that would have been a hit with the hipster crowd back home.

At least, among those who could still stomach real leather.

The smell of tanning got to her, so Barden cooled her heels on track between the two farms as her team split up to gather up their purchases. She told herself it was a good position to keep an eye on the proceedings.

She settled back against a rock that might have been the base of a signpost once upon a time, and stuck her legs out into the rutted track. With her daypack between her knees, she took off her helmet, then cleared and broke down her M27 to wipe down the working parts. Thankfully, not a lot of sand or grit had gotten into it, and she hadn't fired it since the engagements with the elves on Stark Ridge.

Once done, she snapped it all back together, reloaded, then grabbed a piece of fruit that her team had dubbed an Almost Apple. Just like it, but not quite.

They'd caught a break with the little kid. Barden leaned back, took a bite, and closed her eyes.

She knew she shouldn't be relaxing this much, just now, but threats seemed distant for the moment. Everything here by the two farms felt sedate and normal, at least compared to the chaos they had come from back at the FOB.

Farm work carried on like normal. Chickens, or something exactly like them, clucked and scraped in the yard somewhere behind her. In the compound across from her, farmers raised a shed.

She watched as they lifted part of the frame, though all she saw was the top of it rising up over the compound wall. Guy ropes steadied it as they got it upright, reminding her a little of the way the radio aerial was secured at the FOB.

With a radio aerial that tall, a quick job with guy ropes to hold it up, someone could radio the people who had distributed those laminated illustrations.

Guy ropes.

Barden choked on her Almost Apple for a second.

"SHANE!" Barden scrambled to her feet and spit out fruit. "Shane! Get your ass over here!"

Barden slapped her helmet back on and slung her rifle as she

ran for the entrance to the nearer compound, where she had de-
tailed Shane to spread load meat and cheese into the rucksacks.

"Shane!"

"Here, Corporal!" Shane tore out of the compound, her rifle
up to her shoulder, scanning for threats.

"Put that down," Barden said. "Get your camera out. I need
to see your town photos."

"Aye, Corporal." Shane slung the weapon around onto her
back and fished in the front pouch on her vest for the digital
camera.

"You took pictures of the town while we were in Overwatch
position, right?"

"Of course, Corporal." Shane sounded a little offended as she
handed over the camera.

Barden turned it on and started to review the pictures on
small viewfinder screen. She flicked from one to the other,
wishing for a bigger screen just then. But Doc's ruggedized tablet wasn't compatible with the camera, of course, because the
Marine Corps. And the tablet that was compatible was with
Rashad.

"Fuck shit fuck," Barden muttered. She held the camera close
to her face, still searching. Then she stopped. "Goddamnit all to
hell."

"What is it, Corporal?"

"What does that look like to you?" Barden held the camera
up to Shane, her index finger next to a bell tower. Just to the
right of it was another vertical line, with four diagonal lines
coming from near the top, mostly obscured by other roofs and
chimneys. Also partly obscured by the bell tower itself was a
pair of spider-web-looking wires connected at their center by a
horizontal pole, sitting at the top of the vertical line.

She'd noticed the wires, but thought they'd looked like ropes going to the tower, back on the initial overwatch. Without the camera's zoom, after the fact. . . .

"A fucking radio aerial," Shane said, breathless. "It's not ours, is it?"

"If it was ours, it's probably been captured. But my guess is that it isn't ours and never was. That town's hostile. The little girl said it, Peridot the weird Ranger said it. Now we know."

Doc and the rest of the Marines made their way out onto the road, looking over at the two of them with curiosity. A couple of them even had their bags with provisions packed and slung, just in case they had to boogie.

"Two minutes to finish and then we're on the move back to town." Barden walked over and grabbed one of the full packs and hefted it onto her back. She suppressed a groan at the weight of the supplies. Couldn't complain about getting packed up full with supplies after going without for so long. "If you're not on the road in two minutes, you're sprinting to catch up."

Barden wanted whoever, or whatever, the fuck sat under that radio aerial. And the aerial. If there was a working radio, maybe they could call for backup.

If it meant knocking some heads, then that would be just a bonus.

CHAPTER SEVENTEEN

A FEW HOURS LATER, Barden crouched low against a stone wall in the night, her cloak discarded and stuffed into a waterproof sack, together with the others at the base of the wall. The well-shielded alley hid them from ordinary passersby as her team gathered.

Hidden only for now. Once Cale hustled into position with his half of the squad, Barden hoped they would be noticed rather intensely by someone. Or maybe a few someones.

She glanced behind her to see Shane, Jones, and Orley stacked neatly behind her. Doc lingered on her own a little farther behind Orley, providing rear security. Barden and Cale had argued over the radio as to who Doc should go with, but there hadn't been time to meet up and balance the teams out better. Barden had the intel with her on the location of the radio aerial, and that was crucial. If anyone else needed medical treatment, they'd have to wait.

Or not, as the case might be.

Barden keyed her mic.

"Six, this is Five, passing 'Hercules.'" The code word meant she was in position, taken from notebook pages filled with pre-arranged codes. When arranging the operation, Barden had selected two pages, given them to Cale over the radio, and he'd responded with confirmation words.

"Adventures" and "Princess," in this case.

"Roger that, Five," Cale replied. "Give us thirty seconds."

He didn't need a reply, so Barden just held up a single finger, indicating to the others that they would be moving very shortly.

She had to assume the approach to the listening post was being monitored in some way, and that it was possible even their squad radio broadcasts were being intercepted, maybe even decrypted.

Thus, the codes. Even their initial radio conversation had to be veiled, with use of codes and inside jokes.

In a bit of inspiration, she had referred to the possible listening post as a "Hobbit hole" knowing that Cale alone, maybe of all humankind, found Hobbits to be kind of sinister things. Or maybe he just didn't like Elijah Wood as an actor.

Even for Barden, it was hard to tell with Cale sometimes.

Seconds ticked on and she looked down, checking her footing. A thick, black cable ran down from the radio aerial, tucked into the edge of the stone gutter, then snaked up a narrow set of stairs. The stout door at the top looked reinforced by a lock plate. Machine manufactured. From their own side of the portal, not made locally.

Barden had scouted the stone building on the approach. If anyone at all was home, they were lying low.

"Five, this is Six. We are 'Xena.'"

"Roger that, Six. 'Iolaus' in five . . . four. . . ." She held up a hand to her team, three fingers, then two, then pointed forward.

Barden peeked around the corner, raised the compact grenade launcher in two hands, and squeezed the trigger. It bucked, almost out of her grip, and a second later a muffled whump and crash filled the street.

M27 up, she leapt around the corner, gaze trained on the smoking remains of the stout wooden door. Smoldering wood tried to catch fire, growing more orange as she approached.

Shane was a tangible presence at her back as she took the stairs two at a time and rushed blind through the smoke and haze.

"'Gabrielle,'" came the code word through her earpiece as she hit the door, Cale's voice breathy from running.

No one shot her.

No one stirred.

Barden kept moving, rifle up and aiming at any open spaces inside.

A small vestibule, choked with shattered wood, gave way to a large, long room, cut across by a dark, heavy curtain. She spotted a gap and rushed through, Shane still close behind her.

She pulled up short two steps beyond the curtain because there wasn't anywhere else to go.

A narrow table pushed up against the wall held a small rack of radio equipment, with a couple of logbooks stuffed in a file holder to the side. A map of stitched-together aerial photos fluttered against the tape that stuck it to a wall. Assorted other papers lay about the table around a space where a laptop might have been.

To the other side, mussed-up blankets draped off a cot. Barden kicked it over with a boot to find nothing under it.

"Shane, bag up all of this stuff," she said, turning to find the lance corporal already doing just that. Orley and Jones hung back at the gap in the curtain, looking around, eyes wide.

"Are we secure?" Barden asked.

"Yeah, I mean, yes, Corporal," Jones said. "No trapdoors, no spider holes, not even a lousy safe behind a painting."

There wasn't much to the building to hide anything, though she'd been worried about a cellar, attic, or doors connecting to the adjoining building. Barden let out that shaky breath she never realized she'd been holding whenever the lull came after a potential fight. She'd been keyed up, maybe even hoping to get a chance for some payback for the fall of Hammerhand.

Such a basic desire, revenge. But oh-so-human. Advanced training tried to install the intellectual planner in the brain, but at her core, Barden was still a fucking Marine. Kicking down a door and not knowing what waited on the other side scared her as it should, and yet it thrilled her at the same time.

Jarhead for life.

"What about the radio?" Barden asked. "Jones? Someone give me some good news."

"They're not eavesdropping on us—it's their own system," Jones said from where she leaned over the equipment. "Not compatible. We can't use it. Piece of civilian shit. Not military."

Barden tried not to show her disappointment. "Get with Doc on rear security while Shane finishes collecting the intel." At least that was something.

"You going to call it in, Corporal?" Shane asked as the other two vanished again.

"Yeah. Be ready to move in two minutes for either the plaza or the rally point."

"Roger that."

Barden stepped over to the map, studying it as she keyed her mic. Someone had been tracking US military movements on this side.

"Six, this is Five. We are 'Autolycus.'"

————

Exhaustion warred with Rashad's desire not to choke. Every time his knees sagged as he started to doze, his throat pressed against the stock. Each time, he gagged a little and snapped awake. Each time he smacked his head against the upper part of the plank.

Afternoon had turned to evening, then night. They'd all stopped muttering to each other. Even Brust, who never seemed tired of hearing himself talk. The only sounds Rashad heard from his companions were the rustle of baggy cotton trousers as someone struggled to find a more comfortable position, or a muffled curse as they failed.

Even the locals had gotten bored. They had spilled out of taverns when the sun had slipped behind the roofs to taunt and jeer at the Marines. A few of them tossed uneaten food at the stocks, though being into their cups, they'd mostly missed. They moved on after a few minutes, though their guards had looked ready to shove them along if they lingered too much.

Now it was just the Marines, two guards, and a mostly empty plaza.

Rashad smacked his head again, blinked his eyes open, and saw Cale and Barden march purposefully across the square in their full gear: helmets on, the whole thing.

They had their rifles up, pointed at each guard.

"Hey," Brust whispered to him. "Are they busting us out?"

Rashad shook his head. He'd expected Cale to leave the team here for the night to take their lumps rather than risk some kind of incident. Cale, who would have made a great drill instructor, seemed like the type to leave them there just to punish them for getting swept up. Rashad expected a lecture with phrases like "screwed the pooch" and "giving me an ulcer."

The guards drew their swords and held their hands up, palms forward, in command. Their attention remained wholly fixated on the two strangers in strange dress right in front of them. "Sto—"

A well-cloaked Shane ran out of the darkness from the side and clocked the guard on the left with a knife-hand strike from behind, dropping him like a sack of loose bones.

"Rrrrrrreeeecover," Rashad croaked through dry, cracked lips.

His impression of his Marine Corps Martial Arts instructor, Sgt. Delano, was fucking hilarious. But no one heard him. Shane skipped the recovery position after a successful strike, preferring instead to knee the guard in the back as he crumpled.

Rashad slumped and choked himself on the plank again, and missed who got the second guard. He jerked up and smacked his head against the board behind his head. His thighs burned from standing in place for hours. The stocks looked funny on tourist brochures. Rashad fucking hated them now.

He groaned.

"Jesus, let's get you out of here," Shane said from behind him. A metal bolt clanked, and the upper half of the board lifted away. Shane helped him straighten up. Rashad felt like his spine might pop right out of his back, then crawl away to a dark hole to recuperate.

"Shane?"

"Yeah, it's me. I got your shit," she said, then wrapped something around his shoulders. The sound of rifle handguards clacked against each other under her cloak as she thrust his Camelbak into his arms, then pushed the end of the drinking tube into his mouth. He sucked greedily at it.

"You knife-hand chopped the guard?"

"Yeah." Shane pivoted to slip her shoulders up under his left arm. Corporal Barden came up on his other side and did the same.

"You didn't know?" Barden asked. She sounded like she was

teasing him. That seemed unfair, teasing him in his state. "She's a MCMAP black belt. Got to green while waiting for her class to get picked up at the School of Infantry, and happened to have a black belt instructor for a platoon sergeant when she first hit the fleet."

"I thought the knife-hand chop was just something the instructors taught just to mess with you." Rashad kept focusing on that. He was dehydrated from being out in the sun with no protection, and over-exhausted. His mind had to latch on to something, and it had decided this was the important take-away right now. "I've never seen it work like that."

"Gotta be high-achieving in This Man's Marine Corps," Barden said.

"Truth," Shane grunted.

Together, they dragged him toward one side of the plaza. Rashad saw three other groups of cloaked figures moving off in three other directions, each one holding a squad member from the stocks. Everyone was cloaked up now, and moving with purpose.

"Think you can slur your words, maybe drool a little?" Shane asked conversationally.

"Huh?" Rashad asked, mushily.

"That's the spirit!" Barden said. "Now, if we see anyone, you're our drunk buddy, and we're dragging you home. Think you can manage that?"

"Arrrr, Corporal," Rashad said.

An hour later, Barden and Cale stood upwind of a shallow gulley where Diaz and his team were laid out on poncho liners, with Doc monitoring them.

Barden assumed he wanted to debrief her and confer, but Cale handed her his binoculars and pointed toward Hilltown. Candles flickered in windows throughout town, and they could see the occasional flames of torches bobbing around between streets. But something else had caught Cale's attention.

"See those lights?" Cale pointed at the track north of the town. "How far do you think they are?"

Barden pressed the binoculars to her face. She swept up from the dark ground near her feet until she hit the bright pricks of light in the distance.

Her right finger worked the focus until they resolved into headlights. Not flickering torches at all.

"Fuck," Barden said softly as she watched the two sets of headlights bounce a bit as they crept over the landscape.

"Yeah," Cale said, in a tired grunt.

"Five kilometers, at most," Barden said a moment later. "They're creeping along pretty slowly. They won't be US military, will they?"

"Doubt it."

"It'll take them more than an hour to get to town." She handed the binos back to Cale. He waved them off and she tucked them into their pouch on her vest again.

"I'd bet they were coming to pick Diaz and his team up from the stocks, or they're coming in to see who kicked in the door of their little radio station back there," he said, rubbing his chin. "Two sets of headlights. Could be as few as four, maybe eight aboard them."

"Could be two big trucks with two squads each aboard."

"So, either we outnumber them three to two, or three to one—"

"Or they outnumber us four to one."

Cale looked over at her. "Math like that is why I keep you around."

"Right." She was too tired for Cale to be snarking at her . . . and really tired was the only time he started that kind of thing. And they were never both well-rested at once. She wondered what she did while tired that got on her squad leader's nerves.

Barden popped a piece of gum into her mouth and, after a few chews, snapped it between her teeth.

Cale tensed next to her. "How fast can we move?"

"You and me? We can be away over the hills ten minutes from now, but that's not going to help Diaz and his team. They need at least a few hours just to be mobile again."

"Will they be close to a hundred percent by morning?"

"Ask Doc." She nodded back down the gully below them. Privately, Barden doubted it. All of them had needed help hobbling out of the town. Diaz had tried to walk under his own power, bless his thick skull, but Cale had to pull him up into a fireman's carry once clear of town.

Cale grimaced. "Okay. Check the perimeter, make sure we've got defensible positions and keep someone up here to watch those headlights every inch of the way into town."

He nodded and slipped on down the hill toward Doc and the sleepers.

Barden summoned Jones and Orley to the top of the hill and set them on watch over the slow-moving headlights. With them in place, she moved around the rest of their perimeter.

They basically occupied two long sides of the small gully, the seven healthy Marines apart from her and Cale placed in four positions, two on each side. Lomicka was on her own in one position, though when Barden was ready to settle in for the night, she planned to send Shane over there and keep Hassel company herself.

Down in the gully, Doc kept watch over the four sleepers. Barden refused to think of them as casualties, even though they were, technically. Cale set up in the gulley within reach of Wíela. He'd sleep with an eye open on her, Barden knew.

Barden blinked when she realized the little orphan beggar girl Salia lay curled up in the middle of the stacked packs and other gear, fast asleep. They hadn't broken her loose in the middle of boogieing out of Hilltown.

Maybe they could leave her with Peridot, if she could find him. Unlike Salia, who had a knack of sticking right next to her, Peridot vanished at his own will. Not through any magic, as such, as far as she could tell, just uncanny stealth.

"Anyone seen Peridot?" Barden asked.

A dark shadow rose from the ground near Barden's blind spot. Barden instinctively swore, and stepped back.

"Be calm. I mean you no harm; it is only I," Peridot said. "As called upon."

"You're going to get yourself shot," Barden hissed as she crouched down just below the crest of the ridge facing town. She'd circled all the way back to where Cale stood with her just a few minutes before. "And I won't be real sad about it."

"It would be my own fault, should that happen." Peridot's smile revealed improbably white teeth against that tanned, dirty, and scruffy face. "And none should mourn such foolishness."

"Yeah, but I'd probably still get in trouble for it." Barden snapped her gum. The sound made Peridot jump and frown at her.

"Have you observed the others of your world approaching from the north?" He swept his arm at the slowly approaching vehicles.

"Cale and I spotted them ten minutes ago."

"I know not whence they come; no known fortifications of your people lie in that direction."

Barden, for a moment, wondered how much of all that was

the translation spell, or whether Peridot sounded like that even to folks here who spoke his language.

"What *is* in that direction?" she asked.

Peridot made a face, barely visible in the starlight. "The eastern limb of the Sylvene Forest, and the road that runs between it and Mount Grunt."

"Mount Grunt. That really sounds like a Marine named it."

"It is unlikely that those folk came from the mountain itself," Peridot said, "as its keeper is known to me and Lady Wiela and, well, he does not suffer visitors lightly."

"So, the forest?"

"Quite so. The vile villain Chouro may have allied himself with others from your world."

"Same folk who shot down one of our Warthogs during the fall of Hammerhand." Barden took her helmet off and ran her hand through sweaty, oily hair, then dropped it back on her head.

Nope, that made it feel even more gross. The unexpected dunking at the fair glade the nymphs had tried to trap them in felt like a lifetime ago. A nice, soaking-wet, clean lifetime ago.

"When will you be able to move your ailing men?" Peridot asked, cocking his head at them.

"Cale and Doc are talking about that right now." She glanced down toward them, then north again in the direction of the approaching headlights. "Not with any speed before morning."

And once they were up, a grueling march to FOB Vimes sounded like the plan Cale had in mind, though he hadn't laid out the full specifics of his thinking to her yet.

"Very well." Peridot tapped his brow with two fingers in a kind of salute. "I guess I will have to be the rat's tail we all set on fire."

Barden stared at him, wondering if the translation spells had hiccupped. "I think I'm overtired. What did you say?"

"I'll be the rat's tail we set on fire. Did you not play this as a child?"

"No." Barden spit her gum out. "What the fuck?"

"It's more of a common saying. We rarely *actually* lit rats on fire," Peridot offered politely as Barden stared at him in horror. Then, with a determined expression, he changed the subject. "I will go and see if I can cause chaos, to bring your people some time. If they have elven trackers, they will find you, so I will lead them off."

Peridot turned away from her, the light in his eyes shrouded in an instant, and before Barden could open her mouth to ask more questions, he had slithered down the hill and into the deeper dark.

CHAPTER EIGHTEEN

CALE ORDERED THE SQUAD to spend the night at fifty percent, with the exception of the four who had been in the stocks. He partnered with Doc Dooley to split watch over them, as well as over Wíela and the orphan girl Salia.

They needed to hand her off to someone safe. The platoon was no place for a child. But for now, she'd be in even more danger if he gave her over to the night. He'd have to figure out what to do with her tomorrow, because right now just thinking about it made him feel even more tired.

Salia slept the whole night. Cale envied the trusting sleep of a child who didn't have to worry about enemy troops nearby. Even when he was off and Doc took over, sleep came fitfully for him. Like most Marines, he took pride in being able to sleep any-where, at any time, under almost any conditions. Tonight wasn't a good test of that, not with an unknown number of hostiles moving about in the distant darkness.

Itchy and grumpy, Cale slept in twenty-minute blips that didn't help his mood at all.

Doc woke him for the last watch around an hour before

dawn, rousing him out of a confusing, staccato dream in which he clanked around in ridiculous, over-sized armor and carried Salia on his back.

Cale shook his head and looked at Doc.

"How are they?"

"Sleeping like the dead all night, but for all that they seem to be normal. I think we get some water and Motrin in them and they'll be good to go." Doc had used up four of the team's precious saline bags on IVs for the four Marines, which she treated much like Cale assumed dragons hoarded gold. There were about ten or twelve remaining saline bags spread out among the squad now.

"Get them up. I'm going to check on the perimeter." Cale tugged his boots on, laced them up, then rolled up his poncho and liner and tied them up on his daypack. Once he slung it on his back, he crept up toward Barden's position.

She and Hassel peered into the night toward the town.

"Any movement?" Cale asked.

"Nothing so far." Barden had her night-vision goggles down and slowly swept them from left to right.

"Doc's getting the sleepers," Cale said. "We're going to move as soon as they're on their feet."

"Which way are we going?"

Rather than answering her directly, Cale looked over at Hassel. The eager young Marine sensed his gaze and perked right up.

"Double-time, Hassel. Go relieve Shane at her position and send her to us." Cale flicked his fingers and shooed Hassel off.

Hassel slid a short ways down the back of the hill, then shot to his feet and sped off. A minute later, Shane hustled up the hill, sliding a bit in the dewy grass. Her daypack, which had been looking slack as they chewed through ammunition and food over the last week, now fairly bulged with the intel gleaned from the listening post in town.

"You got that map handy, Shane?"

She nodded, not needing to be told which map: the one they had pulled from the listening post had put their own cobbled-together mass of aerial photographs to shame. Some of it was hand-drawn, but in such a way that Cale guessed the person drawing it had actually walked the terrain. A lot more interesting stuff in that pack of hers, and no time right now to paw through it to figure out who was out there in the dark giving RPGs to wood elves, building listening stations in the middle of towns, and driving vehicles around the same landscapes wyverns flew over.

Shane unslung her pack and pulled out the big map.

Cale unfolded it on the grass. Hilltown was rendered on it in crisp detail, very near the center of the map. Bottom left was FOB Hammerhand, with the elves' forest occupying the whole of the map north of that. The Escarpment slashed across the bottom right of the map, with one of the forts there just visible at the edge. The stitched-together photos in that region were fuzzy, though, shot through with opalescent artifacts and blocky patches of unnatural colors.

To the top right was the triangular, rammed-earth shape of FOB Vimes. A road connected the three—Hammerhand, Hilltown, and Vimes—more or less in a straight line.

"They'll be watching the road, whoever they are," Barden said, reading his mind. She had swapped lookout duties with Shane and come to peer over his shoulder.

"Yeah. Roads give me hives, anyway."

Barden snorted. "Typical Staff NCO. So much hate for a nice, flat, gradual route."

"You know why."

"I do." She sighed. "It's where ambushes happen. A girl can dream of an easy walk for once, though."

"You wanted easy walks, you should have joined the Chair Force."

Barden flashed a tight smile. "My recruiter lied to me."

Cale traced his finger along the speckled green bits that looked like trees from the air, and hoped they weren't something else up close. This place could be like that. "I think we parallel the road in these trees here all the way up to Vimes. By the time we run out of trees, it looks like we should be within a day's walk, maybe two. Might be able to radio from there, even."

"What about up this way, by the mountain?" Barden pointed to Mount Grunt, the huge granite bulk that took up a big chunk of the top edge of the map. Skirting along the lower portions of it would bring them within a few days walk of FOB Vimes, though there also appeared to be a road running in and out of view along that top edge of the map.

"There's arrows drawn to it with words that translate to, 'Hell no' and 'Bad place,' if my translation spell is still working properly." Cale jabbed at the relevant spots on the map.

"They'll be much less likely to look for us there."

Cale slowly shook his head at her.

"Fine—" Barden snapped her jaw shut as they both heard a string of muffled pops, followed by the snapping sound of very small projectiles breaking the sound barrier in their direction.

They were under attack. Not by spears or arrows or magical spells. It was gunfire. Automatic gunfire.

"Contact front!" Hassel shouted from the southmost position of their camp.

"Go!" Cale pushed Barden in that direction, and she slid down the hillside, then sprinted over to the southern rim of their little hideout. "Shane, do you see anything to your front?"

"Negative, Staff Sergeant, no movement."

The clacking of suppressed M27s firing echoed all across the dell. To the east, the sky turned from gray to purple. Insects stirred and buzzed and hummed; birds took the sky in full dudgeon, disturbed by the shattered peace.

"Go now, straight across to the eastern position," Cale ordered, his pulse slamming but his breathing steady.

"Aye aye, Staff Sergeant." Shane slithered back, then was up and running the same way Barden had. Cale scanned the ground between them and the town again, saw no movement, then hustled toward their northern perimeter.

Jones and Orley were moving at full tilt toward him already.

"Movement?" he called to them.

"Nothing, Staff Sergeant!"

"South position, reinforce Barden, Hassel, and Lomicka!"

They changed direction and sprinted off. They were open and defenseless on two sides now as Cale had shifted his Marines to bring as much fire as he could against whoever had just found them on the south side. A detached part of his brain wondered what that might invite, but the rest of him had no time to mull it over.

They needed to shoot and scoot right now.

In the bottom of the dell, everyone stood up, fully burdened by the weight of bags of local provisions. Single, aimed shots by his Marines cracked away to the south now that the initial frenzy of combat had passed. By Cale's mental clock, less than sixty seconds had gone by since the first shots.

He sent Diaz and Rashad toward southern position with instructions for Barden to break contact as soon as they were able, then rally to the east of their prior position. Everyone else, he hustled up to where Shane and the others maintained a small security perimeter, weapons pointed in every direction.

"Secure here, Staff Sergeant," she reported.

Damn. He'd sent all three of his team leaders to the point of fighting.

No time to second-guess himself, though. This was the agony of leadership, making decisions and only counting the consequences later.

Cale was just about to shout at them to move out east when the shooting fell off with a ripple and Hassel busted his ass through the growing light of dawn toward them, with Lomicka right behind. Lomicka's left arm was bleeding and her helmet had a worrying gouge in the top, lined with the curled edges of Kevlar fabric released from its stiffening resin by the heat of impact.

"Doc!" Cale snarled the word as silence fell around the dell. But Dooley was already hustling toward the wounded Lomicka, digging through her quick-access bag for a field dressing. She and Cale got to Lomicka at the same time.

"I'm good, Staff Sergeant. Just a flesh wound," Lomicka said, her jaw set and eyes bright. No concussion there, not that he could tell anyway.

"What, are you a corpsman now?" Dooley snapped, a little snarl in her voice. She deftly cut away the bloody sleeve, then splashed some water from a canteen over it to sluice away blood.

Cale let her get on with it and hustled toward Barden's position. The shooting had stopped and the quiet was a little eerie. Not that there had been all *that* much noise to begin with, but still.

"We good?" He slid down between where Barden and Diaz lay prone, and peered out over the brightening landscape. On the other side, Hassel visibly fidgeted with an empty magazine, trying to get into one of his pouches. Diaz slid over to help him.

"Bad guys are down and out for now," Barden said, not taking her eyes off the ground in front of them. Cale saw bodies in the tall grass about a hundred, two hundred meters off.

"Good. Everyone else okay?"

"Present and accounted for, Staff Sergeant." Barden sounded shaky to his ears, but only a little. Bits of earth had been turned over around her, little furrows that he might have missed had he not been looking for them. Intense, but ultimately inaccurate fire.

"Great. Let's move now."

With Diaz leading, they hustled back to the rally point one at a time, keeping their dispersion. Cale brought up the rear, twisting around every third or fourth step to check their six.

No movement at all.

By the time he got back, Lomicka's arm was bandaged and she was already shrugging on her cloak, along with all the others.

Cale pulled Barden's out of her daypack for her, then she returned the favor.

"You okay?" he asked.

"Doing better than the assholes that tried to assault us." Barden turned around and adjusted her gear.

"Take point?" Cale asked, maybe a little too softly. He wouldn't fault anyone for needing a moment. But he wanted his best up front.

"Aye, sir," Barden said, just as softly, knowing his offer for a moment off was genuine and not judgment of her fighting spirit. "I'll take a moment when we find good cover."

And they stepped off. She led them down into a snaking depression that might once have been a streambed, taking them off in a vaguely northeasterly direction.

A kilometer or two away, the first outliers of that band of trees beckoned to them, and Cale willed them to be under cover among them already.

Peridot melted out of the tall grass near the end of the first hour of their march. Cale didn't have the energy to be properly startled.

"What do you want?"

"Your warriors are formidable, Cale of Alpena," Peridot said. "Even when surprised."

"Who told you—you know what, never mind." Cale rubbed his face, sighed, and wondered if he would he ever see Northern Michigan again. Didn't really seem like it, some days. "And thanks. They're good troops."

"You are right to be proud. They killed all but one of the patrol that came upon your team."

"And the other one?" Cale asked.

"That one was mine." A bit of Peridot's uncanny smile showed through the grime on his face and shadows under his hood's cloak. Cale thought about the Cheshire Cat from *Alice's Adventures in Wonderland*.

Yeah, he thought, that tracked.

"The survivor was heading back to town to warn his friends," Peridot said. "I put an arrow through his neck."

"Do you know who they are?" Cale asked.

"The two handfuls I harassed to pull away from your location did not wear uniforms like yours, or have any common token that they wear about themselves. Their manner of clothing and equipment is all very distinct from each other."

"Fucking mercenaries," Cale spat. "Perfect. Where did they come from?"

"That I cannot tell you."

"Fantastic." Cale guessed it didn't really matter who they were or where they came from—what he really needed to know was

exactly how many and how well equipped. But Peridot didn't
know much about their weapons load-out and ammunition.
Just that he'd provoked the mercenaries into firing wildly into
the night and led them around in circles trying to find him
after he'd picked off a few from the shadows.

Cale had to take what he could get. And it was better that
Peridot was on his side than not.

"You're a tracker, right?" Cale remembered how easily Peridot
had found Lady Wíela's trail the day before.

"One of the best."

"How much of a path are we leaving?"

"None at all, once I came up behind you." Peridot smiled that
smile again, then dropped back again, evidently to clean up their
trail some more.

At least he didn't just disappear that time.

Once into the trees, they moved northeast as best they could.
Occasionally Cale sent out scouts to check their distance to the
road, reliably a couple of kilometers off to their right. They ran
across a lesser road, which he hadn't noticed on their map, and
evidently branched off the main one. Lady Wíela dug her heels
in and came to a hard stop.

"What's happening?" Cale demanded.

To their north lay Mount Grunt, a little closer than it had
been all day, lunging up out of the hills. To the south, the road
wound down toward the Escarpment and the tower forts there.

"I will not . . . *I cannot* . . . take another step toward the Corrupted One's lands." Lady Wíela shuddered.

"It's just a day's walk!" Peridot countered.

That was all it would take for them to reach one of largest of the tower forts along the Escarpment, part of the joint US-UN-Kingdom efforts to hold back the Corrupted One.

"If we get to that frontier fort, we might be able to radio FOB Vimes and get us some relief or reinforcements," Cale argued, agreeing with Peridot. Get to the nearest place where other people on your team were. Regroup and strike back out from a place of strength.

Lady Wíela folded her arms. "You do not know if those forts remain in friendly hands."

"If that was true, we would see more of the Corrupted One's forces," Peridot said.

"We saw plenty back around the portal," Cale said, backing off his own position a bit. "Those weren't all rogue wood elves."

Lady Wíela nodded. "Incursions have been growing more frequent, and we know not whence they come."

Cale looked around at his people. "My choices are that I can either just march my squad and you, my Lady, straight up to FOB Vimes, as quick as we can. Or I can try for the Escarpment forts. Or, I can try to get to higher ground, like up Mount Grunt there, and radio for help."

"I would not undertake any of those travels lightly." Lady Wíela looked at the road that led down to the Escarpment. "You are quite correct: those are the only chances we really have to bring your people back into the fight."

Cale glanced at the nearest shadows, where his people waited for his orders, no doubt puzzled at the stop.

"Lady—"

Maybe she could sense the irritation in his voice, as she raised a hand. "If I had to choose, the mountain would be my road."

Peridot started to object. "You cannot possibly—"

"Why not?" Lady Wíela demanded. "The guardian of the mountain is—"

"Not to be trusted!" Peridot argued. "Putting your lives and mission in the hands of the Grumbly Runt? It is foolish, and dangerous!"

"What's a Grumbly Runt?" Cale asked.

Lady Wíela ignored him. "I've known Grunt for over eighty years. He has no greed or thirst or ambition. He only wishes to collect and create. He's a harmless soul, an artist, to all who know him, and good to those who deal with him fairly. Err on the side of caution with Grunt, and you're always safe."

She directed the last few words right at Cale.

Peridot stepped up and looked at Cale. He saw the decision that had formed there, and he threw his hands in the air. "I'm surrounded by souls who wish to kill themselves."

"So, if we go up the mountain, how do we err on the side of caution?" Cale asked.

"We bring him horns and tallow. As much as we can carry."

Cale looked around the crossroads and the forest. "And where do those come from?"

"Gaurus," Peridot said. "You're going to have to kill lots and lots of gaurus."

Cale looked over at the other Marines, the question clear on his face.

"Cow-things, sir," Diaz called out from behind a tree. "You call them cow-things."

Oh. The farmers had them in the fields. They weren't as domesticated as cows, and still had massive horns. Like the aurochs of old.

"Can't we just . . . just go *buy* them?" Cale asked.

"Are you gonna stroll back into Hilltown, and ask for a cartload of horns and tallow?" Barden asked. "We're low on coin as it is."

"Fucking gaurus," Shane mumbled from behind a bush. "I spent summers working on farms. I hate cow-things."

"You need *gaurus?*" Salia asked, peeking out from behind Barden. Cale jumped slightly. The little girl was still with them? Hadn't he given any orders to find somewhere safe to leave her? A small orphan girl didn't belong with a platoon out in the active field. He would need to figure something out shortly.

But, again, Salia had a solution. "I lived a little while with a farmer after I ran away from the castle. He was killed by bandits, and his family fled, leaving their gaurus to wander the pastures of Growal Plain, near the foot of the mountain. It shouldn't be too hard to slaughter them with your magic weapons. I can lead you there."

"Yeah," Diaz said with entirely too much enthusiasm. "Let's go slaughter some gaurus, Shane."

"Mother*fucker*," Shane replied.

Cale had to agree.

CHAPTER NINETEEN

BARDEN SIGHED HEAVILY and leaned on her knees. Then she straightened her aching back, grabbed the two most recently harvested horns, and stalked off toward the collection area. Not only was it grueling and bloody work, it was exhausting in a whole new and different way.

There was no character being built here, just grinding away at a crappy task.

The first few sets of horns they gathered had actually been off beasts already dead from disease or thirst. They had clearly been domesticated animals let loose, with precious few remaining instincts for self-care.

So maybe this was all a mercy, but that didn't make what they had to do next any better. Strolling up to the big animals, shooting them point blank in the head, then making off with their horns and fat.

That seemed like a waste, but then Antoine had to kill a lynx-like thing coming after them, so several of them figured the dead gaurus would keep the cycle of life going.

Barden found most of the rest of the squad already assembled at the collection point she'd hustled over the rise to. The squad had laid the horns out neatly, and gathered the harvested fat up in some spare canvas bags. Smeared pitch outside the bags sealed them.

They had even managed to wrangle up a pair of shaggy mountain ponies from down the slopes of Mount Grunt, and dragooned them into carrying some of the gear and "tribute" for this Grumbly Runt character.

Naturally, the Marines named the ponies Bill and Twilight Sparkle.

"That's twenty sets of horns," Cale said, as Shane dropped hers at the end of the row. "And ten bags of fat. Lady Wíela, do you think that's enough?"

"It will likely do," Lady Wíela said.

Barden couldn't believe that Lady Wíela looked pristine, despite having handled much of the butchery herself. She'd probably had more practice than any of them at actual butchering. In any other Marine unit, back on the other side of the portal, there probably would have been a dozen or more guys and gals who'd grown up hunting and dressing deer. But there were too many nerds on this side of the portal. Only Heath had experience at it, and he was just drenched in blood, though grinning at her and then Diaz.

"Really wish there was somewhere we could wash up now," Heath said.

At least *his* cloak was still clean. Barden was a mess.

It made her twitch a little. But with that damn Barbie nickname, she wasn't going to say anything about the matted strands of hair. Cale owed her one after the firefight and she wasn't above cashing in, but she could see that he was pissed at the delay and had made up his mind about moving on with this plan.

"We could head back to the glade with the nymphs for a rinse . . ." Dooley said.

"Doc, we're too far away," Cale said.

"As a medic, I have to say that everyone is at higher risk of infection with gauru blood and gore all over us."

"We're going up that mountain," Cale said. "That's the plan. Straight up."

"Besides, I've smelled worse," Heath said.

"Yeah, you *have* smelled worse," Shane agreed.

Jones aimed an accusatory finger down toward the plain, which still appeared to be sunlit. "Did anyone see snow on the mountain down there? I know I did *not* see any snow on the slopes when we were down there."

They had been on the mountain most of the day now, following their successful horn-and-fat hunt, and the arduous climb had just gotten ridiculous.

"Looks can be deceiving, Jones," Barden said.

Jones shook her head. "There was no snow."

Whether there had been or not, snow now swirled all around them. They trudged through it almost up to their knees, and lumps of the stuff rolled down the slopes.

"Suck it up, Marine," Barden said.

"Aye aye, Corporal," Jones replied, and gritted her chattering teeth.

But in truth, Barden was just as dispirited as Jones appeared to be. They didn't have cold-weather gear. At least, not Arctic-level. The wind cut through their cloaks, and a chunk of ice in Barden's collar was slowly, ever so slowly, melting its way down to the small of her back.

Things were not looking up.

Behind them both, Twilight Sparkle trudged through the

snow, looking just as dispirited as Jones. Hanging out on a narrow ledge a thousand meters up from the plain was no place for a pony, either.

Cale had said he wanted quick. Cale was also paying a lot of attention to the mysterious dark elf. Barden just hoped that didn't lead them off to their deaths.

She was just grumpy. That chunk of ice was making her really grumpy. This cold wind made her even grumpier.

The trail they climbed wound narrowly and switched back repeatedly across the steep western face of the mountain. Sunlight streamed toward them, and a few of the Marines popped sunglasses on. Hand it to Mother Nature, or Gaia, or whoever: the out-of-season snow on the mountainside was weird, but with the westering sun it sure was pretty.

"How you feeling about a full pack now, Corporal?" Orley asked.

Barden ignored him.

The switchbacks scrunched closer and closer together, until it got so that when she struggled up one turn there were still Marines on the path below her, working their way up. Bill was down there somewhere, in Brust's keeping.

The ponies turned out to be a good choice. Tireless, they climbed the narrow paths with a steady, surefooted pace.

When they all arrived on a shelf that had been partly worn, partly carved into the mountainside, and the trail finally went up no farther, Barden gasped with relief. She hadn't been sure she could keep on walking.

All that PT, and going up the mountain had kicked her ass.

She looked at her team, red-faced, puffing, dragging their feet, but first up the hill and looking less wobbly than just about anyone else other than Cale.

Barden dragged Twilight Sparkle all the way to the back of

the shelf as fat snowflakes continued to drift down out of the darkening sky. Everyone groaned as asses hit rock and packs dropped.

"Alright, quiet, listen up." Cale waded into the center of the open space, Marines crowded around him both for warmth and word. Two of their favorite things and all. "There's still a lot of mountain over our heads."

All the full creative swearing Marines could muster filled the air, and even Cale didn't try to stand against the torrent. Though, at some point, they realized Salia, all wrapped in heavy blankets, stared at them from the back of Bill.

The swearing tapered off.

Barden blinked. How had the child still ended up traveling with them? She needed to check with Cale about that; she couldn't remember a specific order about Salia.

Salia smiled at her, and Barden gave the little orphan a reassuring wave, then focused back on the platoon.

"I'm done mountain climbing," Jones said into the increasingly calm air. "If I wanted to be a fucking mountain climber I would have been white, had dreadlocks, and spent a lot of time in parks on the West Coast."

As he let everyone vent, Cale counted off heads. "Where the hell is the Ranger? I was in the rear. Who last had eyes on him?"

Lady Wíela cleared her throat. "I believe Peridot intended to go on to the Escarpment forts. When we disagreed, he followed his own counsel and left. We no longer have his company."

"Jesus. He just left us alone?" Orley asked.

"He's not under my command; nothing I can do about it." Cale turned to Lady Wíela, a tired look on his face. Mysterious Rangers came and went as they pleased, apparently. "Now what?"

Cold wind whipped at them; it ripped at their cloaks and

battered them with snow. The vast arch above them and the cavern seemed to trap the bitter cold gusts.

It was a place to stand and wait, but not a good one.

"It won't be long. We wait," Lady Wíela said, but whether it was the cold or something else, her teeth were on the verge of chattering and her lower lip quivered.

"We wait?" Cale growled.

Lady Wíela stepped back from him.

"Seriously, though, my lady—" Cale's *my lady* dripped with sarcasm. "Where is his door? I know you said he could be touchy, but we're not going to get anything done for you, or us, if we freeze to death."

And, where the hell could someone live up here? Barden reached in to touch her M27, but the metal was so cold it startled her.

"Just point us to the front door, okay? If we have to climb some more, it's okay. I'll go knock, and we'll sort this shit out."

Lady Wíela gave him a funny look for a moment, lips pursed, brow scrunched down. "What do you mean, 'front door'? We're there. This is his stoop, his front porch. We're waiting for him to come greet us."

Barden looked up at the top of the rock cavern, far above them.

"Stoop?" Cale asked.

A loud, shuddering thunk of falling rock made them all jump. Then a thudding vibrated through the soles of Barden's feet. Rhythmic, deep, it got stronger, and stronger.

She looked behind Cale, down the cavern and into the snow-flecked darkness behind. A long way down, and in the dark. Maybe. She'd thought it was all rock and shadow, but had something changed?

"Staff Sergeant!" she shouted, her voice breaking slightly, and

Cale whipped back toward the yawning blackness in the face of the mountain. Only now, high up in the dark, a spark jiggled around, casting a little orb of light around it.

The glow filled the darkness, and now she could tell they weren't standing in a scoop-out of the mountainside, but at the front of a tunnel twenty meters high, and almost forty meters wide, as though the entire back wall had been rolled aside by some massive force.

"Spread out! Spread out! Take positions!" Cale shouted.

Cold and darkness and fatigue were forgotten as adrenaline coursed through Barden. But adrenaline could only do so much, and she staggered, dropped to a knee, and lifted the cold M27 that her fingers screamed at her to drop. Her vision swam as she peered through the optical sights of her weapon.

"Troll!" someone shouted.

The massive gray-green bulk of a troll reeled into focus. A tangled lantern dangled from one upraised fist.

It was coming for them!

"Concentrate fire on the head, we've only got one chance at this!" Barden shouted.

"Oh man, I smell like gauru guts!" Heath babbled, off somewhere to the left.

"On my command," Cale screamed. Barden could hear the horror in his voice. Salia was screaming and her pony reared up from the pile of snow around its legs.

The last time they'd fought trolls, they'd barely been able to retreat. This thing was going to just toss them off the side of the mountain.

Lady Wiela threw her arms out and sprinted toward the ravenous beast, right into the line of fire.

"Don't harm him! Don't shoot! This is Grumbly Runt! This is Grumbly Runt!"

Snow swirled into the air between them all as everyone took a breath.

"Weapons down! Down!" Cale snapped.

Barden lowered her M27.

But someone else fired. Just a single shot. Maybe panic, or reflex, or fingers too numb to follow commands.

The sound of it echoed all throughout the cavern, bouncing off rock and dancing around them as they stood there in increasing horror.

A puff of rock dust hung in the air next to the troll's squat neck where the bullet had hit.

The piece of ice working its way down Barden's back slipped through her waistband and into her underwear.

CHAPTER TWENTY

"Owwww," said the troll.

The rest of its words sounded like grinding rocks, so much so that Barden looked up at the mountainside overhead, certain it was about to come sliding down on their heads.

Wíela had frozen, her eyes wide with sudden fear. Everyone else made like statues too. Barden swallowed hard.

"We are very, very sorry," Wíela said. "We come with supplies. Would it be possible for one of your people to very slowly, very calmly, open the sacks to show Grumbly Runt that we come with gifts?"

"Heath," Cale growled from the side of his mouth. "*Slowly* get it all off the ponies. No one else so much as breathe."

They all remained still, hardly blinking, as Heath moved in slow motion to pull the sacks off the animals.

One of the bags clattered loudly when it slipped out from a web of ropes. Barden forced herself not to close her eyes but to stare at the mass of rock and moss that dominated the cavern right in front of them all.

A loud huff of hot air, and the troll raised the massive, flaming torch to look at the bags. It thundered in that other grinding rock of a language.

"What's it saying?" Orley croaked, lips not moving. "Why can't we understand it?"

"Shut up," Cale said.

Troll tongue. Not in the language spell they'd gotten hit with on first arrival, along with all the shots and medical exams. Even Lady Wíela was using some kind of creole or trader tongue. Barden's fatigued and fogged brain recognized some patterns in the sounds, though, outside of any help the language spell gave her.

She took a hesitant step forward, then another, to get a better listen. Occasional, recognizable words floated through the grinding speech, like "forest" and "guardian" and "beast."

The troll beckoned to them all, then Wíela turned to them and did the same.

"Grumbly Runt will receive us," she said.

All eyes turned toward Cale.

"Let's go," he said after a moment's thought. "If we're going to die, I think I'd rather be warm."

"Sure," Orley said. "Let's go spoon a troll."

"Shut up, Orley," Barden said.

They hauled their hard-won trophies up onto tired backs and stumbled toward the massive cave mouth. The troll and Wíela walked inside, quickly engulfed at the threshold by a curious gloom darker than night itself.

Evil magic had to be the reason for that, Barden thought, since the gloom did not let up as they approached. When Barden stepped through, she thought back to striding through the Central Park portal for the first time, because suddenly she found herself in a different world.

Dozens of twisted, gnarled fixtures fashioned from bone

and horn filled the cave with warm light of more bright tallow candles that dripped wax waterfalls than Barden could count. Organic chandeliers blazed from the ceilings, and the hewn-rock walls glittered with hundreds more sconces far over Barden's head.

"It's bright as day," Barden muttered as they all shuffled into the light and warmth to deposit their burdens in a heap before the troll. Barden could tell that he, or maybe she, stood twenty meters tall. And that was with a slouched back and sagging knees. Fully standing up, the troll might have been closer to thirty.

Barden noticed a very discreet Shane reach for the camera in her vest pouch and snap pictures with Wíela near the thing, for scale.

"They were never that big in the movies," Heath whispered beside her.

"They were all sizes in the movies," Antoine said. "And all sizes in the myths Tolkien was strip-mining for material. In the old Scandinavian stories they could even be human-sized and look completely ordinary."

"They must have been thinking of the ones on the internet," Shane said.

Under Lomicka's direction, Ysbarra and Brust arranged the tallow and horns in a relatively neat array. Cale was having another intense chat with Wíela and the troll was paying close attention to the two of them.

Barden took the moment to have a bigger look around the cave. Bigger really might not be enough, though. The place was damn enormous and *really* well lit. The only exceptions were the huge opening they had come through, and another, slightly smaller opening across from it, though they were a good hundred meters apart. The floor was flat, either carved or worn smooth by troll pacing.

"Where you headed?" Antoine caught up and fell into step beside her.

"Recon. This place is huge."

"Big as the parade ground at the Recruit Depot in San Diego."

Barden shook her head. "Lance Corporal?"

"Yes, Corporal?"

"You are a genuine goddamn Hollywood Marine."

"Yes, Corporal!" Antoine agreed readily. "It was all sunglasses and suntan lotion for 'beach runs' and homoerotic volleyball games!"

In reality it would have been much the same in California as in South Carolina. Climbing hills versus dealing with sand fleas seemed to be the real distinctions.

Or so Barden had heard.

Some small, jealous part of her still assumed San Diego had to be better than Parris Island.

Antoine was looking back over at the massive creature in the middle of the cavern. "Goddamn, Corporal. When that troll appeared I just about shit myself."

"Who *was* the nervous shooter?" Barden glanced at Antoine. "Our boot?"

"No." Antoine looked down.

"I'm not looking for punishment, just to check on them. It wasn't anyone on my team."

Antoine walked alongside in quiet for a long moment before saying, "It was Hassel. Lomicka's talking to him."

Sure enough, Lomicka was crouched down next to Hassel, both of them murmuring.

"He's been a little gung-ho," Barden observed.

"For a moment, he thought he got us all killed. He's pretty shook."

Hassel leaned into Lomicka, and she grabbed his shoulder.

Lomicka was dead set on trying to get a promotion, always gaming the system for her and her team. But she was clearly doing the human thing here, making sure Hassel was going to be okay.

Maybe the doc could get in on that. Barden scanned the cavern and saw that Dooley sat cross-legged at the edge of it, staring into a wide pool of water that looked like it might be a cistern or well.

"How long's Doc been doing that?" she asked Antoine.

"Since we got here. Probably waiting for the nymphs to show."

That was another problem they needed to keep an eye on. Dooley was ready to drop anything for a body of water now.

"Those nymphs did a number on her," Barden muttered.

"I didn't know she played for the other team. All that time with our minds in Tactician's Weave and she didn't show us her cards?"

"Not that it's any of your business," Barden said.

Antoine shrugged. "We're always in each other's business, Corporal."

True. This many human beings, jammed up against each other elbow to elbow for multiple tours, they all ended up knowing quite a bit about each other.

"It may not even be that she's gay," Barden said. "It could have been the impact of the nymphs. She got the closest to them." No one was going to care which way Dooley swung, Barden just didn't want her drowning herself in the next open puddle they encountered.

A loud clatter from Cale's direction got Barden's attention. The troll rooted through the supplies.

Cale pointed and shouted. "Barden! Get over here!"

Barden headed over, but carefully kept the piles of gauru stuff between her and the troll, Lady Wíela's assurances notwithstanding.

When she fetched up next to Cale, he held up a hand to her and half-turned to Shane, who he'd also waved over. "Looks like we have an arrangement. Get everyone else on rack ops right now. We need shut-eye. Seems like Grumbly Runt here is pleased with our haul, so we're safe for the night, at least."

"Aye, Staff Sergeant," Shane said, and trotted away.

The troll spoke up, voice like tumbling rocks and crunching gravel. Wíela smiled up at him for a moment, then looked to Cale.

"Grumbly Runt is very pleased with your offer of trade. He seldom gets down the mountain these days, as the land is in turmoil and his old friends in the countryside have been driven off, killed, or worse."

"Worse?" muttered Barden.

"Shh." Cale nudged her.

The troll carried on. He motioned down and away, out the wide door, then to Lady Wíela twice.

"In fact," Lady Wíela continued, "the last time he was down the mountain, he was in the forest of my people, looking for deadfall to use in his carving. He makes the most ornate pieces."

The troll crouched down and held out a huge, gnarly hand. A delicate, carved hummingbird balanced in his palm.

"It's . . . nice," Cale said, not even looking at it.

Lady Wíela and the troll waited.

Barden leaned closer, studied it closely, and then announced, "The craftsmanship is stunning. It's so tiny, it must have been an incredibly challenging project."

Lady Wíela translated, and Grumbly Runt huffed happily and put the piece down on the floor in front of Barden.

A slimy fingertip scooted it toward her feet.

"For me?" Barden looked over.

"A gift for the appreciative," Lady Wíela said, ignoring Barden but staring coolly right at Cale.

Now, Barden thought, was not the time to be measuring dicks with a troll. The human was always going to lose.

Cale saw he had to play diplomat and not drill instructor and said, although mechanically, "We thank you for your carefully crafted piece of art, and our people will treasure it always."

Lady Wíela continued talking with the troll and translating its words for them. "He tells me when he was down looking for wood, he witnessed the uprooting of the Tree of Divine Power. He was shot at and harassed out of the forest by those who would see great harm come to the peaceful elf clans of the forest."

"That must have been a lot of firepower," Barden muttered to Cale.

Lady Wíela continued, "But he saw the Great Worm come, just as it was also described to me by my attendants, roaring and grinding the very earth, lifting the Tree in its great maw, and carrying it to the Silvene Citadel nearby, where it was plunged into a deep cavern beneath the castle."

"Weren't you there, too?" Cale asked her.

"No," she said. "What I know of that day myself, I heard from those loyal to the rightful rulers of the wood elf clans. I have not been there in many years, myself, not since the slaying of the Queen in battle. Chouro, who pretends to rule now, was only meant to be a steward—"

"So how big is this tree?" Cale interrupted her before she could tell them all the history of the many kingdoms. The last thing the Staff Sergeant wanted was a live, in-person performance of *The Silmarillion*. Barden suspected Cale would slice his own ears off before he'd let it come to that. "If you think we can recover it, get it away from this worm, I assume we'll need to get it back to where it belongs."

"Yes," Lady Wíela said.

Grumbly Runt held his hands out wide to indicate the size of the Tree. Lady Wíela smiled at Cale, and Barden's bullshit alarm started blaring.

"Six of your kind could carry it."

Grumbly Runt's crunching-gravel voice got a lot more tumbling-boulderish. Wíela waved whatever he was saying away.

"Sir?" Barden grabbed Cale's arm. "Mind filling me in?"

"We can try the radio again, up in that snowy mess. Or we can keep trying to hump our way over to FOB Vimes."

"Or?" Barden didn't like that there was an "or." They'd changed plans enough, and she didn't want to be the Hermione Granger of the squad, but her command position meant she did have a duty to speak up before the order was actually given, make sure Cale had counsel to consider.

"Or we can help Lady Wíela get that holy potted plant back right now in one quick move, which both ties up the mission and gets us the backup we need. The entire forest that she'll rule."

"They move it . . . again . . . soon." Grunt worked the words out slowly, probably in Elvish, though to Barden it just sounded like English. That was the bummer about the translation spell they were all under. The troll could have been gargling out French or Arabic, but they would never know the difference. Unless she could read Trollish lips which . . . no.

"We have very little time," Wíela pleaded with Barden.

"We can't be going on a raid to help the mystery queen of the forest here, can we, sir?" Barden asked.

Cale wrapped his arms around himself, a sign of insecurity that Barden had never seen before. "Grumbly has apparently seen dark forces in large numbers, breaking through the Escarpment line into our route to Vimes."

"So, we'll shoot our way through the bastards and get home," Barden said. "We're stocked on ammo and food."

"We almost got flattened by trolls, killed by walking skeletons, and half my people almost drowned at the hands of water nymphs."

"That's three almosts, Ray. We're still standing and we can still kick some ass." She swallowed as his head jerked up, and realized she'd fucked up, using his first name.

But he shook his head, and it slid past.

"We're cut off, alone, but we also always have a bigger picture to think about." Cale took a deep breath and relaxed his arms to his sides. "If we take the time to trek to FOB Vimes, and bring the fight back, we might be too late to help Lady Wíela. It's a major setback for the entire coalition out here. The Corrupted One's forces will have time to consolidate their position."

Barden looked over at Lady Wíela, whose dark eyes glittered in the torchlight as she watched them hawkishly.

"Ask the troll this question," Barden demanded. "Why is it helping us out? What are we going to owe Grumbly Runt beyond the gifts we gave it today?"

Lady Wíela hesitated and looked at Cale.

He nodded.

The question was asked, and troll language grated against Barden's ears.

"Grumbly Runt only desires to be able to return to the forest, unmolested, and collect wood for carving. That will be reward enough." Wíela smiled and spread her hands in beneficence. No doubt she would be happy to let the troll pick up whatever it wanted if it gave her a shot at the throne.

"Staff Sergeant." Barden put a hand on his shoulder. "Think it through, right?"

He laughed at hearing his own advice given back to him. He clapped her on the upper arm with the side of a fist. "Always, Corporal. Always."

Well. Here we go. Time to fall in line and follow orders. "Then I'm there with a spare, Staff Sergeant."

"Okay." Cale turned away to look at the troll and the elf. "My Lady, how do we get to this castle safely? There are mercenaries from our side out there, and the Corrupted One's agents all across the land."

"You . . . use . . . back door." Grunt struggled the words out, but he did not seem to want Wíela translating for him anymore. "Avoid all. Is how I go get wood in elf forest."

"Excuse me, back door?" Barden asked.

"Dwarf Mines of Khrelburaladram." The grinding, bouldery voice returned, though maybe Dwarvish kind of sounded like that too. "All dwarfs leave. Furnace wrong. Miss them. They make nice lights."

"How do we go through these dwarf mines?"

"Doors there." Grunt pointed off through the arch at the far end of his cave, opposite the entrance from the mountainside. "Bad moving furnace make it hot, sometimes. You go through quick, squishy ones, you be okay."

"Want to clarify that moving-furnace translation?" Cale asked Lady Wíela.

She looked pained and spread her arms and also shrugged. "Sometimes it's rather complex to get a full and exact meaning across when dealing with troll tongues. Will you not go?"

Cale looked up to the roof.

"We'll do it," Cale finally said, committing. "We'll do it."

"Our people need rest first," Cale said. "And food and water. Then we'll head down through these mines and back to scout and see if there's anything we can do. No guarantees."

"Of course," Lady Wíela said, all too graciously. "And thank you for considering being my champions. Together we shall wrest this land back to its rightful state."

Barden bit her tongue. The squad's nerds would no doubt tell her that nothing good came of walking through abandoned, dwarven mines. And they wouldn't need to tell her twice: even *she* had seen that movie.

CHAPTER TWENTY-ONE

Despite being unnerved by the concept of sleeping near a troll the size of a Transformers robot, Cale found he slept decently in Grumbly Runt's chandelier-lit cavern. He needed it, and the weariness had been put away for the time being, at least.

Barden had been a bit distant since she'd pushed back at his decision. But there was always something about making a firm call that set things in motion for Cale. It even got his blood going, a spring in his step, as he woke up and got ready for the next move.

Everyone had been briefed, they'd done inventory, the machine that was the Marines was oiled and ready.

There was some morning grumbling as tired people got moving, but the team leaders did their junior-drill-instructor routines and kicked a few feet, and the platoon spun into gear.

The last watch said that Grumbly Runt had gone back out on the mountain ledge to see off the last of the night. Some troll thing, waiting until that first deadly hint of dawn came before coming inside. The troll had urged them to go on without him.

"Let's move out!" Cale ordered.

The warm radiance of hundreds of tallow candles gave way to a much cooler dimness as they walked on deeper inside. Cale realized a fainter light came from within the cave, a pervasive green glow. Phosphorescent lichen with writhing roots, like the end of some far-off tree, clung to the walls. Spotted mushrooms grew in the crevices and emitted their own nauseating glow.

"This so don't look like the right way, Staff Sergeant." Ysbarra trudged along just behind him.

"It's not like there's a bunch of branching tunnels or anything. This is it."

"I'd be happier in daylight, Staff Sergeant."

"I'd be happier eating a steak at a shitty chain restaurant, but here we are."

The deeper they went, the brighter the green glow, lighting them up like the view through a pair of night-vision goggles. The only difference was the lack of weird retinal reflection in people's eyes, but that just made it creepier, as everyone's eyes looked dark and empty.

Drips echoed loudly in the darkness, matching time with Cale's steps. The cavern opened wider, and the heights of it were lost in shadow as the glowing lichen only reached up a few meters.

Massive doors of stone coalesced out of the greenish gloom as they approached. Shadows flickered and writhed in the half-light. Cale put the stock of his rifle into his shoulder and scanned up, aiming up out of a sense of duty to all those years of field-of-fire drills.

"We not getting through that, Staff Sergeant," someone shouted from farther down into the gloom.

Doors and corners were where the surprises came. Didn't matter if the door was a wooden one in Fallujah or a massive stone one over here.

The thought had barely formed in his head when a phosphorescent glob of something dropped out of the gloom of the cavern's high ceiling and struck Brust. A few meters to Cale's left, Brust dropped to the ground as glowing goo sizzled and smoked on his chest.

Cale scooted over to where Brust, on his back, struggled with his gear.

"Spread out! Down!" Cale shouted as he swung his rifle around onto his back and started fumbling with the clasps on Brust's gear. The phosphorescent glob had struck Brust square in the chest and was in the process of eating through the layers of Kevlar and ceramic on his upper torso.

"Jesus! Jesus, get it off get it off *getitoff*!" Brust shouted.

They got his Load Bearing Vest out of the way, then ripped open the Velcro seals on his body armor. Brust slithered out, trying not to touch more of the vest than he had to. By the time he was clear, the goo had eaten through the whole Kevlar-and-ceramic front panel and was about to go to work on the thin inner Kevlar layer.

Brust stood there looking down on it for a moment, oddly slender in just his helmet. Then he swept the helmet off his head and spiked it on the ground near what was rapidly becoming a *puddle* of ultra-modern ballistic protection.

"Fuck this!" he shouted. "Fuck the Marines, fuck the portal, fuck the monsters, fuck all this nonsense."

"Brust—"

He whirled and pointed over at the green wall. "And fuck you, you Lovecraftian shitgibbon!"

The thing that spat at him descended out of the darkness into the half-gloom of the floor with them. Tentacles writhed and a beak-like mouth opened and snapped at them.

Cale was on the cusp of making a decision about whether

to retreat, or engage the thing, or just nuke it from orbit, when Grumbly Runt strode heavily into the gloom from the direction of his cave.

"Why awake?" he asked, boulders grinding in his landslide cacophony of a voice. "*You* not be awake now!"

The troll clocked the thing hard with a massive fist to the beak. It squealed and scampered back up the wall into the gloom above, the yelping squeak receding for quite some time as it crawled back into deep tunnels within the mountain. Grumbly Runt stood there for a moment, looking up into the dark after it.

"Naughty," the troll said.

Then he shook his head and moved toward the immense doors. He pushed them open, stone grinding on stone so loudly it made Cale's teeth ache.

"You okay?" Cale asked, looking at Brust now that the Marine had calmed down a little. The man's body armor sizzled in a little pool of bright green by his feet.

"I'll live, Staff Sergeant." Brust gathered up his LBV and weapon and strapped them both back on. The LBV hung loose on his lanky frame without the bulk of his body armor underneath it.

"Guardian of the Portal worries you not, now," Runt said, standing aside from the door. Jones scrambled to get out of his way as he nearly trod on her as he backed up.

It was dark on the other side of the door. No bioluminescent lichen out there.

"Go," the troll gestured. "Elfland on far side."

The troll had said the way was marked with misshapen antlers that didn't make the cut for his massive chandeliers.

Easy enough, right?

Cale waved Barden forward, and she pushed Rashad out on point. The young Marine took a moment to steady himself, looked at everyone, and then moved forward into the deeper darkness beyond the huge doors.

Jones hurried up to Cale's side as he fell into the middle of the column.

"I got a bad feeling, Staff Sergeant," she said.

"You said that when we were stepping off in Central Park."

"I was right then, Staff Sergeant."

"I know this looks like a road of shit. But it's a road of shit toward mission accomplishment. I'm not going to throw the squad off a cliff, though. If it gets too hot or nasty or whatever, we boogie back and knock on the doors. Runt will let us back in."

Jones looked long up at the huge doors as they passed through. They had to be stone, maybe a foot thick, with huge, iron bands holding the slabs up and binding them to great hinges.

"Yeah, Staff Sergeant," she said. "But how do we knock on those?" The door knockers were well out of human reach, and too big for any of them to lift without a crane's help.

Cale pondered it as they walked. Explosives might do it, maybe a couple of grenades, or one of the two 66mm light anti-tank rockets they had with them. Or both of them. Or every scrap of boom-pow they had with them. Maybe that would get Runt's attention. If they needed to.

As he ran through the possible plans in his head, though, the last of the squad crossed the threshold and Runt swung the doors closed behind them with a titanic boom.

Rashad picked his way carefully over the rough ground, the bright xenon flashlight mounted to his M27 stabbing a cone of white light into the smothering darkness. Everyone had their lights on, as the night-vision goggles soon proved useless. The goggles worked on enhancing ambient light, and there was fuck-all for them to enhance this deep inside a mountain.

Every few hundred meters, a chasm opened up, or some rocky pillar sprouted up from the living stone. Well ahead, on point, Team Three was prowling around, checking their path, finding piles of rocks or large pots of wax that Runt had used to guide himself through the dwarven mines.

And mines they were, certainly, no rectilinear dungeon or picturesque subterranean city. Filthy, abandoned camps could be seen at the edge of their flashlights' glow every now and then. Runic graffiti covered some walls.

Rashad figured Diaz could probably decipher it, but Team Two was too far back for him to ask.

An hour into the dark, they found a narrow bridge, which should have presented a challenge to Grumbly Runt, as big as he was. No railings, no curbs on either side, and *maybe* wide enough for three to walk abreast, if they were brave. Everyone stayed scrupulously in the center as they shuffled across it.

"Well, now we know the fucking Mines of Moria ain't OS-HA-compliant," Jones said, close behind Rashad as they started down the far side of the narrow, arching bridge. Rashad didn't point his flashlight down off the side as he went, resolutely keeping his eyes forward. He did *not* want to see the edge of the light disappear into the dark.

"Yeah, well, that's the thing, ain't it?" Orley asked. "You wouldn't want to be crossing this thing if shit went south."

Team Two remained on the near side in a defensive semi-circle while the rest of the squad shuffled across.

"It's a great choke point for stopping anyone with bad ideas," Orley said.

"Iron Age armies, maybe," Jones said. "But man, you pound the far side with a couple of M-240 machine guns and lay down some mortar fire, you can probably stroll across by the time the defenders put the pieces back together."

"Yeah, maybe," Orley looked back at it. "If the defenders don't have all that stuff, too."

Rashad thought about that Warthog going down to a Stinger missile fired by one of the attacking wood elves back at the base. Someone else on this side of the interworld portals had advanced weapons, and they really needed to stop thinking they were the only ones with modern munitions. That was "gets you dead" complacency shit.

Ass-umptions make *asses* out of all of you, his drill instructor used to say.

At the bottom of the bridge, Cale waved everyone impatiently on. He seemed even more tense than usual, which Rashad hadn't thought possible.

Team Two boogied across the bridge and Barden moved Team One into the point position, relieving Team Three. Rashad prodded at the darker corners of the little paved plaza at the end of the bridge.

"Where the hell are Runt's signposts?" Orley asked. He was on point, waving his flashlight around. "I can't see anything."

Barden frowned for a moment, then aimed her light up the nearest wall. Sure enough, there was an antler jammed into a fissure in the rock, drizzled on the end with melted wax.

"Look up," she said. "Runt's twenty meters tall."

Orley started craning his neck as he walked.

"But watch your feet, Orley!" Barden snapped. "No bottomless chasms, got it?"

"Aye aye, Corporal."

He moved off into the gloom, with Barden close behind him. Rashad followed, with Jones behind.

"You okay back there?" Barden asked.

"It's getting hotter and I can't see shit. I think my batteries are dying," Rashad confessed.

"Stay close behind and watch my light," she said, half-turning her head. "Is your solar charger in your daypack?"

Barden and her full load-out. "Yes, Corporal."

"Make sure to recharge next time we're out in the light."

"Shit."

That was Jones, all the way at the back. Rashad swiveled to look.

"Something's moving toward us," she said.

In the far distance, Barden spotted a flicker of orange flame. She frowned as it dimmed, then flared up again. The ground sloped down, which could only mean good things, at least as long as they didn't keep going down below the level of the ground around the mountain.

"Jones? What do you see?" Barden asked.

The occasional tunnel branched off left or right, but nothing that Runt could have fit in. Above, near what must have been the top of Runt's reach, the walls of their present path flared out and embraced a dark openness. This path must have been a central route for ore and whatever else was mined in the upper reaches, which was then sent down to smelting furnaces. That was likely what lay ahead.

Only, there were no rail lines here. Just . . . shadows of where lines had once been.

"I don't know." Jones pulled out a laser thermometer and waved it around.

"Picking up the furnaces ahead?" Barden asked.

"Something hot. Are you sure that what's up there? There

aren't any people living here anymore—Runt said it was abandoned."

"I hope so." Barden shrugged her shoulders, as much in uncertainty as a desire to resettle the weight of her armor, vest, and pack.

Jones looked back off into the dark as she waved the thermometer around. "Furnaces don't usually move, Corporal."

"Move?"

"Watch . . ." Jones said, and waved the laser thermometer left, then right, the numbers dipping, climbing, then dipping again. Then she held it still, and the numbers rose and dipped on their own. When Barden looked up, the orange light off in the dark flared brighter.

Then a tongue of bright flame lanced out in a straight line, followed by the roar of fire and the press of a giant bellows.

Or—

"DRAGON!" shouted Orley from the front of the squad column.

The bright spot grew rapidly, growing clearer as the deep and constant fire within a great dragon's open mouth. It looked, Barden thought, like some mix of a flying Godzilla and angry, giant iguana with wings. Everyone dropped low and the creature flew above them an instant later, another bright line of flame striking out to smash a finger of rock over their heads. Molten clumps dripped down the wall and lit the Marines up in a soft orange glow.

"Scatter!" Cale shouted, and everyone split left and right. Barden saw Cale hunched over Heath, who had dropped on his back to point his automatic rifle toward the distant ceiling of the cavern. It was classic dragon-overflight-immediate-action mode.

Barden dodged right, pulling Jones with her. Cale went right, Heath left as he scrambled to his feet. From overhead, a head-pounding shriek dizzied Barden and fire lashed the path they had just stood on. Barden's face reddened with the near heat.

She and Jones ran with Cale and Diaz into one of the side tunnels and crouched. The line of fire left by the dragon continued to burn, setting up a wall of flame between them and the Marines who had gone left.

On the other side of the curtain of fire, Ysbarra stepped out of a tunnel with an opened LAW propped on her shoulder. She triggered it, and the missile leapt out of the collapsible tube and shrieked up into the dark of the cavern. She scuttled back inside just as a new blast of fire splashed the rock by her feet.

"What can we do to bring these down?" Cale shouted. "I never trusted that immediate-action shit. Diaz?"

"A black arrow in the right spot?" Diaz offered, gritting his teeth and aiming down the tunnel toward the fire.

"Didn't the dwarves dump molten gold on that dragon in *The Hobbit*?" Barden asked.

"That's not canon," Diaz hissed. "It takes air support or surface-to-air missiles to tackle a dragon. Ysbarra's got the best idea. I don't know if it's powerful enough to penetrate all that scale, though."

A new blast of fire sent them scurrying farther back. Cale kept them moving deeper into the tunnel, as fire completely blocked the other end. They ducked left and right, following the tunnel, then taking what forks and crossing tunnels might bring them back to the central path, or down to another one.

The radio didn't work through the rock, only when they were back out in the open. They couldn't raise anyone else, other than in shouted fragments and echoes.

They popped out into a narrow passage, then turned and ran downslope, finding cart rails there unmelted by the dragon. They ran down them until they found a crossway. One opening led them out into a wide plaza, fronted with a tall colonnade, though it held up no roof—as here the ceiling reared high up as it had on their previous path.

"Do you see it?" Cale spun in a tight circle, aiming upward. "Anyone see it?"

Barden swung in a slow circle, keeping the others at her back, scanning right and left, up and down. Jones was at her shoulder, her M27 up, grasping both the laser thermometer and the foregrip of the automatic rifle in one hand. The dayglo-yellow instrument bleeped.

"Jones?" Barden hissed. "What's it telling you?"

"There!" Jones and Cale shouted the words together. Bright flame blossomed under a tall, stone arch. Barden felt someone grab at her daypack to pull off the squad's other LAW.

The dragon crawled over the ground, long neck craning about as it looked for anything moving to barbecue.

Diaz ran forward at it as he extended the rocket launcher's telescoping tube.

"Diaz!" Cale shouted.

"I got this, Staff Sergeant," he said without looking back.

"Fucking idiot," Cale grumbled, but they all hustled after him. Two hundred meters from the arch, Diaz skidded down to his knees.

They were all, painfully, out in the open.

The dragon turned to regard them, the armor around its black eyes crinkling as it squinted in anger.

"Backblast area clear!" Diaz shouted, and the other three swerved off to the right of him. The rocket flared bright in the dark as it shrieked out of the tube. Angled up slightly, it flew straight, no wind or updrafts or anything in the still dark of the mine to divert it.

And it missed.

Barden's heart skipped a beat as the missile flew high of the dragon as the beast awkwardly walked under the massive arch.

The arch's keystone shattered, turned to gravel by the anti-tank round. The crumbled stone pattered down on the dragon's back, followed a moment later by tons of stone. A brief belch of flame flared out, then darkness and sulfurous stench settled hard in the open plaza.

"Is it down for good?" Cale asked.

"Probably not, Staff Sergeant." Diaz shouted far too loud, overcompensating for his own likely ringing ears.

"Let's move, then."

"Should we try to track everyone else down?" Barden asked. The place looked like a dungeon maze to beat the worst of Gygax's imagination. No telling where the rest of the squad was, or how many of them had survived the dragon.

"Find a way out, first, then we can try backtracking. Everyone else knows we're trying to get out."

"Which way then, Staff Sergeant?"

"I don't care, just not back the way we came. Otherwise, my sense of direction is truly fucked."

Barden led off. She spotted the tunnel they had come through, ninety degrees around the huge square from where the dragon lay mostly buried. Leaving the thing behind them felt like a bad idea, but they had no idea if they could kill it, or if it was even safe to try.

She picked the colonnade directly opposite where they had come in and hurried through it. Jones had chalk out, and tagged the walls with directions and intel, hoping anyone who came behind used it.

Behind the columns, a series of arches led them into a wide arcade, but a false turn led them into a rough mining area, covered in the graffiti of dying dwarves who had no doubt been in the same position. They backtracked and down the other end of the arcade, which led into another wide plaza.

She took them down only three other false turns before she caught a whiff of fresh air. Within a few more steps they all sensed it and hurried on, breaking from a cautious shuffle into a trot. Dazzling daylight hit them and they burst out onto a wide balcony cut into the side of the mountain.

For a moment they panted and looked up at the sky, appreciating just being out of the dark.

In the distance, a fortress rose up against the far blue sky, towers looking as though they had been grown from the boles of great trees. Finger-like branches curled out, offering parapets on which an archer might stand to shoot down at attackers.

"That must be it. Looks wood-elfy enough," Jones muttered.

The towers themselves stood on pyramid bases, thrusting up like great collections of roots, to push the tree-towers to the sky. The greens and browns of the towers and roots glowed in the noon sun. Below them, maybe fifty meters down the mountain slope, a road had been carved into the craggy face of the mountain, terminating somewhere off to their left, and shortly along to their right jutting out from the mountain along the spine of a great spur of stone, leading off toward the distant fortress.

The radio crackled. It was Lomicka.

Barden leaned over the balcony, cautiously, as it was crumbling. Marines below her were spilling out of a cut in the mountain and onto the road.

CHAPTER TWENTY-TWO

THE CLIMB DOWN from the balcony nearly killed Cale.

It wasn't an especially challenging climb, but all they had was that 550-pound test cord. It was strong, but thin. All they could do was tie loops in it for hand- and footholds, and use that to climb down. Each grip dug into Cale's hands, down even through his gloves and calluses, and half the time he felt like he was tipping backward off the rope or wobbling too much.

On the ground, most of the rest of squad, including the Lady Wíela, had gathered to watch them all awkwardly clamber down.

When Cale had massaged the feeling back into his hands, he looked up at Lomicka.

"How did you get out?"

"Luck of the draw, Staff Sergeant. We zigged when you all zagged and the tunnels barfed us out on some kind of main street. We heard the cave-in and thought you all might have bought it."

"No such luck." Cale looked around and did the head count. "I don't see Shane or Rashad, or the kid."

Lomicka shook her head and Cale sighed. They both glanced in the direction of the other two team leaders.

Each of them was one down; each of them had been forced to leave the rest of their teams behind in the tunnels. Lomicka had organized almost all of the rest, including their High Value Asset, and pulled them out of the fire.

"If the cutting scores are not in your favor when we link back up with the company, I'll be putting you in for a meritorious promotion, Lomicka."

She gave him a half-smile and shrugged. He didn't need any more thanks than that, and the squad knew it well enough. The promotion was his thanks to her, after all, for making sure he didn't have to live with losing his entire squad.

"Did anyone see them go down or anything?" he asked.

"No, Staff Sergeant. I saw Rashad grab the girl, and Heath says he saw Shane push them both down a tunnel. But we couldn't find a connection to them, the radios couldn't get through the rock, and the fire was too hot for us to get around by the main way."

"Yeah." Cale glanced over at Antoine. Part of his sleeve had burned away, flashing into dust when the flame got too near. Doc had him sitting on a rock, tending to the small burns he had suffered. "Get your team in order and get me an ammo check. Spread load if anyone is running critically low."

"Aye, Staff Sergeant." She drifted back to her team, leaving him alone by the side of the stone-paved road.

"What are we going to do about the three of them?" Barden asked.

It was the question Cale had been avoiding drawing up an answer to as he mulled the situation. *Leave no one behind.* Or, get the job done and go find your missing people with the full resources and might of the USMC and its local allies behind the effort.

"If they come out on this side, the radios will work." Cale had to hope that. Or he'd have let them down. Rashad was just a boot. You had to look out for the new ones. That was *the job.*

Barden crossed her arms. "And if they don't come out on this side?"

Cale propped a foot up on one rounded lump of rock and leaned forward, looking out toward the looming, sylvan fortress. The elves' woods stretched away from the fortress base to the west, then tapered down to scattered trees and undulating plain to the east. He couldn't answer her right now, didn't trust his voice.

Lady Wíela stepped up beside him. "If they stay close to the little girl, they'll survive. She has walked through tempests unscathed, and knows this land better than they do."

"If she survives," Cale said slowly, "it'll be because my Marines bring them through."

"Perhaps." Lady Wíela shrugged. "Will you still help me on my sacred path to regain—"

Cale straightened and called out, "Three minutes, then we need to move."

He didn't want to talk to her about her sacred *anything* right now.

"Aye, Staff Sergeant," everyone replied.

Barden leaned in. "But we're coming back, when this is all over. If we don't hear anything."

"We'll come back with the whole platoon, a month's worth of food, and a truckload of batteries for the flashlights and NVGs," Cale said. He would bring the entire goddamn Marine Corps back out here if he had to. "Lieutenant Chucklefuck owes me at least that much."

Barden laughed as he caught her off guard. As if, Cale thought, he didn't know what the junior Marines called their platoon commander, Lieutenant Nacklebuch. Like he hadn't been a lance corporal once himself.

"Okay, Staff Sergeant," she said. "Okay."

"Go on. Get Jones and Orley moving."

Barden nodded and hurried back to her reduced team. He looked after her for a moment, then shook his head. It was time to get their minds right, and time for him to put his own bullshit behind so he could face what needed to be done next.

"Squad! School circle!" At his words, they all perked up and hustled in his direction. He faced them, his back to the fortress and forest beyond. They spread in a semi-circle, most of them dropping to one knee and looking up at him.

Cale looked them each in the eye, trying to summon every bit of advice and learning he had gathered from Staff NCO school. But no one in NCO school had told him what to say when your people had been scattered by a dragon deep in the mountain, two of them being led by an oddly knowledgeable child probably toward who-knew-what, while you prepared to launch an assault on an elvish tree fortress.

"I know this sucks," Cale said. "I know we're all tired and hurting. I know we miss those two knuckleheads still inside the mountain. But you know how it goes. The fastest way out is through. We get that magical tree back for the lady, we get the right—or at least the less wrong—people in charge of the elves standing between us and the portal home and a pile of reinforcements. We do this one bit, and I guarantee Captain Hobbs is going to bring the whole Fifth Marines back through here if she can."

They didn't smile. But their looks hardened. Shoulders straightened.

"Everybody got me?"

"Yes, Staff Sergeant," they chorused back at him.

"Good. On your feet, let's get this done. Team Two lead, Team One slack." Diaz nodded sharply at him, then pointed at Heath, who positioned himself down the road. The rest fell in behind him.

"You sure about all this?" Doc sidled up beside him, a worried look on her face.

"Very," Cale lied firmly. "Now fall in."

They stepped off smartly, moving quickly down the road. He felt exposed out here, especially to a dragon, but there was no sign of it anywhere. He wondered if an elf sentry could see them from the distant tower.

Maybe.

He couldn't worry about that now. The road down the mountain was the best way, otherwise the face of the mountain fell sheer down into unforgiving gullies. No way to go down the slope, and in most places it was as bare of vegetation as the road.

So, they hustled down.

Once they dropped onto more level ground, Heath guided them off into the fringes of the forest and off the road. There still wasn't a great deal of cover: the trees were spaced out widely as though there had been a fire in the last five years or so and not much had grown up among the survivors.

Then the forest thickened, and the fortress loomed larger. If the towers were meant to be trees, they were a monument to the largest trees that had ever grown anywhere. Ever. Bigger than California redwoods, certainly. When they paused within a thousand meters of the fortress, the towers loomed like the mountain, set upon the pyramid tangle of stone roots, cleverly carved into embrasures and walks.

In a small stand of trees, they low-crawled to a slight rise in the ground, hopefully hidden from all but the keenest eyes. Lady Wíela lay prone beside him on one side, Barden on the other with her binos up, looking over the fortress.

"Can they see us from here?" Cale turned to glance at Wíela.

"Some, perhaps. If they're looking right at us. We see well, but we cannot see through walls."

"Comforting." He glanced back at the rest of the squad, holding set in their perimeter. Lomicka anchored the far side of the circle. Then he turned to Barden. "What can you see?"

"Bad fucking news, Staff Sergeant."

"Tell me."

"Elf sentries, armed. A couple of wood trolls of some kind ambling around. But we expected that. The bad news is. . . ." She pulled the binos away from her face and looked at him. "It's the fucking mercs. I can see them."

Cale knew it. He'd guessed it from their encounters, even though they hadn't gotten close enough to put eyes on them. "A bunch of dipshits who couldn't cut it in the military, or wanted a bigger payday, strolling around with their tacticool M-4s, dripping with GI Joe accessories."

"Yessir. They're teaching some of the elves how to shoot. Badly."

"Which outfit?" There were a half-dozen corporate names he could think of.

"Can't tell." She put the binos back to her face, even so, as though trying to puzzle it out. "It's not like they're wearing uniforms. *Assholes.*"

"You jealous?" Cale held his hand out for the binos and she handed them over. He squinted through them and dialed in the focus.

"Fuck no, Staff Sergeant. I got those dope Marine Corps blues that pull all the boys to *my* yard."

Cale quickly found the cluster of mercenaries trying to teach elves to shoot. They seemed unfamiliar with it, and at one point an elf dropped the black rifle as if it had burned his hands.

He scanned slowly left, then right, and found something curious: a small clutch of people in white hard hats, working what looked like surveying gear. Not the GPS-enabled stuff they used back home these days, but then there wasn't any GPS system here, was there? Just talk of mounting shit to blimps that made the rounds once a week or so, but had yet to materialize.

He handed the binos back to Barden.

"Frontal assault isn't going to cut it, is it boss?" she asked.

Cale didn't think so. Not if the enemy had automatic weapons as well as magic ones.

Lady Wíela had slithered up next to them. She stiffened, then looked around.

"Who just broke a branch?" she asked, her voice slightly panicked.

Cale followed her frantic glance, worried that she spotted some threat, but she was only looking around his small circle of Marines. Then she stared at Brust, trying to quietly snap a branch out of the way so he could prop up his rifle and get a better firing position.

"NO! Stop!"

Lady Wíela's warning came too late. The tree shifted, and a huge limb reached down to grab Brust around the waist. Screaming, he flailed as it lifted him high in the air. His M27 clattered to the ground as the tree opened a mouth, gaping and dark like the entrance to Hell, and roared.

"Shit-fuck-shit." Cale scrambled to his feet, bringing his weapon to bear.

Another nearby tree stirred into action, then another. "Back, back, fall back!"

Barden stumbled back, looking up, aghast. A leafy limb swung at her and she rolled away, just out of reach, then sprang to her feet again.

"But . . . but ents are supposed to be *nice!*" Barden sounded equally pissed and shocked.

Cale had no idea what the fuck "ents" were.

CHAPTER TWENTY-THREE

"THE GODDAMN TREE got Brust," Heath hissed to Cale.

"I saw it," Cale said. "I saw it."

They hunkered back in a copse of trees, the non-moving kind, thankfully. Brust and Jones had been snatched up, but the rest of them had gotten away from the monster trees, thankfully.

"In the movies, that one tree-guy helped the Hobbits, right?" Heath said. "What the hell is going on?"

"We don't have time for me to give you a lecture on the elemental nature of ents and huorns and how *this isn't that fucking movie*," Cpl Diaz snarled out the last few words.

Something large crashed through the undergrowth nearby. "We smell you, you fucking rats. Shit-stained little fuckwads, clinging to your weapons of metal like the lice-infested vermin that you are."

"The ents are *salty*," Orley whispered.

"Your fuckwitted kind come to our world, clear-cut our homes like the cock-gobbling shitstains you are, and presume then to break off our branches? Vile motherfucking ass-faced bastards. We'll find you and crush you like shit-eating bugs." The walking tree paced around the copse, seeming to zero in on them.

"They got the wrong guys," Diaz muttered. "We haven't clear-cut shit."

"I imagine we all look the same to them," Antoine replied. "Also, cock-gobbling's a bit homophobic, yeah? I know they're not as woke in medieval world, but you'd think walking wood would respect—"

"Diaz, when he's on the far side, pop an illumination round. When he zigs, we'll zag." Cale looked around at all of them to make sure they understood, and Heath nodded when the Staff Sergeant locked eyes with him. "Good."

They all listened to another minute of the tree's foul-mouthed diatribe. It was enough to make even a drill instructor blush. Some humans, maybe these mercs, had really, really pissed off the trees by doing something . . . all too human.

If the ents ever crossed through a portal and saw a city, they'd be *livid*.

Diaz blooped an illumination round from his grenade launcher. The little parachute popped on it and the phosphorus flare ignited and it started to drift down. Cale got up and ran.

Three strides out of the copse, he realized he was first out. He was overeager. And the creature hadn't had time to react to the distraction just yet.

Cale tried to swing his M27 up to bear on the angry, walking tree that now turned to look at him running by instead of the flare. A huge limb batted the weapon out of his hands. Strong branches closed around his body and yanked him off his feet, surprising a scream out of him.

"You little shit-for-brains ass-licking fuckstick." The words growled out at him from deep inside the bark. From within the branches he could perceive dark, hateful eyes as the thing lifted him off the ground.

"That wasn't us!" Cale snarled.

"Shut up." The tree curled more branches around him.

The suppressed chatter of an M27 filled Cale's world. The tree swore and turned, whipping Cale around so fast his vision faded.

It dropped him to the ground and charged Heath, who stood his ground to make sure Staff Sergeant had time to get to safety as rounds blew chunks of wood and splinters into the air.

"Run! Run, you asshole!" Cale shouted.

The next moment Cale blinked, the tree had swooped over Heath.

All around, Marines opened fire, and the tree retreated toward the fortress with the Marine tightly held in its branches.

Diaz got hold of Cale's drag-strap and pulled him to his feet, helping him stagger out toward another ominous line of trees.

Barden led them across the road back to the mountain and off the far side. The land fell away a little to the east and north, much like the land they had seen east of the mountain. They were clearly on the edge of whatever geological formations had given them the hills and badlands around the FOB. Few trees dotted the plain and greenery seemed to fail completely a kilometer or so in the distance.

She spotted a small hill that reared up just over the level of the road and separated from it by a hundred meters or so. They all made straight for it, the remains of the squad scrambling up behind her. At the top they found the mossy foundations of an old observation tower. It would once have commanded a good view of both the road from the mountain and the expanse of the plain.

It would serve them well the same way, but it would also be easy to surround.

Barden didn't think they could linger there. But maybe it could give them just long enough to plan their next steps.

Marines arrayed themselves in a perimeter, though most of them laid out on the side facing the fortress. The threat would come from there.

Cale crouched down beside Barden, panting heavily, which was unusual. She noticed even Doc had taken a position on the perimeter, her M-4 snugged up on her shoulder and Brust's rifle slung across her back. Cale had grabbed Heath's weapon from the ground once he was able to walk on his own again. But it had been close. Barden had screamed at Heath to get the tree's attention.

She'd ordered him to take it on, and it had tossed Cale away for Heath.

That was fucked up, she thought. Really fucked up. But Heath hadn't blinked. He'd known what she was asking.

Or at least, she really hoped so.

"It's a shit sandwich, Staff Sergeant." Barden locked eyes with Cale. His face was pale. The tree had tossed him around like a chew toy. It was a miracle he was walking.

"Down five Marines now, and how many mercs out there?" Cale asked. She could hear the pain in his voice.

Doc heard it too. She pulled out some painkillers and a canteen.

"Guess at about forty," Barden said. "Plus maybe a hundred, hundred-fifty wood elves. All they got is bows, but we're running out of bullets."

"And they know we're coming, now." Cale swallowed the two pills and drank heavily from the canteen.

"What's our next move, sir?"

Lady Wíela crept over and crouched beside them. Her gown, which had already been dirty when they'd pulled her from the crashed Osprey, was now completely filthy. Yet it did not seem to have lost a single stitch. Elven workmanship.

"Complete your mission and get me to the Tree," she said softly. "The moment I'm returned to my power I can bring forces to bear, Cale of—"

Cale pinched the bridge of his nose and closed his eyes. "Where is the cavern entrance, the one Runt said they had taken the tree into?"

"On the far side of the fortress, to the north. A wide gap in the rock supporting the fortress, which can be secured with swinging gates, though rarely it has been in all the years of relative peace."

"We'll have to sweep way out and around the fortress to get there. And if they're smart, they'll send out patrols." Cale frowned and opened his eyes to look off to the north, then to the west. "A few hours yet until sundown, but I don't think night is going to bring us any advantage against elves on their home ground."

Barden looked up at him, then back out to the west. She caught flickers of movement between the trees, though still at least a kilometer off. "We've got movement."

Cale looked pained. "We need a plan, but we do not have nearly enough time or intel. And all my choices have gone to shit so far."

Barden leaned in. She grabbed the front of his armor and pulled him until they were nose to nose.

"We've made it farther and come through more than we should have, and that's because of you. You kept a level head and got us through more than anyone should expect of any rifle squad. We're not Force Recon, or SEALs, or Delta, and I doubt any of them could have done much better than this."

He was feeling the pain of not getting Rashad through the mountain, and damnit, so was she. But they had to move on, they had to see this through, or there would be no chance of going back for the kid. No one would even know where he was lost if they didn't finish . . . whatever came next.

Cale grabbed her wrist. "Corporal, I have to be honest. I'm feeling a little out of my depth."

"You just got hit in the head." Barden looked around and lowered her voice. "Ray, you told me once, when it all fails, get them all running right at the problem with fresh ammo."

"I was joking."

"Were you?"

"Staff Sergeant, big squad approaching the road." Orley struggled to keep his whisper from becoming a shout. "Mixed mercs and elves."

Cale let go of her. They both stood.

"Hassel, on point, down the back of the hill, let's go." Cale straightened his shoulders and snapped the order out. Whatever momentary despair that he had shown was gone, dispelled either by her words or the imminent threat. Perhaps both. "There's no way in, now that they know we're coming. They'll be doubling up the security. Or just running away."

Lady Wíela was looking at the sun, covering it with a hand and deep in apparent thought. She ignored the Marines moving around her. "If we retreat and hide, in a few weeks with the new moon, there will appear another way into the caverns under the fortress."

"What?" Cale turned back to her.

"Few, even among my family know, about this entrance, much less these interlopers." Lady Wíela clutched at Cale's sleeve as the squad started to move on his order.

"Why the fuck are you just telling us this now?" Barden growled. "We could have just gone straight to the back entrance, *Lady*."

Lady Wíela winced. "Some secrets are not supposed to be mine to share. And . . . it will not be open just now. I knew time was not on our side. It can't be opened until the new moon."

"We'll find a way, with explosives if we need to."

"It is not that easy. There is seasonal magic involved."

"Show us the fucking way." Cale's voice brooked no argument. "Show us this way, and we're right behind you. If not, we have to leave. Make your choice."

Lady Wíela stared at him for a moment, weighing her options. Then she nodded. "The Crescent Door it is."

She ran to the far side of the hilltop and slipped down the side. Cale ran after her, and Barden followed right behind Cale.

CHAPTER TWENTY-FOUR

"WHERE NOW?" Hassel asked from beside the bole of a huge tree.

Cale had seen Hassel check it a few times before approaching, and they saw no sign that it was anything other than an ordinary tree, doing ordinary-tree things. Like shifting slightly in the wind, or attracting moss. Still, they all kept nervously glancing up at the branches.

The lady elf hunched over Hassel's shoulder, her grimy gown still glittering a little in the late evening light.

"To the left—the standing stones there, do you see them?"

"Check it out, Hassel," Barden ordered.

Hassel threaded through a narrow and stony track in the woods, trying his best to slip through the underbrush without much noise.

Tracking side to side across the path, he moved into the deep shadow of the stones, through the narrow gate between them. The circle was clear, floored with springy green turf and open to the sky. But trees, ordinary trees and not stomping monsters by the look of them, ringed the circle beyond the fence of stones.

To Cale it looked like the pictures of Stonehenge, but more

precisely cut and intricately carved. And smack in the middle of a forest instead of a grassy field.

With the trees and brush growing around them, the place seemed all but impossible to find from outside, unless someone took the path they had. Hopefully the shitheads and the elves back behind Cale would take a little while to find them in this thick copse, though that seemed like hoping the rain wouldn't be quite so wet, or the sun all that hot.

Barden, as if reading his thoughts, was looking behind them now that she'd scoped out the magical stone circle. "Not a bad blind, sir, and easy to defend, while the ammo holds out."

Cale couldn't meet her gaze right now. Not since she'd had to pull him to his feet and give him a little pep talk earlier. Yeah, she was ready for that next level of leadership. She could drive her very own platoon nuts insisting on full packs, map memorization, and extra mags of ammo.

They might call her Barbie behind her back, but Barden was high-speed low-drag and cool under pressure.

But what would he do without his corporal?

He didn't want to think about that. It wasn't something that needed solved right now.

So, he pointed at the stones and said gruffly, "Spread 'em out, Corporal Barden."

Then he made his way across the circle, maybe fifty meters, and crouched beside one of the upright stones. Marines crept through the gate and fanned out around the perimeter, though like him, they could not hope to push through the brush and actually guard the perimeter.

"Alright, what now?" Cale asked.

"Now?" Lady Wíela asked.

"Yes, now. What now? Where do we go from here?"

Lady Wíela closed her eyes and lay her head back, looking

up into the slowly darkening sky. Just to the east, the sky had started to go purple, a few bright points flickering to life in the heavens.

"Well?" Cale prompted again.

"According to the stars," she said, and peered off toward the east, over the tops of the trees on that side. "It is three weeks until midsummer. On that day, we must watch the upper faces of the leaning stones. The one on which a lizard scampers upward, then widdershins, at the moon's highest light, will mark our way in. The earth under will have aligned—"

"We don't have three weeks." Cale leaned his back against the cool stone. He was in a foreign land with foreign rules. Don't just smack your head against the door, he thought back to his leadership training. Understand the problem first. Learn everything you can about your situation if you have the time for it. *Then* make a plan of action.

"Is it just a hidden door, or is there some kind of portal that opens?" Cale's voice was calm. He was surprised by that.

"Portal?"

"Like we came through, to get from our world."

"No, no, it is a regular tunnel entrance. My grandmother carried me out through here when her husband the King was slain in his sleep, beginning this unholy struggle."

"You've been right here before? You know this castle, and you know the grounds, then?"

"Well enough to get you this far, and inside, if we can survive long enough for the door to reveal itself."

"We can't—that's not going to happen. We may as well wish for Shane and Rashad and Peridot and the little squeaky orphan girl and Grumbly Runt himself to come on down here, guns blazing, and rain hellfire down on all the elves and human mercenaries between us and the tree." Cale had a grim smile that caused the normally implacable Lady Wíela to take a step back from him.

"Perhaps we can lead our enemies away from here? Maybe back into the woods, or down onto the plain. We can circle back in stealth when the time is ripe?"

Cale shook his head. "No, that's a good plan for a wood elf who can hide here, and a shit plan for us. We'll wear ourselves out, might get caught in the open and fucked up. And we can't waste a bullet from this point on."

No, if they were going to do something, it would be now.

"Perhaps. . . ."

"No more *perhaps*." Cale shook his head and patted his vest pockets absent-mindedly, then stopped. "Are you sure there's a real door somewhere here? And the problem is just finding it?"

"Yes. But it cannot be opened until a midsummer's moonlight is shining on it and—"

"Yeah, yeah." Cale dug out night-vision goggles and strapped them on. He clicked the goggles down and took a look around.

"Cale of the Marines, what *are* you doing?"

The stones glittered faintly, their intricate designs catching starlight. Or maybe they glowed a little from within, he couldn't say. Looking up and down, Cale examined the stone nearest Hassel, then moved on, working clockwise around the circle.

"Cale of the Marines?"

Ninety degrees away, facing east and out toward the plains, he stopped. Then he stepped back, then forward, closer again.

"Well, well," he breathed softly, noting just a slight hint of light. "What do we have here?"

He slipped his bayonet out of its sheath, now with everyone watching him, and fixed it to the muzzle of his M27. He thrust the blade through the overgrowth on the far side of the stones, and the sharp clink of steel on stone echoed across the circle.

Now everyone stood and turned in that direction.

Cale moved the bayonet around, testing the edges of what he had found, checking where the blade kept going, sinking deeper into overgrowth. Once, it stuck into the bole of a tree and he had to yank it back out. When it seemed he had the shape of it, he stepped a pace or two off, gesturing for everyone to join him.

"Who's got C4?" Cale asked.

"Two bricks, but no blasting caps," Barden said, and shook her head. "Rashad had them."

"We used all ours on the Ospreys." Diaz said. They were not at all equipped for this kind of thing. Hell, they were only still on their feet thanks to their ability to buy provisions near Hilltown. Otherwise, they would have run out of food days before. Ammo and everything else expendable was running way low. With all of four full drums of ammunition, Hassel was their only gunner capable of suppressing fire. Barden was down to a magazine and a half.

"Same," said Lomicka.

"Alright. Let's plant what we've got. Barden, Diaz, and Lomicka, one round each of high explosive." Three grenade launchers firing on the C4 should give them a crude blasting cap. "Fire on the same mark, and let's see if we can blow the door."

"It'll draw a lot of attention, Staff Sergeant." Barden wasn't arguing, exactly. But she had a point.

"Hassel," Cale barked. He was starting to see everything form up in his head. That clarity and energy that came with seeing the path ahead sizzled inside of him. "You're fastest. Hunker down in the path outside the circle. When we blow it, chuck a willy-pete grenade out into the woods as far as you can, then run after us. If we're lucky, they'll think the explosion here is a distraction for whatever we're doing with white phosphorous over there."

"Aye, Staff Sergeant." He had one of the incendiary grenades, and cadged another one from Antoine. Waiting only for Cale's nod, he slunk out to the circle's gate and beyond.

Cale ordered everyone behind the stone slabs for cover, backs to the blast, while Doc Dooley packed bags of saline around the C4 to direct more of its force against the stone.

"As soon as you fire, drop flat," Cale told Barden, Diaz, and Lomicka. Fifty meters away was outside the lethal range, but it was going to ring some bells.

Any farther away, they might miss.

His team leaders looked at him expectantly. Barden, hair slightly caught in her straps, Diaz, dark brown skin smeared with mud and a slight grin of being resigned to whatever happened next, and Lomicka, a snarl on her lips.

"Let's keep our jaws open like the mouthbreathers we are!" Cale shouted. "The moment you see open tunnel, move by team."

Then he held up a hand.

They all waited in the silence of the stone circle for a moment, until Cale heard the explosion and thump of a distant grenade.

"Fire," Cale ordered calmly.

The soft triple-foomp of the team leaders' grenade launchers broke the peace of the glade, followed half a second later by over-lapping blasts—one sharp, then another one enveloped by the deep, throaty bass of C4 detonating, then a third sharp explosion nearly lost in the cacophony.

Cale was tossed back against the soft grass, mouth open. His helmet smacked the ground as a cloud of saline and rock shards flew overhead between him and the stars.

CHAPTER TWENTY-FIVE

CALE BLINKED AT THE SKY. He watched as Orley ran over and hauled Barden to her feet. As he tried to gain his bearings, he saw Antoine grab Diaz. Ysbarra was lifting Lomicka up.

Cale staggered up and wiped a bloody nose with the back of his hand.

"Move!" he ordered as he took point, unsteadily pushing into the billow of smoke and nastiness his team leaders had created.

"On your right, Staff Sergeant." That was Dooley beside him. The doc had Brust's M27 up in her shoulder, looking more like a badass SEAL than Cale had ever seen her.

The stone door's pieces and shards choked the entranceway, along with faded machinery that glowed with magic. Cale kicked them down with a boot. The debris tumbled inward in a cloud of dust. The Marines had apparently destroyed whatever ancient magic gizmo had once powered the secret entrance.

Dooley had to duck to get in, and Cale pushed the ruins of a shattered wood frame aside to clear the way for the others trudging after them.

A crystal light glowed in a brass sconce just inside the door, the bright glow that the night-vision goggles had picked up through a slender gap in the stonework. Cale grabbed Dooley by the upper arm to stop her from charging any farther in. "Stay here, and count them through. I'm going to scout ahead."

"Aye, Staff Sergeant," she hissed.

Cale scooted through the scattered rubble, finding the tunnel's downslope rather gentle and easy, even with the broken stone underfoot. Once he cleared the worst of the steam, smoke, and airborne debris, he spotted a T-junction in the tunnel up ahead. The walls and ceiling were hewn from rock and decorated with tree-like carvings along the way. The floor had evidently been excavated out, then paved with close-fitting stones of some other kind, not matching the stone around him.

Hugging the left wall, he moved down to the junction. Left and right, the way looked empty, though he doubted that would last, unless there was no one within five hundred meters of the blast. He had no doubt the sound of their breach had carried down the tunnel a ways.

Back along the tunnel, the squad was moving to join him. Barden, Diaz, and Lomicka all looked more alert now and were under their own power, though speckled with blood and grit from the explosion.

"Barden, move up, left-side branch. Lomicka, block the right. Diaz on me."

The three moved to obey and brought the remnants of their teams with them. Hassel had made it back from his diversion attempt, looking a bit dazzled. The bright flashes of the incendiary grenades must have fucked with his night vision something fierce.

"What's up, Staff Sergeant?" Diaz gritted his teeth, visibly fighting pain, but not enough to take him off his feet.

"I need you and Antoine on rear security," Cale said. "Move up when we make a turn. Conserve ammo, all that good shit."

"Aye, Staff Sergeant." He leaned a little on Antoine as they moved back up to the blasted entrance.

Cale turned to Wíela, who'd eagerly followed them. "Now where?"

"To the left." She pointed down the passage, helpfully. "To the right are storerooms against a siege."

"Hopefully we won't need those." They had no hope of holding out against even a half-hearted counterattack. Their plan was to get to this Tree of Power. The Lady would then be able to take control of her people. All she had to do was touch, she'd said. Then she'd be their queen. That was how it worked here. "Barden, go."

Barden stepped off with Orley, creeping up the passage as fast as they dared. Dooley followed with Wíela, then Lomicka and Ysbarra.

So far, so good. No contact yet. They were conserving ammo.

With the drums for the M27 automatic rifles, they had maybe 1,500 rounds among them. It always sounded like so much, but Cale regularly reminded them that they could easily spend thirty rounds for every target hit in combat situations. And they were facing far more than fifty mercenaries and elves.

Barden moved smartly ahead, half-crouched and measuring her steps. If she weaved or wobbled, she got her shit together again immediately. Orley paced along just behind her, staying off her heels, but only just. The suppressor on the front of his M27 was almost even with her shoulder as he moved.

If they could get to this damn magic tree before—

Orley and Barden fired twice each. The sound banged off the rock walls around them, and a couple of mercenaries in jeans and ridiculous tac vests tumbled to the paving stone floor of the passage.

"Clear." Barden and Orley only paused for a moment to make sure the mercs were out of commission.

As they moved farther in, the carvings grew more intricate, the crystal sconces closer together and brighter. The tunnel sloped down, then up. Cale stepped over more dead mercenaries as Orley and Barden cleared the way ahead.

"We've got compatible magazines." Lomicka stopped to strip the bodies of spare ammo and their radios.

She and Ysbarra hustled to catch back up when they were done, and passed out the scrounged magazines. They were fancier than the government-issued stuff his Marines all carried, but fit the M27s well enough.

"We must move faster," the Lady Wíela urged.

Barden had the point well handled, so Cale fell back to check on Diaz and Antoine bringing up the rear. The dull thump of a couple of hand grenades reached him, then the sound of Diaz's launcher popping off twice.

"Diaz!" Cale shouted.

Antoine came running up first. He had been shot dead center, a smart hole drilled in the front of his vest, and the pocket that held the ceramic strike plate looked misshapen. When Cale raised an eyebrow, Antoine simply nodded.

"Diaz?"

"All clear."

More shots came from up front, and now the snap of supersonic rounds passing them in the wrong direction filled the passage. Cale ranged back up toward the front. The halls were widening, growing more expansive.

"We gotta be under the fortress proper by now," Orley shouted.

Arrows pinged down the passages as well. One stuck in Ysbarra's armor, the shaft wobbling about like a porcupine quill. Another sliced through Orley's sleeve. Barden's rifle chattered, and the team shouted at each other as they kept fields of fire swept clean.

"Clear!"

Wíela scooped up a bow and quiver from a dead elf as they moved forward again. She started shooting arrows back into the dark.

Their pace picked up. Wíela moved to the lead, drawing fire but ducking it as well, twisting her body and running through the gauntlet like Legolas on speed.

One of the mercs in the shadows ahead threw a grenade, and Lady Wíela reacted before anyone else. She batted it back down a crossing corridor with her bow, then stepped out of the junction just as it blew. A cloud of black smoke and glowing shrapnel cut her off from Barden and Orley for a moment, then it settled and cleared.

Everyone paused for a second, caught off guard.

"Move!" Cale shouted, shattering the still of the moment.

They popped out into a wide tunnel, carved from stone with much less delicacy than the passages through which they had come. Lady Wíela snarled as she looked around, clearly upset with what she saw. Cale figured this all must be new, recent, and an abomination to her. Human-made. Humans from his side of the portal, at least.

Three dead mercs lay just beyond the threshold into the tunnel, one of them with a smoking ruin where his chest should have been, thanks to a grenade from Diaz's M-203. The other two looked to have been eaten up by the blast. What a waste. To cross a portal illegally into a strange, far-off world just to die for gold.

Everyone limped out, hugging one of the rough walls. They curved away in both directions, as if they were at the top of some great circle.

"Your leg," Dooley noted.

"No time now, Doc," Cale said. Shrapnel and stone chips had peppered his left thigh from a near-miss, and he had twisted his ankle at some point coming around a corner.

They were all beaten up, though. Blood soaked Barden's right sleeve. Dooley caught a double tap to the chest that had shattered her strike plate and probably cracked a few ribs, along with a slice to the side of her neck from an arrow.

But they were all upright and mobile. And if Lady Wíela's urgency was any indication, they were close.

"Lady Wíela. . . ." Cale looked at his charge with sudden horror. The wood elf held her side tight, and dark blood oozed from between her fingers. "Doc!"

"Your people can't heal me," Lady Wíela said with a grimace.

The right side of her face dripped with so much blood from a head wound she looked like a ghoul, or an extra from a zombie movie. But she sure as hell didn't shamble like a zombie when she started to run again with nothing more than a faint grunt.

"Keep up with her!" Cale snarled, pain shooting up his leg as they ran after her.

"Not far ahead now, not far!" Lady Wíela shouted at them as mercenary fire flashed again.

The stench of cordite stung Cale's nose. It mingled with the smell of spilled blood all around him as his team lit the crevices up around them with firepower.

A light bloomed ahead out of the darkness of the tunnel, dazzling him.

How much ammo had they used already? Cale was running low.

"Steady on, Marines. Suck it up, we can do this." Cale shouted motivational nonsense bullshit like he was some kind of demented walking recruiting poster.

The quickest way out was through, though. He knew that well enough, recruiting poster nonsense or not. There was more danger in stopping now, trying to rest, or trying to hole up, than in pushing on. Aggression was now their only hope.

"We'll take it down, whatever this great worm that Grumbly Runt heard is, we throw everything we have at it as fast as we can so we can get the Lady to the tree."

"Worm?" Wíela shouted back at him. No one could speak in anything but shouts now. Her normally calm voice was strained. "No, that's not the exact word. It's off."

Something had been lost in translation by the spell. Cale had heard "worm" several times, hadn't he?

The bright light filled Cale's eyes, actinic and pure. But nothing shot at them. There was a moment of calm, other than the impossible, intense light up ahead that was blinding them all.

This was what they'd crossed the land to face. This was what Wíela had risked everything to try to get the Marines to attack.

Cale checked his rifle, steadied himself, and then gritted his teeth.

"Forward!" he snarled, and they advanced.

From behind the eye-watering light, something loomed in the abyss, three stories tall, colored a sickly yellow. Cale moved closer. A huge, black, gaping maw appeared, and it held the root ball of a massive tree, itself at least forty meters tall and far beyond the ability of the squad to lift, even when they were whole and unwounded.

They moved in closer.

The bole of the tree leaned back against the thing's great yellow neck, from which hydraulic hoses protruded at every joint like greasy, black coils of guts or sinew. Massive treads supported the squat shape, and a catwalk circled it just above the treads. From there, a set of stairs rose to an upper deck, and a glass-fronted control cabin perched on the very top, just to the right of the long, hydraulic neck.

They all stopped.

"Oh," Barden said. "Not a worm, but. . . ."

Blazoned on the side of the machine in meter-high letters: CATERPILLAR.

CHAPTER TWENTY-SIX

"WE ARE HERE," Lady Wíela said under her breath. There was far, far too much blood dripping from her robes.

How was Cale going to explain dead royalty in the after-action report? Or court martial, as he envisioned it, now that things were going south.

"Is that the tree?" Cale asked.

Lady Wíela didn't lecture them about the Tree's provenance, or tell them about any Mystical Powers it held. She just nodded, exhaustion plain on her face.

She tried to reach for it, straining to hold one hand up into the air, but she could barely reach the bucket.

"Up the ladder," Cale said, and slipped under her shoulder.

Together they limped around toward the backside with the rest of the squad, then clambered up the ladder there onto the catwalk around the machine.

They were all winding down, low on water, low on ammo, trying to keep adrenaline pumping long enough for them to achieve some kind of nominal security.

Now was not that time or place, not yet.

"Find good firing positions. Let's make sure we have three-sixty awareness," Cale ordered as he pulled Lady Wíela up after him.

"I need to get to the Tree," she whispered. "Before I die."

"We'll get you there," Cale promised. But first they needed to get the tree out and to a secure location.

Then he could fulfill a promise to a dying elven princess.

"Let's get it secured!" Cale shouted. "Then let's get the hell out of here."

Barden got Dooley to the forwardmost position, right next to the glassed-in cab, while Orley got into the cab and started to look over the controls. Lomicka and Ysbarra went right-rear, and Diaz and Antoine took left-rear, right over the ladder up.

Cale pulled the ladder up behind him and locked it in place. But he already had another problem: Lady Wíela had closed her eyes and folded up on the catwalk. She looked like she was sleeping.

Shit.

He headed up the stairs to the cab. "What's the word, Orley?"

The young Marine glanced up at him, face a mask of confusion. "No idea how the fuck to make this thing go, Staff Sergeant."

"Well, let's see if we can figure it out together." Cale started pulling out binders tucked into plastic slots. Data sheets for hazardous materials, safety bullshit, more safety bullshit. Idiot manual with pictures in a binder!

Cale opened it.

"Okay, got it!" Orley hit the Initiate Power On Cycle button before Cale could point it out from the diagram in the second binder.

Somewhere deep in the thing, a giant diesel engine turned over and rumbled to life. Must have been a big enough block to drive a train, the way it sounded.

As it spun up, screens came to life all over the inside of the cab. Three of them were arrayed around the seat where Orley sat, several more mounted to the overhead, at least two for Orley to see, and four more for a seat up behind Orley's.

"Uh. . . ." Cale flipped pages. "Look for the transmission default state initiator. . . ."

"Never mind, Staff Sergeant. It's got a dummy screen." Orley pointed at one of the three screens in front of him lit up with big buttons that offered just a few options.

He skipped the testing and diagnostic startup and went straight for the operational go. Warnings flickered down the side of the screen about the low fuel state.

"Let's hope we can at least get it out of the cavern, Staff Sergeant." Orley tapped at a screen that had filled with computerized dials, one of which was their fuel gauge. Not much there. The computer estimated less than an hour of running time.

"Get this thing into gear and get us turned in the direction of the entrance." All the new carved-out tunnels that Wíela disapproved of had been carved out so that the Caterpillar could carry the divine tree-thing in here, where it could be protected by mercenaries.

"Aye, Staff Sergeant."

Cale popped back out of the cab to take Dooley's position and send the doc back to look Lady Wíela over, just as a round snapped by his head and pinged off the metal roof of the cab.

"Contact left!" Cale scrambled back over the upper surface of the huge machine and lay flat, peering out.

Cale saw a merc, all in black, hunkered near the cavern's entrance. The man fired a few more times, and as he did so two more mercenaries ran out of the tunnel, hugging the near wall, trying to get around the right side of the machine.

Barden fired once, dropping one of them, while Dooley sprayed the other one with rounds. Both down, neither moved.

"Good shooting, Doc!" Cale shouted. "But make 'em count. One shot, one kill. Let's conserve ammo." He had no idea how long they had to make it last. They had to be down well under a thousand rounds for the lot of them, maybe as few as five hundred. Most of their grenades were gone.

Whatever Dooley might have said in reply was drowned out by a sudden rev of the huge machine's engine.

It lurched forward and started to turn over to the left. The big leafy branches of the tree in the bucket shook. Lady Wíela leapt past Cale and Dooley in a jump from off the catwalk, moving quickly and unsteadily along the huge, hydraulic arm to the point where it bent into the bucket. She left bloody handprints as she clambered along.

"Lady Wíela!" He'd get her to the tree when they were safely out of here.

His shout was utterly lost in a clatter of fire that came from all around the cavern and the engine noise. Sparks flew from the metal around the wood elf's bare feet, as bullets stitched along the metal arm.

Cale felt his breath catch as Lady Wíela flinched, blood sprayed the air from two shots, and she wobbled.

If she fell now, she'd fall to the ground.

But then she grabbed a branch, pulled herself up into the shaking foliage, and disappeared.

Barden slid along the upper level of the giant machine as it jerked around.

"Orley, you asshole, don't knock us all off," she hissed.

Dooley slid over into her more than once as the thing turned, even heeling over a little. It did one complete circle of the cavern, and the tree's branches slapped the ceiling several times as Orley struggled to straighten the thing out. Shots pinged off the steel here and there, even some arrows skipped off the vehicle's skin and threatened to skewer the unlucky or incautious.

They had to be careful, as the team was getting a little slug-gish. Barden and the rest of the Marines were tired. Bone tired. The last time she, or any of them, had slept was high up in Runt's mountain hideaway. That was, what, twenty-four hours or more prior?

They were all wounded, too. Even Doc was bleeding from a wound to her hip.

The machine heaved around again, moving at little more than a walking pace. Orley got it more or less aimed at the entrance to the tunnel. Mercs and elves swung into view, and Barden backed herself off the edge of the top as much as she could. She fired, aiming for a merc and missing him with the first few shots. Then her M27 locked back on a dry magazine, and she cursed.

"Keep up the fire, doc!" Barden shouted. "I'm reloading."

Dooley picked her shots now instead of wasting her maga-zine, so that was something. Barden pushed back farther from the edge and rolled to her side. The magazine pouches on her chest were empty, but for one. She opened it, snatched out the last magazine and swapped it into her M27.

Twenty-eight bullets. No more.

She'd have to make them count.

"God damnit!" That was Cale.

Just as Barden closed the bolt, she heard a high, single piercing note that shifted into a fluttering melody.

Barden rolled over to look at the bucket loader just as Lady Wiela popped up out of the foliage, near where the leaves stopped and the heftier lower limbs converged on the bole of the tree.

Cale was low against the railing, looking like he was going to try to jump the hydraulic arm to go after her.

Lady Wíela raised her blood-slicked arms. Last Barden had seen her, she'd looked ready for a dust-off, and a date with a doc of her choice.

But now she *glowed*.

Literally. The very air bent around her, and the light that peeled off her seared the air so radiantly it made everything else around seem like it had been in deepest darkness all this time.

The crystals in their sconces faded, and Lady Wíela's voice boomed out as if she had a throat mic and the cavern was wired like an arena for sound.

"I am she! The one rightful ruler of all the wood elves!" Her words echoed all throughout the dark.

Even Barden felt herself instinctively snap to attention at the authority lying just under the words. She had to actively ignore Lady Wíela's voice in order to concentrate on the situation around the machine.

"I am Wíela te-Corunna and I command your loyalty! Bow down to me or I will strike great vengeance upon you with furious anger; and you shall know that I am the Queen, when I shall lay my vengeance upon you!"

Dooley scooted back beside Barden, both of them looking on toward Wíela. "Was that Samuel L. Jackson's line from *Pulp Fiction*? Where'd she get that from?"

"Don't know." Barden was too busy sighting on the elves stepping out from behind the rock that were bowing, scraping, and groveling before the bucket loader. They raised interleaved fingers over their heads. "Watch out for the mercs!"

The mercs, though stunned, did not grovel. They were immune to the light. One aimed his M-4 at Lady Wíela.

Barden twitched her rifle his way, but before she could squeeze a burst off, a great beam of light lanced out from Lady Wíela's hand at the man. He sort of evaporated in a swirl of flesh and fabric.

"Holy shit," Dooley said, eyes wide.

The merc fire started up again, but it was more sporadic as they were trying to remain in solid cover to avoid Lady Wíela's lethal return fire. And then, after a few confused moments, that fire became panicked as wood elves turned on the mercs firing at Lady Wíela.

The human screams echoed around them all as the mercs faced the knives, arrows, and even sharp teeth of suddenly madly enraged, almost-possessed wood elves.

Orley drove the machine into the tunnel past groveling elves that darted out of the way.

Several mercenaries threw down their weapons and cowered beside the elves when they saw Lady Wíela vaporize anything, elf and human, who resisted her. Mists of blood that had once been bodies rushing the machine hung in the air as they passed.

"Give me what you've got left." Barden had run dry and held her hand out for the rest of Dooley's ammunition, which amounted to one partial magazine. "Go check on everyone else—we might be winding down here. I don't want anyone bleeding out this close to being done."

"Got it." Dooley nodded and crawled off toward the rear of the machine.

Barden stared forward at the tree. They'd known Lady Wíela had a claim to power, but Barden hadn't been ready for the light show. It was clear that she meant something around here. And if a true heir could wield *that* kind of power with the tree, it was no wonder the enemy had tried to tuck it away deep under a fortress.

The end of the tunnel yawned in front of them, a pale gray

light dawning outside. Barden scanned forward of the machine, but nothing moved, and no one opposed them.

As they cleared the end of the tunnel, she saw why. Three Ospreys hovered fifty meters over a cleared space in front of the fortress, blazoned with block letters that said ROYAL MA-RINES on the side. Each of the Ospreys had their tail ramps lowered and British Marines were fast-roping down to the ground. Men and women in distinctive British camouflage had already rounded up prisoners.

They didn't stop. The great big 'dozer kept moving on as if it didn't see the Royal Marines stepping out of its way.

"Orley!"

Barden slid down to the platform beside the cab. She yanked open the door.

"Orley, you can stop. Orley?"

Orley sat upright in the driver's seat, fingers clutching the control stick. His chest was a mass of scarlet, the Kevlar vest and strike plate hit by multiple rounds before it gave up. But he hadn't. He had steered them through the tunnel with the last of his strength, and brought them safely outside.

"Orley . . ." she whispered, and the name caught in the back of her throat.

Barden pressed two fingers to his neck to be sure, but there was no pulse. His eyes stared lifelessly ahead, and the weight of his body kept the control stick pushed forward, arm locked in place.

She pried his fingers away from the stick, and the machine shuddered to a halt fifty meters short of where the Ospreys hovered.

CHAPTER TWENTY-SEVEN

THE COMMANDER of the Royal Marines detachment approached as the Osprey hovered over to a landing site that had been cleared out near the massive excavator. Cale raised a hand in greeting at the rangy, rugged-looking soldier. Ginger wisps of hair escaped from under the suspension band of his helmet, plastered down on his forehead.

"Are you Staff Sergeant Cale?" the commander shouted.

Cale shook his hand. "Yes, sir. Might have been nice to see you a day or so ago, but we're excited to see you now. How did you find us?"

The commander pointed back to the Osprey. Heath jumped out of the side of the aircraft and waved at Cale. "Your people called it in. Elves didn't understand the importance of radio kit when they locked them up in the fortress's towers."

The angry trees had dragged Heath and the others back to the fortress by the elves, who'd locked the Marines in with some of their equipment until the mercs dealt with them. The trapped Marines had apparently gotten busy. The calls for help had been buried in static, the commander told Cale, but knowing that some Americans had gone missing prompted the Brits to scramble some aircraft to find out if they could get a clearer signal.

"What about the rest of your people?" the commander asked.

"Beat up, sir, but nothing serious. Other than Orley, I think we'll be fine with some Motrin and a few days' rest, and maybe a lift." Cale cast a significant glance over at the idling Osprey.

The officer nodded. "Wouldn't dream of making you walk back, Staff Sergeant."

"Thank you, Captain. . . ."

"Captain Sharpe."

"Thanks, Captain Sharpe, sir."

"Wheels up in thirty minutes, Staff Sergeant."

"Aye aye, sir. We'll be ready."

They nodded to one another—Marines the world over observed the taboo against saluting officers in a combat zone—and headed their separate ways.

Cale joined the rest of his squad propped against a low retaining wall along one path to the fortress. Heath hobbled over to join them, with Jones close behind.

"Brust?" Cale asked.

"The British medics are treating him for shock," Barden said.

"He didn't do well with getting dragged around by a tree that cussed him out the entire time, Staff Sergeant." Jones was never not matter-of-fact.

"How the hell did you get up on the radio?" Cale asked.

"It was touch-and-go," Jones said. Dooley made the rounds with the squad, assisted by a Brit medic, as Jones explained to Cale how they had cobbled together a working radio out of everything that had been smashed when they'd been captured. The trees and elves knew to take away their guns, but had left the radios.

Jones had spent hours, channel by channel, calling out their position. By the time Jones got to the point where she described all three of them standing in front of the tac radio at the last minute to shield it from a suspicious guard right as the Royal Marines responded, they all sported field dressings and bandages. Diaz sat with his right leg extended, boot off, and an ice pack taped around his right ankle.

"So then Heath started screaming and frothing at them, and they dragged him out for a beating," Jones said, wrapping up. "After that, we dangled some ChemLights out the barred windows and spun them around to make a buzz saw that the Osprey could see from above."

Cale settled down between him and Barden, leaning back against the retaining wall.

"Good thinking."

"Thank you, Staff Sergeant!"

Cale fumbled with his gear for a moment, frowning at the bandages Dooley had applied to his right arm. The one on his neck itched something fierce.

"Look at this." Barden tapped his foot with hers. She pointed toward the fortress.

Lady Wíela approached them, looking radiant. Gone was the limping, shot-up wood elf that Cale had last seen struggling up into the tree. She had bathed and changed into a clean gown. A pendant hung around her neck, silver glinting on her camouflage skin. Inside the clear crystal disk at the center was a large splinter of wood. Three elves trailed her respectfully, expertly balancing trays of fruit and pitchers of some liquid. Walking trees stood just as respectfully in the distance.

Cale started to rise again, with a groan, but she waved him back down.

"I come to offer you my thanks, Staff Sergeant Cale. You and your Marines did me, my family, and my people a great service. We shall not forget it."

"Glad to help." Cale squinted. "There was *some* mutual self-interest involved."

"I know the problems you faced. For the part that my people played in causing those troubles, well, let me say they will trouble you no more. We will ally deeply, and formally, with the Marines of the US."

Well, that was a little better than Cale had been hoping for. "And the portal?"

"The elves who held it against your people have withdrawn and the servants of the enemy who had accompanied them will trouble neither you, nor anyone, again. Please accept this small hospitality as a token, but not a fulfillment, of my personal thanks." Wíela gestured at the trays of food and drink, and the elves bore them forward, helping each Marine take what he or she wanted, then piling the remainder on one tray and leaving it for anyone who desired more.

The drink turned out better than water, and not really wine as he knew it, so Cale figured he was getting something like ambrosia. Didn't make him feel godly at all, or anything like that, but it sure went down nice on a dry throat. At least as nice as a cold beer, if not better.

As they munched on strange fruits and wood elf refreshments, another British Osprey landed. A handful of Royal Marines escorted a line of prisoners, mercenaries with their hands bound behind their backs, blackout goggles over their eyes, and their ears covered with the big earmuffs that aircrews used to protect their hearing. Maybe twenty or thirty of them were herded aboard the Osprey with their Marine guards, and seconds later it was off again, heading toward FOB Vimes.

The Marines finished off the food given to them, everything

the elves had left behind, and then drank the pitchers dry by the time a couple of Royal Marine loadmasters came to beckon them onto one of the waiting Ospreys.

Cale got them squared away, then hustled them up to the yawning cargo ramp.

He counted them off as they trotted by, remembering that Brust was already aboard. And of course, Rashad and Shane still had not turned up. Lady Wíela said she and the elves would watch for them around the fortress and the forest beyond. But she did not have much hope that they had been able to fight clear of the mines beneath the mountain.

Cale would be back with fresh troops to search soon.

He settled into one of the seats, and moments later the Osprey swept up into the air. The huge proprotors tilted forward once they climbed a hundred meters or so above the treetops and zipped off toward the forest's edge.

He looked from face to face and heaved a small sigh. Really, he should be thankful that so many of them were still in one piece. Delta operators, or SEALs, might have been able to do it better, but not by a whole lot. The losses stung. They always stung. They weren't the first he'd known not to come home, and he knew they wouldn't be the last, either.

Still didn't make it easy, or normal, or something he'd ever really get used to.

They swung from their southerly heading a little more east now.

Diaz and Antoine ripped MREs open. Cale stared at them. "We just ate the wood elves out of a home. We drank ambrosia?"

Or at least, he thought it was ambrosia.

"Still hungry," Antoine grumbled.

The battle cry of a Marine, Cale thought.

CHAPTER TWENTY-EIGHT

OUT OF THE GLOOM, a light flickered into brightness. Step by trudging step, it drew closer. For a moment, the brightness washed out all detail, just glaring there in agonizing contrast to the darkness.

Then details resolved. First, a dark triangle of sorts near the bottom, then a slight dimming on the left side. The triangle resolved further into a green shape, furred on the edges. The fur sharpened into needles on a pine tree as the light grew larger.

Rashad had never been happier in his life to see a tree.

Shane groaned and hitched the little girl up in her grip. She threatened to keep falling to the hard stone floor of the tunnel. Rashad, just behind her, noticed that Shane's arms threatened to give out. Her palms slicked with the sweat of exertion.

"Do you need me to take her?"

Shane hugged little Salia higher up in her arms. "You carried her for three hours, at least, Rashad. I got this."

"It's been six since then."

"I got this. And I outrank you." Shane gritted her teeth and kept moving.

The light looked like it was only a hundred meters away.

Rashad bit at the nozzle of his Camelbak, sucking on it and getting a scanty drop of water as a reward. Over a day since they'd last seen a hint of drinkable water, and he only knew that because Shane's watch was still ticking and she'd told him. Otherwise, they would have lost all track of time in the dark beneath the mountain.

A warm breeze wafted in, and only then did he realize how chilly it had been in the dark.

Step by step, the end of the tunnel grew larger and more details resolved themselves as their eyes adjusted to the light. A steeply sloping rock face to the left, furred with trees and greenery halfway down. The big pine tree in front of the tunnel's mouth, others peeking out here and there in the distance. Tall grass waving around the edges. A tiny curl of smoke in the distance.

Shane stumbled coming out of the tunnel, and only a quick grab by Rashad kept her from tumbling head over heels down the steep hillside they'd just wandered onto. She clutched at Salia, who stirred and mumbled through dry lips at Shane's chest.

Down below, the ground crinkled in interesting ways around a watery inlet of some kind. At the farthest point inland, maybe a few kilometers away, a small village clustered around the water. Fires burned in several chimneys.

It looked charming and pastoral.

Rashad gazed around and spotted a dirt road winding up the valley away from the village and in their general direction. He glanced left and right, trying to find some sign of it nearer to them.

"You think they're friendly down there?" he asked Shane.

"It's not a goddamn mine, it's not a dragon, it's not those chitinous shitheads we ran into the day before yesterday. Those look like human cottages down there."

"Chitinous Shitheads is the name of my next band." Just seeing what could be help had lifted Rashad's spirits.

Shane laughed.

They stumbled on together, not daring to split up for anything, as they trudged through the thick undergrowth. They paused once, and Rashad gathered some rocks and laid them out in an arrow. Shane looked on in fuzzy-headed confusion for a moment, then nodded.

Then they got to their feet again and stumbled on until they found the road within another fifty meters. It was broad enough for Humvees to pass in opposite directions, with a little room to spare, and it ran down toward the water, or up to the narrow end of the valley, where a pass had been carved out.

They both looked up the road, then at each other, and shook their heads in unison. They turned to face the village below them and started down, stumbling and weary.

"Wait." Shane put her hand on Rashad's chest. "You got binos?"

"Yeah," he replied, and slapped at his gear pouches. Fatigue clouded his thinking and conjured up a warm and comfortable inn to rest in, maybe food to eat, a real hearty stew. . . . "Got 'em."

He pulled out the little foldable binoculars and tried to adjust them into position. Then he flipped them over, realizing he was looking in them the wrong way around.

"What am I looking for?"

"Out on the water. Left-hand finger of the mountain. Angular black shapes."

"O-okay . . . yeah. I got . . . what the fuck?" Rashad blinked and looked again. "Three . . . four patrol-boat-looking things. They're flying a flag, white and blue, I think."

"Holy shit," Shane muttered. "Track back toward us, along the finger of the mountain."

"Okay." He kept the gray stone and fir trees on the very left side of his view and followed the line back. Water. Water. Docks. Another patrol boat. Different flag. Blue, black, and white? Farther. A new path of some kind. A fence. And then. . . .

"A camp. A whole-ass camp. GP tents, some trucks. . . ."

"Flags?" Shane asked, her voice strained. She was struggling with Salia's inert form.

"Yeah. I see them now. Blue cross on a white field. Then a blue bar, black bar, white bar. Then like . . . magenta with a horizontal white stripe. Then a yellow bar, a green bar, and a red bar." He looked over at Shane, but she was already moving, stumbling down along the road. She pointed at the dirt and let out a little whoop.

Rashad's gaze followed as he struggled to put the binoculars back in their pouch. Tire tracks. Wide ones, like Humvees. He started moving his legs as quick as they could, a hysterical giggle bubbling up in his throat.

"Who . . . who are they?" he asked as he drew level with Shane again.

"Finns and the Baltics."

"The name of *your* next band?" He could barely process the words.

"Finland. Estonia. Latvia. Lithuania. Fuckin' NATO!" She let her own little giggle slip. "That must be Camp Peikko. Holy shit, are we far from home."

Shane relinquished her burden to Rashad. He stumbled as he gathered Salia in his arms, holding her with her head over his shoulder. His weapon clattered at his back as he walked, now. But he wouldn't have to walk far. A couple kilometers maybe? Not more than three.

Unencumbered now, Shane got her little squad radio out and flicked it on. Batteries were still good as a little burst of static issued from the speaker.

"Any station, any station, this is . . . this is Echo Three Sierra Longshanks, over." She listened for a moment, then pipped a button, and the tone of the brief squelch of static seemed to change.

"Come on," Rashad muttered. They could use a win.

"Any station, any station, this is Echo Three Sierra Longshanks, over." Shane released the talk button. "Fuck, what's the trouble signal?"

"Rolled a one?"

"Funny, but no." Then her eyes lit up. "Got it. Any station, any station, this is Echo Three Sierra Longshanks, we are CUMBERBATCH, say again, CUMBERBATCH." A squeal of static as she let the button go, and silence.

Then: "Echo Three Sierra Longshanks, this is Moomin Six Actual, we have eyes on you and QRF is on their way." The voice was oddly accented, but absolutely fluent in English. More fluent than more than a few Marines Rashad had known. "What is your status, over?"

"Separated from Longshanks Actual, Moomin. We are Echo Three Sierra, Echo Two Romeo, and one local civilian child. Hungry and thirsty, but on our feet, over." Even as she clicked off, they could see the first military vehicle creep around the corner of the final cottage in the village, then accelerate up the road toward them. Two more followed, and Rashad recognized them as Land Rover Defenders, though kitted out for military service.

"Understood, Longshanks. QRF will be on you in a moment, over."

"We've got eyes on, Moomin, thank you."

It didn't take more than two minutes for the three Defenders to cross the distance, and Rashad was content to wait for them, feeling like his legs never wanted to move again now that a ride was imminent. The vehicles quickly surrounded them in a rough triangle, and the outboard troops dismounted and fanned out into a protective cordon. Didn't seem particularly necessary, but Rashad appreciated the gesture.

One of the troops on the inner side of the vehicle cordon got out and stepped up to them, the white-and-blue flag of Finland on his right shoulder. They could see the suppressed officer's insignia on the front of the man's body armor, but like all Marines in the field, they resisted the impulse to salute. Rashad's hands were full, anyway.

"Good morning, Marines," the officer said. "I'm Lieutenant Sinisalo. You are a very long way from home. How did you get here?"

Rashad looked over to Shane to answer, and she opened her mouth to speak, but then Salia pepped right up.

"*Luutnantti*, is that you?" She rubbed sleep from her eyes as she twisted in Rashad's arms to look at the Finnish officer.

"Salia? What are you doing here?" He was surprised, and clearly confused, but not unhappy to see the child.

"We found her in Hilltown a few days ago, sir. She helped us out of a spot, then tagged along. She and I got separated from our squad while in some dwarf mines under Mount Grunt, then found PFC Rashad here. We tried to link back up, but kept taking wrong turns after the dragon attacked."

Sinisalo's eyes were wide as Shane recounted the bare bones of their recent struggles, but it seemed his expression grew a bit more amazed every time he looked at Salia.

"We heard about the fall of Hammerhand a few days ago, though I gather it happened a bit before that. But that's over six thousand kilometers away. How did you cover all that distance?"

"Most of it was underground," Rashad said, while frowning about the "six thousand kilometers," which made no sense in the moment. "We went into the mines just north of Hilltown, and came out of them just up the valley here, sir."

"Alright, let's get you back to camp. Commander Oksanen is going to try to raise someone to let them know we have you, but communications are difficult."

"We're going to see Oksy?" Salia asked.

"We sure are!" Sinsalo replied, but shot a strange look at Shane.

Rashad couldn't spare a lot of brain cycles to work through the implications, but the Finns were clearly a little unsettled to see Salia again. But not so unsettled that they were kicking her out of the Defender. He piled into the back seat of one of them with Shane, and the Finnish soldiers they displaced clung to the outside, holding on to the roof rack and standing on pegs that unfolded from the bases of the doors.

Within moments, they were heading back into the village, and Rashad leaned his head back to rest his eyes for a moment.

CHAPTER TWENTY-NINE

CAPTAIN HOBBS WAITED as they unloaded the Ospreys. No MPs with her, no higher-ups. The tight, clenched feeling in Cale's stomach faded. A chewing-out from the Captain was something he could take. She was intense, but fair.

"Barden, get everyone taken care of," Cale said. "I'll go face the music."

"Aye, Staff Sergeant."

He waited for the Ospreys to take back off, and for the dust to settle, before approaching Hobbs.

"Captain Hobbs, ma'am. Good to see you." The sounds of Marines and Seabees putting the FOB back together meant he still had to shout.

"Staff Sergeant. It's been a busy twenty-four hours." She pulled him by the sleeve toward a hastily built command tent. The flaps did fuck-all to drown out the sound, but it created the illusion of a private debrief. "What happened out there, Ray?"

They stood next to a table of paper maps, scrolls, and a staff with a glimmering orb grasped by wooden fingers at the top that casually held the papers down. The Captain's personal weapon. Thick operations manuals peeked out of a set of crates improvised into a bookshelf along one "wall" of the command tent.

"We improvised, adapted, and I think we overcame."

"And the whole report?"

Cale looked at her, tired, his eyes drooping with exhaustion. "Can I get a coffee, first, ma'am?"

She looked annoyed for a second, opened her mouth to say something, then changed her mind. Her features softened.

"Horne! Coffee, pronto!" she shouted.

There was a flurry of movement from the other side of the tent flap.

"It won't be any good," Hobbs said. "We just got here."

"It never is," Cale said flatly.

A reedy assistant sporting heavy, black-rimmed glasses with all the aesthetics of plate armor slipped in a few minutes later with a tongue-blistering metal cup of instant coffee.

It was, Cale thought, the real ambrosia.

"Let's hear it, Staff Sergeant," Hobbs said, after giving Cale a few seconds to sip and wince.

How to summarize all this? He spent the better part of an hour trying. Securing the asset, multiple times, against fantastic odds. *Fantasy-like odds.*

". . . and Shane and Rashad are still missing," he finished. "I need fresh people and more resources to go back and get them."

"Put a pin in that. The orphan girl. You have a name. Salia?"

"Yeah." Cale sipped his coffee and rubbed his face. "We really should have gotten her to someone safe for her to stay with. I don't know why it kept happening that the best choice was to keep her with us, but things kept getting strange—"

Hobbs scrambled through the chaos of papers and folders on the table as he spoke, and pulled out a single folder. She flipped through it, selected out a single, glossy photo, and handed it to Cale.

It was Salia. Unmistakably. Same shape, same face, same hair, damn near the same smudges of dirt *on* her face. But instead of the streets of Hilltown, Salia was picking her way through the blasted terrain below the Escarpment. A battered-looking human soldier of the local variety stood behind her, sword drawn, as though to protect her from an unseen attack.

"Where did this come from?" Cale asked.

Hobbs took the photo from him. "Electronic observation post along the Escarpment. Divisional intelligence sent it down, along with a couple of other photos of her from other places. Intel came in that she was in the area of interest. We're supposed to observe and make note if anyone spots her, but *not* approach if we see her."

"Damn it, ma'am, this would have been good to know before."

"I just got it handed to me when we were cooling our heels on the other side of the rift. I was going to brief platoon commanders on it tomorrow."

Cale ran a hand through his greasy hair and picked through the other photos in the folder. Same girl, *absolutely* the same, riding in the open back of a British Land Rover, out near FOB Vimes by the look of it. Another of her among a small passel of children being protected by Army Rangers in a firefight. The Rangers were operating almost two thousand kilometers away in this world, near a rift that connected the world of elves and trolls and magic to Seattle.

And then the photo that made the hair on his neck prickle. Salia standing among the hazy air of the collapsed Empire State Building, Manhattan skyline behind her, and a troll off to the right of the frame. Was it protecting her? Or about to attack?

Salia looked out at the devastation with childlike curiosity.

Nothing here was ever what it seemed. Elven queens could vaporize enemies and pledge their loyalties, a troll could offer them help, Rangers could melt in and out of the shadows, and a little girl could be maybe something vastly more powerful than he'd suspected. "What do we know about her? Are Rashad and Shane in danger? Who is she?"

"We have no idea. The other units that encountered her indicate that she can be a shit magnet." Hobbs shrugged. "And that's probably putting it charitably. But we don't know if she's Chaotic Evil, or just Neutral."

Cale leaned against the table and took another sip of coffee. "Shane's the intel specialist. She had the combat camera with her, and a ton of shit from the elves we fought on Stark Ridge, plus everything from the merc listening post in Hilltown."

"Well, here's where we have some good news. Ten minutes before you landed, I got a call from NATO. Shane, Rashad, and Salia popped up near Camp Peikko this morning."

"Camp Peikko?"

"It means 'troll' in Finnish, I guess. But they're not trolling. I got a video clip of the three of them in their camp medical station."

Cale set his coffee down, grabbed the edge of the table, and just looked down at it for a good long minute. They were okay. They'd made it out. They were . . . where?

"Hang on. Camp Peikko? That's like—"

"In a fjord on the other side of the continent." Hobbs brushed some papers to one side, revealing a huge, hand-drawn map. Unnervingly big swaths of it were just blank, but they had the general shape of the continent, and at least a hundred square kilometers around each NATO base. Hammerhand near the bottom right of the map, Peikko up and center left. A continent the size of Eurasia, at least. If Hammerhand were in Paris, Shane and Rashad were practically in Siberia.

"What the fuck?"

"Good question," she said. "The Finns are going to try to

separate Salia from Shane and Rashad, and ship them back here through the portals." Made sense. Helsinki to New York was way fucking easier than trying to cross all of that uncharted business, even in the air. "But no one wants to bring Salia through a portal."

Hobbs tapped the picture of Salia in Manhattan. Cale understood. They didn't know *what* Salia was, so bringing her to Helsinki with Shane and Rashad was an unwanted risk.

"If intelligence wants her, I'll just have to head back to those mines and see if we can figure out how they teleported across the continent."

"Jesus, Ray." She drummed her fingers on the table. "I don't like having to send you out there again, particularly knowing there are mercs out there. We have some idea who they are, and their numbers."

Cale stiffened. "You have ID on those assholes?"

"Private contractors. Security for the bases and roads they're trying to build." It turned out it was hard as hell to move a modern, mechanized army around a medieval road system. Some of the equipment lying around the FOB came from those same damn contractors, Cale knew. They were getting paid on both sides of the conflict. "But the rumor is that they're trying to help companies get the mineral rights locked down. All the resources here are unused. It's a resource gold rush."

"Can we shut them down?"

"Official complaints are being lodged. The legal teams are swinging into action."

That could mean weeks. Months. Hell, if politicians got involved, years. "I want back out as soon as you can authorize it," Cale said.

"Things are getting hectic around here. It'll be hard to get that for a few days. Your little maneuver with Queen Wíela of the Sylvene Elves put us on good terms. She's ready to take the war to the Old Man in the Cursed Realm. It tilts things away from us all sitting about, waiting for the right moment." The US military and all its allies had been pushing against Realm Forces and not getting very far on this side of the portals for a while. "State Department is sending some people to talk to her to make sure she doesn't go off half-cocked. I mean, she does have her own house to get in order yet. I think they might want you there. Personal connections, and all."

"I don't want to get involved in that stuff, ma'am. It's way above my pay grade."

"Amen. I'll do what I can to keep you clear and get you back out there. But the higher-ups are sticking their fingers in it down here." Hobbs leaned against the table and tapped her staff idly. "One last thing. I'm making you platoon sergeant, and you're getting a promotion to Gunnery Sergeant."

Cale stared. This had not been the direction he thought things would go. He'd really been expecting his career to head the other direction. "Ma'am."

"I'll be really busy with the new push against our enemies here, and I need Lieutenant Nacklebuch helping me with ops. You'll be effectively running First Platoon, most of the time."

"Understood, ma'am." Cale paused. "Are we going to be getting any replacements?"

"Corporal Marcel will be coming back in a few days, and you're getting a boot, but that's all. Any other requests?"

"Yes," Cale straightened. "Barden to Sergeant, and Lomicka to Corporal."

"Two meritorious promotions?"

"They earned them."

"Okay, done. Well, paperwork and shit, but I'll let you know when it's close enough and we'll pin them together."

"Thanks, ma'am."

"Get some rest, Ray. I'm sure the other platoon commanders can take it from here."

Cale snorted. "Maybe."

He took the pause in conversation to drain the last of the now-cold coffee in the cup. He was thinking about how to turn everyone around and cash in some favors to get a ride on one of those supply Ospreys back to the mountain. Resupplied, they could get the retrieval operation up and running days early. Maybe get Rashad and Shane back before they headed through the portal to Helsinki.

Hobbs hadn't said anything, so Cale took that as a dismissal. He turned to leave the tent, but she skewered him place with a look.

"Don't go off base after your wayward souls, Gunny," she said with a sigh. She held up a hand. "Don't lie to me and say you aren't thinking about it. I would. I can see it on your face. Give us three days, tops, to get situated. Get Marcel back and get your boot folded into the team. We'll have more truck support by then, and they're talking about dropping a diesel depot up near that town you resupplied in. Maybe an airfield, too. We'll be able to truck you over to the mountain in no time, and you'll be able to bring plenty of supplies for an extended exploration of those mines."

"Anything could happen out there in three days."

"I need three days, Ray. You know how it goes. If we don't wind up with any exigent circumstances. . . ."

"Semper Gumby," Cale sighed. "Always Flexible."

Or, maybe more accurately, Always Shapeless, Malleable, and Slightly Disturbing Putty, he thought.

"The Finns and Estonians are going to treat them well," Hobbs reassured him.

But they were in the company of a shit-magnet little six-year-old that might already be drawing who knew what kind of danger to them. Besides, they belonged here, not with the Finns, as good and reliable as their allies were. Cale opened his mouth to relay his thoughts, then closed it again as Hobbs frowned him down.

Then someone shouted, clear above the chaos of the base: "Troll sign!"

Cale could hear the sound of the base kicking into gear outside the tent.

"Not again." Cale hustled out of the tent without asking permission, downhill toward the northeast gate, where the call had come from. Hobbs grabbed her staff and followed.

The Marines on the gate hugged the walls to either side of it, now made from HESCO barriers—essentially giant sandbags in steel baskets.

He saw Barden pulling on gear across the dirt from him as she ran. "Too tired for this shit, sir," she said.

"What can you see?" Cale asked as he ran up to the gate.

"One big-ass troll, Staff Sergeant," Harper, from 2nd Platoon on the .50-cal said. "It looks like he's carrying some antlers?"

The Marine turned toward him in confusion as he racked a round.

Cale laughed and let his rifle drop down. "Stand down, it's Grumbly Runt."

"What the fuck's a grumbly runt?"

"Don't shoot!" Cale shouted. "No one shoot. It's a friendly."

Hobbs repeated the order, and the riled-up base ground to a nervous halt.

Cale ambled through the open gate and out onto the path to the road, his M27 dangling in one hand at his side. The troll stomped up slowly, looking around. If he had started off from his mountain around nightfall, he'd made good time.

"Runt, what brings you by?"

"I hear. . . ." The voice that sounded like boulders tumbled out of his mouth. Cale winced a little, but gave no other reaction. Either the translation spells were getting better, he thought, or Runt was using another language. "Your people are back in their little mud fort. But it is so dark here now, and I bring light."

He proudly held out his two meaty fists, each the size of a Humvee. Chandeliers dangled from both of them, some of them looking like they had been made from the antlers the squad had scavenged from those gaurus near the mountain.

"That's mighty nice of you, Runt." Cale smiled widely. "Come on in, and you can help us hang them up."

And there were a few other things that the troll could help move around the base as well. And the faster things got back in order, the faster Cale could get to retrieving the wayward members of his platoon.

CHAPTER THIRTY

Two days later, the skies opened up and pissed down rain. Everything in the FOB turned to mud, except for the helipad and the beginnings of a central street through the FOB that some dwarves had started laying the night before. They had shown up out of the blue, told the Captain that more were coming to pitch in to make up for the crimes of their undermining cousins. Seabees worked through the rain to get things put back together, but mostly from the relative comfort of all-weather heavy equipment cabs. Marines tried their best to stay out of the rain, grumbling into motion whenever strong backs were needed here or there.

Until, that is, those magical words were bellowed across the living area: "MAIL CALL!"

Marines and sailors boiled out of the tents, hastily pulling on ponchos and Gore-Tex jackets. Two big seven-ton trucks labored up the hill toward the helipad, churning through the mud. The call had gone out ahead of them from the sentries at the gate, though one glance would tell what the trucks bore. The big orange AFPO bags on the back were a dead giveaway.

As the trucks shuddered to a halt next to the helipad, NCOs were busy putting the jostling Marines in order.

Cale stood back, letting the squad leaders do that work for him. Barden had taken charge admirably already, keeping a firm hold over the Marines in her squad. They were salty now, much more seasoned than a week-plus ago, with what they had endured. They looked different, held themselves different than the others.

Other Marines popped up from the backs of the trucks and began calling units out by squad while handing the orange sacks over the sides. The sacks were passed from hand to hand, piled together, then gathered up once all of a squad's mail had been unloaded. One by one, the clusters of Marines broke up, bearing their mail away like hunters after felling a herd of prized, orange prey. As his platoon's squads all scampered away, Cale sauntered toward the trucks.

Corporal Dale Marcel hopped down from the back of one of them, another Marine stumbling down right behind him.

"Good morning, Staff Sergeant!" Marcel shouted over the thrum of the trucks' engines and the steady beat of the rain.

"Gunny now, Corporal. You missed me getting pinned yesterday." Cale raised his travel coffee mug.

"Sorry, Gunny! Hell of a wet-down you're having." Marcel shot him a lopsided grin and raised his gaze, if not his face, toward the sky.

"Yeah, it'll do for now, Corporal. Who's this?"

"PFC Elena Koestler. Fresh drop from ITB."

"Good morning, Gunnery Sergeant!" She shouted the greeting, stepped forward, and popped to a parade-ground perfect attention, apart from holding her rifle wrong in its tactical sling. He waved off the criticism and her formality.

"Call me Gunny, Private."

"Aye aye, Gunny."

Cale took a sip of his coffee and looked back at Marcel. "I'm running all of First Platoon, and Barden is getting another stripe. She'll be in charge of the squad. You're going to run First Team now, and take Koestler here with you. It's just Jones, otherwise. Orley. . . ."

"I heard about Orley, Gunny."

He nodded. "And Rashad is TDA with the Finns right now. We're going to go figure out how he and Shane fucked off across an entire continent . . . soon."

"I'm ready when you are, Gunny. And Koestler will be ready." He glanced over at her, then nodded again at Cale. Then, as if remembering, he gave Koestler a look. Her eyes widened and she scrambled onto the back of the truck again, then slithered down with a box in her arms.

"This came for you, Gunner—Gunny," she said, handing over the box.

"Thanks, Koestler. You two go get settled in the squad tent. Chow in two hours."

With a stereo rendition of "Aye aye, Gunny" the two hustled off, Marcel leading the way. Cale hefted the box, feeling the solid weight of it, then carried it toward his tent. They had pitched a new one, properly, and kept the chandelier, though it looked ridiculously large with the lower headroom. He skirted around it, then sat down on his cot. The tent flap fluttered closed, and he picked up the barbecue lighter and reached up to light a few of the candles. Rain thrummed on the waterproofed canvas roof, making the chandelier shake and sway ever so slightly.

He tossed aside his poncho, then set his package back on his knees. The cardboard was sturdy, proof against all but a torrential downpour. He took the folding knife out of his pants pocket, flicked it open, and cut the tape slowly and carefully. He opened the flaps and shook off a few raindrops. Two big air-pillows were just under the flap, added protection against the rain, it seemed. He tugged those out of the way and popped them with his knife.

Then he slowly extracted the books. The first was a sturdy, leather-bound volume over a thousand pages long. *The Lord of the Rings* had been embossed on the cover in gold. Below that, another thick volume, bound in glossy cardboard. A huge, green dragon lunged at some heroic knight, under the words "D&D Starter Edition." Cale weighed them in his hands, then set the Dungeons & Dragons manual aside.

Soon there'd be a new mission. There would be a reuniting of his people.

But right now, for the next couple hours. . . .

Lying back on his cot, he propped *Lord of the Rings* up on his chest and started to read by the flickering candlelight.

ACKNOWLEDGEMENTS

THEY SAY WHEN WRITING that your first audience should be yourself, the writer. Write the story that you want to read, first and foremost. And that's what we did when we wrote a short story together called "The Rules of Enchantment" for the anthology OPERATION ARCANA, edited by John Joseph Adams. Months after that story saw print, we kept telling each other that we'd left fun material on the table. "We could write a scene where . . ." and the other would say "Or what if. . . ."

To a very certain extent, we kept writing the story because, well, we wanted to see how much we could continue to entertain ourselves with the setting, characters, and concepts.

And entertain ourselves we did.

It didn't all happen right away, of course. Writing doesn't always happen like that. But we kept talking about "the novel" when we got together at cons and such. We planned an extended weekend outlining session that got us about two-thirds of the way through the story, and otherwise noodled around with the ideas in our own brains that we'd excitedly email each other. When Dave unexpectedly lost a job, though, we jumped right into finishing the outline so he would be able to start working on a draft alongside looking for gainful employment.

And then he *did* get a new job almost immediately, and things wound their slow way along. That first draft happened in the nooks and crannies of a busy life—the last third or so of the first draft, in fact, was composed between scenes of a small stage performance of *Romeo & Juliet*, in which Dave played Chorus/The Prince. From there, Toby worked his magic on it, then passed it back, and on it went until we were happy with it.

Over a number of years we kept revising it, fine-tuning it with the help of our agent, Hannah Bowman. Finally, after many twists and turns of publishing fate, it ended up in the hands of Jacob Weisman at Tachyon Publications after a late-night conversation with Toby about "this crazy, but fun, book we wrote together that we just adore," and the rest is, as they say, history.

Which brings us to the people we'd like to thank. Collectively, we're very grateful to Jacob Weisman, Jaymee Goh, and the whole awesome team over at Tachyon. They do amazing work, and our work is certainly better for being in their caring and capable hands. We'd also like to thank our agent Hannah Bowman, her assistant Lauren Bajek, and everyone at Liza Dawson Associates, who have been tireless champions of our work.

On a personal level, we'd very much like to thank Charles Coleman Finlay, who introduced us to each other at the Detroit-area convention ConFusion, way back in the early '00s, when we were all just sort of starting out. He seemed to recognize immediately that we were kindred spirits, and he was absolutely correct. Two decades of friendship have borne that out.

Individually, Toby would like to thank Dave for going along with him in this zany experiment. Co-authoring can be a complicated friend-ending experience, but if anything, we've gotten closer over the years we spent tinkering with this manuscript.

All that time trying to get a laugh out of each other as we gently poked fun at our favorite fantasy, gaming, and RPG tropes that we love from decades of marinating in our favorite genres was time well spent. Toby would also like to thank Emily, his wife, for all the usual patience a creative's spouse has with their "here-but-not-here" energy as they daydream their way through daily life, and his daughters Thalia and Calliope, who push him toward more and more creative wordplay as they force him to up his game.

And Dave has a huge list of people to thank, but he'll try to keep it short. First, though, are the Marines and sailors of Alpha Co., 1/24 and Kilo Co., 3/24 for guidance, inspiration, and generally putting up with his nerdy self during his enlistment. Specifically, though, Matt Wright, who was a constant companion in uniform and kept Dave sane through a difficult deployment, and remains a lifelong friend. And then there's Toby himself, of course, for being a friend and collaborator—lo, these many years. He'd also like to thank John Scalzi and Mary Robinette Kowal for the mentoring, collaboration, encouragement, and friendship they have shown in the time he's known them. And last, but certainly not least, is Dave's family: his wife Tarri, who does her level best to keep up with his various creative pursuits and, along with Toby's wife Emily, showed superhuman patience with our late-night con conversations. Tarri is a supreme constant in Dave's life, and he's not sure how he could do it without her. And of course, Dave's kids, one of whom chose to remain nameless in these acknowledgements, so they all get the anonymous treatment. They're great kids, growing up to be amazing adults, and he draws inspiration from them every day.

Called "violent, poetic and compulsively readable" by *Maclean's*, science-fiction author Tobias S. Buckell is a *New York Times* best-selling writer and World Fantasy Award winner born in the Caribbean. He grew up in Grenada and spent time in the British and U.S. Virgin Islands, and the islands he lived on influence much of his work.

Buckell is the author of the acclaimed four-volume *Xenowealth* series, which begins with *Crystal Rain*. He has also written five standalone novels and almost one hundred stories. Buckell's works have been translated into twenty different languages. He has been nominated for the Hugo, Nebula, and World Fantasy Awards, as well as the Astounding Award for Best New Science Fiction Author. His most recent novel is *A Stranger in the Citadel* (2023).

Buckell currently lives in Bluffton, Ohio, with his wife and two daughters, where he teaches creative writing at Bluffton

University. He is also an instructor at the Stonecoast MFA in Creative Writing program.

Visit Buckell online at www.TobiasBuckell.com.

Dave Klecha was born in Detroit and grew up in the Metro area, bouncing around to 5 different school systems before graduating high school. It was during high school that he started writing, at first to stave off boredom, then with an eye toward publication when he realized he might have a knack for it. Since that plan didn't turn to immediate riches, he embarked on paths more and less conventional for a kid from the suburbs.

He studied Russian and history at university, joined the US Marine Corps Reserves, and at some point started graduate school. To keep food on the table, he's delivered pizza, fixed computers, worked front desk at a hotel, fixed computers, consulted on computer systems, and fixed computers. These days, computers are almost too easy to fix, so he's given that up in favor of just breaking them in ever-more-creative ways.

In addition to writing, Dave engages in a number of other creative pursuits, including acting, set-building, scriptwriting, and extreme amateur landscaping. His fiction has appeared in *Subterranean Press Magazine*, *Clarkesworld*, and various anthologies.

Dave currently lives in Rochester, Michigan with his wife and three children.